PLATINUM MAGIC

Bruce C. Davis

Brick Cave Media
brickcavebooks.com
2018

Copyright © 2018 Bruce C. Davis

ISBN-13: 978-1-938190-39-1

All rights reserved. No part of this publication may be reproduced, stored in a retrieval system, or transmitted in any form or by any means, electronic, mechanical, recording or otherwise, without the prior written permission of the author.

Printed in the United States of America.

Copyright 2018 by Brick Cave Books
All rights reserved.

The characters and events in this book are fictitious. Any similarity to real persons, living or dead, is coincidental and not intended by the author.

Cover Illustration by Thitipon Decruen [xric7]

Brick Cave Media
brickcavebooks.com
2018

To my wife Michele,
my partner in all things.

For Jean

PLATINUM MAGIC

The magic is real!

Bruce C. Davis

Brick Cave Media
brickcavebooks.com
2018

CHAPTER ONE

"Breaching team in position," Haldron Stonebender whispered through the silver Far-Speaker receiver clipped to Simon's left earlobe. "I'm not too keen on the new Fire mage, though. He's a tad shaky."

Simon lifted the leather and moonstone bracer on his left wrist to his lips and spoke into the faintly glowing gem. "Give him a break, Hal. It's his first raid. He'll be fine."

"He'd better be." Hal's Dwarfish burr grumbled through their private FS connection. "We only get one chance at this."

Simon shifted his weight and brought the D'Stang pneumatic bolt thrower up to a ready position. The short-barreled weapon, slung from his tactical vest for easy deployment, could be shifted out of the way if the fight came to close quarters. Simon hoped it wouldn't. "You have eyes on the door," he said. "Your call."

His double-edged Bonecleaver Mark 3 was within easy reach in the rear sheath of the vest. The short sword had been a gift from Hal's wife, with the admonition that he watch her husband's back. Simon's sword skills were marginal at best. He had no desire to face the wrath of a Dwarven widow out for *were geld* if he failed to protect his second in command.

"Make ready," Haldron rasped over the FS tactical web. "Breaching team, by the numbers."

"*One, ready.*" Hamish McPhee, the team's armorer and Simon's rear cover.

"*Two, ready.*" Jack Ironhand, in place to cover the door.

"*Three, uh, ready.*"

Simon smiled. That would be Liam Aster, their new Fire mage.

His turn. "Five, ready." He was careful to keep his tone neutral. If his confidence in Liam turned out to be misplaced, Hal would never let him forget it.

A gibbous moon shone down through the bare trees that surrounded the old farmhouse. The land around them had been subdivided and sold off to developers long ago. The half-acre parcel on which the original farm buildings sat had been preserved as a bucolic island in a sea of suburban sprawl. In the wan light of Midwinter's Eve, it looked more sinister than pastoral.

Simon loosened the Bonecleaver in its sheath and raised the pneumatic to his shoulder. He flipped off the safety and felt the slight vibration as the Air spell spun up in the cinnabar rod encased in the ebony and aluminum stock.

"Take the door, Three," said Haldron. "All others, on my lead as soon as the door is down."

Simon tensed as blue flame swirled in front of the door. Within a second, the spiraling flames funneled down to a narrow point that struck the doorjamb just below the lock. The jamb disintegrated with a burst of molten iron and a flash of burning wood.

Haldron dashed forward and hit the door with a flying kick, smashing it inward. "King's Agents!" he shouted, identifying the team. He had his own pneumatic up as he stepped into the darkness beyond the threshold.

Simon rushed in right behind Hal, swiveling left and right, sighting along the D'Stang's barrel, seeking targets. He felt rather than heard Hamish trailing behind him. Simon heard a rattle of gear as Jack took up station to cover their exit. He knew Liam would wait outside to provide anti-air cover in case their quarry had access to a flyer.

Hal gestured to his right and Simon split off that way into a modest-sized sitting room dominated by a large stone hearth. The room was dark. With a practiced shake of his head, he flipped down the brass-framed seeing stone mounted on the rim of his helmet so that he looked through it with his right eye. He muttered the incantation and the room seemed to light up with a soft green glow. The stone washed out all color and there was a slight distortion at the edges of his vision, like looking through warped glass, but at least he could see.

Simon caught a glimpse of movement near the hearth and swiveled the pneumatic to cover it.

"King's Agent!" he shouted. "Get down on your knees. Hands where I can see them."

The thing by the hearth cocked its head at Simon's command. It was squat and broad, like a full-sized man whose legs had been shoved up into his torso. Its long muscular arms reached almost to the floor. Its head was human in outline but flattened on top, as if the skull had been sheared off at the brow line. It was hairless, naked and sexless, the space between its short legs smooth and featureless.

Simon cursed and fired two bolts as it growled and bared long, fang-like teeth. He dropped the bolt thrower and it swung down beside his left hip on its harness. He drew the Bonecleaver and shouted over his shoulder toward Hal, "Golem!"

The creature rushed him, the two cold iron bolts from the pneumatic protruding from its chest. The bolts didn't even slow it down.

Simon swung his sword at the thing and the double-edged blade sliced deep into its left shoulder. It roared and spun to its right, nearly wrenching the sword out of his hand. He backpedaled away from the golem, bringing the Bonecleaver up to a high overhead ready position.

The golem snarled as it lifted its nearly severed left arm with the right one, until the edges of the sword wound touched each other. The thing's flesh seemed to melt and flow as the arm reattached itself. The golem flexed its biceps and rolled its newly healed shoulder as if loosening it. It snarled at Simon again and crouched to spring.

Simon shifted to the balls of his feet and made ready. Even though he was expecting it, the thing sprang at him so quickly he barely had time to react. He swung the Bonecleaver in a powerful arc aimed at the golem's thick neck. His aim was off by a fraction, but it was good enough. The blade struck the golem just above the angle of its lower jaw and sliced through the base of its skull, cleaving most of its head from the rest of its body. It went limp and dropped at his feet, the putty-like flesh sizzling and foaming as the spell that had created it dissipated. Sword now at low ready, Simon swept his gaze around the rest of the room.

"Clear!" he shouted and backed out into the entry hall.

"Clear!" Hamish's shout came from the room to the left.

"Hal!" Simon called. "Hal, sound off!"

He pulled the D'Stang up in a one-handed grip with his left hand and clutched the sword in his right. The broken front door faced a narrow corridor leading toward the back of the farmhouse.

Jack stood in the doorway facing outward. "Hal went toward the back of the house," he said over his shoulder. "The door closed behind him and he hasn't checked in on the tactical web."

"Cover me, Hamish," Simon said as he started down the hallway. It ended at a heavy, iron bound door. It was closed and a faint glow of red light shone beneath the lower edge.

Simon released the pneumatic and slung it near his left hip as he felt Hamish's hand on his back. He tightened his grip on the Bonecleaver and reached out with his left hand, feeling along the doorframe until he found the handle. He shifted to his left to give Hamish a clear field of fire through the door. Hamish tapped his back twice to indicate he was ready.

Simon turned the handle and felt the latch give. He kicked the door open, slamming it into the inner wall of the room. Golems surged toward him. The Bonecleaver whistled through the air, taking the head off of the closest creature. Simon dove under the grasp of the second, clearing the doorway and slicing off one of the golem's legs with a backhand stroke. It went down in a smear of greenish fluid, tripping the one behind it. Simon cut upward, and the third golem fell in two pieces, still animated but unable to move. Simon stabbed downward at the golem with the severed leg, driving the sword through its head and into the wooden floor.

Behind him, he heard the hissing buzz of Hamish's D'Stang slinging bolts into the room. Two more golems fell with explosive bolts through their skulls. Hamish had switched from cold iron to Fire-charged ammo after hearing Simon's initial warning.

The strange red light filled the room, seeming to come from the air itself, like a glowing fog. Simon flipped the seeing stone out of the way as his eyes adjusted to the low light.

"Hal!" he shouted, struggling to his feet and wrenching the Bonecleaver free of the floor.

Haldron lay on his back in the middle of the room, apparently unconscious with a deep gash in his scalp. Two golems held him down by the arms. Above him stood a man-sized figure robed in black, a full hood covering the figure's head and face. It held a long dagger in its right hand and a small shield, like an old-fashioned buckler, in its left. The dagger glowed with a blue light that shimmered like moonlight on a deep lake. For a second, Simon thought he heard a high sweet song, like the voice of a temple virgin singing the first notes of the moonrise hymn. He stood still, listening, as the black figure raised the dagger above Hal's chest.

Hamish's voice cut through the spell cast by the sweet voice. "King's Agents. Drop the blade and stand away from my teammate."

Simon shook his head, clearing it, and raised the Bonecleaver to full guard. "Drop the blade," he repeated. "On your knees, hands behind your head."

The figure in black said something in a harsh, hissing language that hurt Simon's ears with its discordant sounds. The two golems started forward and the figure raised the dagger.

Hamish's bolt thrower buzzed again. The Fire-charged bolt struck the man in the center of his chest. The impact released the Fire containment spell on the copper arrowhead and all of the energy of its forward motion was instantly converted to heat. The man's chest exploded from within, throwing him backward into the far wall and showering Simon with bits of flaming flesh and bone. Then the first golem struck his chest, sinking three-inch teeth into his vest.

The Earth spell embedded in the steel mail of his tactical vest withstood the bite but the impact threw him back into the wall. He struggled to fend off the sinewy arms and stubby hands that clawed at the vest, seeking an opening to his bare flesh. He reversed the sword and worked it between the vest and the golem, under the thing's left arm. He thrust upward. It was awkward and lacked power, but it was enough. The steel blade sliced into the golem's head and the animation spell was broken.

Simon pushed the already disintegrating golem away from him and swung to face the spot where Hal lay. Hamish stood nearby, the foaming remains of the final golem dissolving at his feet. The glowing red mist dissipated, leaving the room bathed in moonlight. Haldron stirred and moaned.

Simon rushed to his side and helped him to sit up. He pulled a battle dressing from the pouch at his waist and pressed it to Hal's scalp. Hamish swept the rest of the room, sighting along the barrel of his bolt thrower before signaling all clear. Only then did Simon notice the glowing symbols etched into the floor. They seemed to crawl in front of his eyes like living things. Their red glow faded as he tried to focus on them and read their meaning.

Simon was no mage, but all King's Agents received broad training in magical practice. Part of the job, after all, was running down bootleg conjurers. You had to recognize illegal magic in order to know whether there were grounds for an arrest. The old days of the Magisterium were long gone and even criminals had rights under the Commonwealth Accords. Simon was pretty sure these symbols had something to do with an Earth spell, but they were unfamiliar to him. There wasn't much question about the guilt of the dead mage, though. Creating golems outside of an approved laboratory was illegal, not to mention the assault on a King's Agent.

Hal groaned and touched the battle dressing on his head. "What in the name of Stone . . ."

"Are you all good?" Simon asked, looking into his friend's eyes. They were clear. Hal blinked several times, glancing rapidly around the room.

"Aye," Hal said. "Head feels like a bloody bass drum, pounding away, but I'll live. Is the house secure?"

"We're clear here," Simon said. He touched his bracer to open the Far-Speaker web. "Jack, Liam, all secure outside?"

"All clear." Jack's voice was steady, but the relief was evident in his tone.

"What happened in there?" asked Liam. "I felt a huge energy surge. Earth spell, I think. It almost nullified my containment. Don't want to think about what could have happened if that failed."

Simon understood. Fire mages worked at the very edge of safety when operational for a raid. The spells needed to conjure their particular medium were lengthy, so most kept a potential store of flame within a magical containment bubble ready for instant use if combat demanded it. If the containment failed, the flames would consume the mage and most everything else within a few yards' radius in an instantaneous fireball.

It was one reason why Fire mages had a reputation for being a little twitchy.

"We're not sure yet, Liam," Simon replied. "The perp is dead, but he was into some strange shit. Stand down your containment. I don't think we'll need more flame tonight."

"Aye, sir," said Liam.

"Once you're secure, get Lieutenant Gulbrandsen on the mirror and join us inside. I want his eyes on this scene."

A clanking sound interrupted Liam's acknowledgement. Simon felt vibration in the floor beneath his boots.

"Ham," he said. "Give us some light over here."

Hamish stepped up beside him and drew a torch from his utility belt. He muttered a Fire incantation and a blue flame flared within the torch's small crystal globe. The light revealed a trap door set in the floor and a small windlass anchored next to its edge.

Simon glanced at Hal who nodded and drew his own sword. Simon pried up the front edge of the trapdoor with his Bonecleaver until he could get a grip on the wood, and then heaved it open.

An Orc stared back at him, wild-eyed. He struggled against the chains that bound him to a flat stone slab and grunted unintelligibly around the rubber ball gag that was stuffed in his mouth.

"Easy," said Simon, sheathing the Bonecleaver to hold out his empty palms. "Take it easy. We'll get you out of there."

He looked at the edges of the slab. Heavy metal cables ran from eyelets set in the stone to a winching mechanism bolted to the underside of the floor. Hal looked over his shoulder, and then took hold of the windlass and gave it a turn. The mechanism was well oiled and turned smoothly; the stone slab began to rise. Hal continued cranking.

When the slab reached floor height, Simon noticed locking bars set into its surface. He slid them out and Hal let go of the windlass. The bars held, keeping the slab level with the floor. Symbols and glyphs were etched into the grey stone, many of them matching the symbols drawn on the floor.

Simon removed the gag from the Orc's mouth as Hal went to work on the manacles that bound him to the slab.

"Don't hurt me," the Orc begged. "I'm just a poor farmer. I don't know anything. I won't tell anyone. Please let me go."

"Calm down," said Simon. "We're King's Agents. No one wants to hurt you. We'll get you out of those chains as quickly as we can." He looked at Hal.

"Can't get through the manacles without a cold chisel," the Dwarf said. "But I think I can manage the chain links." He spoke to the Orc. "Pull your left arm tight against the chain and look away."

The Orc's voice trembled, "What are you going to do?"

"Just do as he says," said Simon. "He won't hurt you. What's your name?"

"Gripple," said the Orc, keeping his eyes fixed on Simon. "Gripple Swampwater."

"Do you live in this house, Mr. Swampwater?" Simon saw the look of disgust on Hal's face but ignored it. He well knew about his friend's hatred for Orcs, even if he didn't understand it.

"No. I farm a shareplot down Fernhill way, just outside the Reservation fence. Ten acres are all mine, though." The pride in his voice temporarily masked his fear. Hal's sword came down with a clang, severing a link in the chain about six inches from Gripple's arm.

The Orc cried out and jumped against the remaining chains. "Durlash's Beard," he squeaked. "Give an Orc some warning."

"Shut up and I will," Hal said. "But only if you promise not to jump around like a toad on a mudflat."

"I won't move. I promise."

Hal moved quickly around the slab, repeating the procedure on each of Gripple's chains. The Orc sat up and rubbed his wrists and ankles. He was smaller than a man, no taller than Hal, but slight of build with spindly limbs and long fingers that ended in thick black fingernails.

Hal examined his sword and grunted. "Lucky for you I didn't notch my blade. It'll take an hour at the grindstone to restore the edge, though."

'Thank you," Gripple offered meekly.

Hal just grunted again and turned away, walking over toward the mage's body.

"Don't worry about Agent Stonebender," said Simon to Gripple. "He's always cranky after a raid. The golems getting the drop on him didn't help his mood, either."

Gripple shrugged. "He's a Dwarf," he said, as if that explained everything.

"Simon," Hal called from next to the body. "You'd best be having a look at this."

"Can you help Mr. Swampwater?" Simon asked Hamish. "Start taking his statement and as soon as Liam gets a mirror up, we'll have him talk to the Lieutenant as well."

"Right," said Hamish as he reached down to help Gripple to his feet.

Simon walked over to Hal. The Dwarf looked up at him, frowning. "Mr. Swampwater, is it now?"

"He may be an Orc off the Reservation, but he's still a citizen," said Simon.

"Too bad for him," grumbled Hal. "His kind should stay where they belong. The Magisterium had a few things right."

Simon sighed. Old grudges and racial hatred were supposed to be a thing of the past. Hells, Simon had more reason than most to hate Orcs. But he had walked a beat for three years in the worst Orc slums of Cymbeline. He knew them as well as any Human could. He couldn't hate the mass of them for the acts of a lone terrorist.

"What did you want me to see?" he asked.

Hal reached down and pulled back the hood of the mage's robe. The first thing Simon noticed was the fine platinum blond hair, slanted eyes, and exquisite facial features of a High-born Elf.

The second thing he noticed was that she was a woman.

"Oh, shit," he said.

CHAPTER TWO

"Tell me again how your team had no choice but to kill a High Elf." Lt. Gulbrandsen's voice wavered with the slight distortion of a field-expedient magic mirror. Liam stood behind the mirror, half seen through its flickering light, muttering a steady stream of incantations. The unstable combination of Fire and Water magic that created the mirror was hard enough to maintain in a physical object. Conjuring one from thin air required constant adjustment and a higher than average level of magical aptitude.

"She was holding a knife on one of my team, sir," Simon repeated for the third time. "She didn't comply with instructions to stand down."

"That's not a reason to use a Fire bolt on a sentient, Sergeant. Cold iron would have been as effective and likely not fatal to an Elf. The Havens will be screaming for blood. They're sticklers for the letter of the Accords."

"We were fighting golems, sir. Hamish likely saved my life with those bolts. What was he supposed to do? Change magazines in the middle of a melee?"

Gulbrandsen sighed. "I don't doubt your account, Sergeant Buckley. Swampwater's statement confirms the presence of golems. But, damn it, Simon, a High Elf? What in the Seven Hells was she doing in Bowater? Her kind hardly ever leaves the Cymbeline High Street."

Simon had no answer for that and sensed the Lieutenant didn't really want one. "Did her ear pattern show up on any of the identity registries?" he asked instead.

"Not yet. She's a pure Elf. No fingerprints or scars to track. If she was never imaged outside of the Havens, we may be stuck with aura analysis to try to identify her. And if the Haven Consul gets wind of this first, he'll claim the body and whisk it off to Tintagel, in which case, we may never find out who she was."

"But, sir, she was clearly an illegal conjurer. The golems alone are a hanging offense, not to mention the assault on a King's Agent and the kidnapping of another sentient."

"Since when do the Havens give two shits about Orcs?" Gulbrandsen scoffed. "Even in a Commonwealth Court, the kidnap charge would likely be reduced to unlawful detention. The golem charge might have stuck, but only if we could show probable cause for the armed raid. How secure is the warrant on this one?"

Simon hesitated a moment before answering. "Secure enough. Justice Severna himself issued it."

Gulbrandsen nodded. "Good. I may have to go to the ring with the Haven Consul on this one. Keep the scene under Veil until the CSA mages get there. Turn the physical evidence over to them and get your team back to the House as quietly as you can. Gulbrandsen out."

"Aye, sir," Simon said and nodded to Liam who dropped the spell that maintained the mirror with a cutting motion of his left hand.

"When do we tell the boss the warrant was for a search only?" asked Hal.

"When we get back to the House," Simon said. "Hopefully by then the mages will have an ID on the Lady and we can show that she was connected to the Azeri."

"This wasn't about conjuring Fire bombs for a bunch of half-assed terrorists," said Hal. He traced one of the symbols on the floor with the toe of his boot. "This is some deep Earth magic, way beyond anything I've ever seen."

"It was your informant who gave us the tip on this one," Simon reminded his partner. "Where did he get the information? And why did he say it was connected to the Azeri Liberation Brigade?"

Hal glared at him for a second, then made a wry face.

"Snick has always been straight with me before. He's reliable, for an Orc," he said. "He told me his cousin had delivered a hundred-weight of aquamarine dust to this place, along with three rowan logs. That implies Fire conjuring in my book. And that same cousin was a known affiliate of several Azeri clan enforcers. Two and two seemed to add up to four. At least Severna thought so when I applied for the warrant."

"I hope Gulbrandsen agrees with the good Justice. Severna's an easy touch when it comes to the Azeri."

"I know," said Hal. "That's why I took the information to him in the first place." To Simon's inquiring look he went on. "I scouted this place on my way home last week. Something about it bothered me. The Stone seemed rotten somehow."

"So, we mounted an armed raid on a suburban farmhouse based on a deliveryman's second hand report and your sense of Stone?"

"The Stone didn't lie," insisted Hal. "It just didn't tell me what the real threat was."

"I know, partner," said Simon. "I just wish I had something more solid to back up my decision to mobilize the whole team. I trust your Stone sense, and you were right about the threat level, but I don't know if we can sell this to Gulbrandsen or to the Haven Consul."

"Sarge?" Jack's voice came over Simon's FS receiver.

"Yes, Jack."

"CSA team is here. Should I send them in?"

"Yes. How's the Veil holding up?"

"No problems. The emitter has almost a full charge. It should hold until daylight."

"Good." Simon nodded to the head of the Crime Scene Analysis team as he entered the room. "We don't want any nosy neighbors calling the newsies before the Lieutenant can get ahead of this. Keep me posted if anyone gets through the Veil. Buckley out."

The Veil wouldn't physically keep anyone away from the farmhouse, but would mask the team and the CSA mages from outside view. The last thing Simon wanted right now was to have to add crowd control to the team's duties.

"Sergeant Buckley?" asked the tall mage who approached Simon with his hand extended. "Good meeting. I'm Kyle Evarts, CSA."

"Simon Buckley. Good meeting, Mr. Evarts." Simon took the proffered hand. Evarts' grip was firm but not overly strong. He had the slim build, fine features, and long narrow hands of a Half-Elf.

"So, what have you got for us?" the CSA mage asked.

"One dead perp over there—a High-Elf, by the way—the remnants of a bunch of deanimated golems, and a very frightened Orc. That, and the makings of what my partner tells me is some potent Earth magic. We're hoping you can ID the perp and tell us something about the spell she was trying to cast."

"She?" Evarts raised an eyebrow but kept his voice neutral.

Simon nodded. "Female. That didn't keep her from controlling half a dozen golems, or trying to stick a knife in my partner's chest. You have a problem investigating an Elf?"

"No," Evarts said. "It's just unusual for an Elven Lady to leave the High Street, much less be involved in illegal conjuring. Interesting."

"Her ear pattern isn't in any of the usual registries. The Lieutenant is searching the military and anti-terrorist registries, but it will take time. Do you think you can get anything from an aural analysis?"

"How long has she been dead?" Evarts asked.

Simon checked his pocket timepiece. "About thirty minutes, maybe thirty-five."

"Sure," said Evarts with a shrug. "If she's ever done any commercial or government casting, her aura pattern will be registered. I can get a reading up to twelve hours after death if the body is reasonably intact."

Simon gestured toward the corpse. "Whenever you're ready."

Evarts turned and gave some orders to the two other members of his team, then followed Simon to where the Elf lay. Simon knelt and pulled the hood away from the corpse's face. Evarts' sharp intake of breath made him look up.

"Damn," whispered Evarts.

"What?" asked Simon.

"I'll do the aural analysis for official confirmation," said Evarts. "But it isn't necessary.

Her name is Glendowyn Hightower. She's a Professor of Earth Magic at Caledonia University."

"You know her?"

Evarts shook his head. "Not really. I attended a couple of her seminars on Quantum Magic Theory last year. She was supposed to be on sabbatical back in the Havens, last I heard."

"So how does a University Professor end up in . . ." Simon paused. "Wait. Hightower? As in the Steward of Tintagel? That Hightower?"

Evarts nodded. "Her brother, I think. She's the youngest of her line and a bit of an iconoclast. She actually believes Humans are as intelligent as Elvenkind."

Simon smiled wryly at that. "That must make her popular with her kin." The Hightowers were well known Traditionalists, absolute believers in Elven superiority in all things.

"I suppose it's why she teaches at a Human university rather than at the Academy in Tintagel," Evarts said. "What was she doing here?"

"No idea," Simon replied. "We mounted the raid on a tip that someone was making Fire bombs for the Azeri in this house. Instead, we find an Elven Lady conjuring golems and kidnapping Orcs. Can you take a look at the symbols on the stone slab over there and tell me what they mean?"

Evarts took one last look at the dead Elf before turning and bending over the stone slab. He traced a few of the symbols with his fingertip, muttering under his breath. He glanced up at Simon, his expression puzzled. "Were there other symbols around the room?"

Simon nodded. "On the floor. They were glowing when we broke through the door, but faded after Hamish shot Professor Hightower over there. You can still see some of them if you look carefully."

Evarts stood and rubbed his fingertip on the hem of his jacket. "I'll cast a Reveal on them after we've collected the evidence so that my imaging tech can capture them." He stared down at the slab. "If I'm right, this was some kind of Portal spell. But that doesn't make sense. Portal magic has been a dead end for almost a century. I can't see a scholar of Hightower's caliber working on that kind of nonsense."

"Why not?" asked Simon.

"Well, for one thing, it's Blood Magic. Requires a living sacrifice to activate a spell. Very strange for an Elf Lady to be messing with this type of thing."

"Portal to where?" Simon asked.

"No way to know," said Evarts. "I wouldn't want to go through, no matter where it was supposed to go."

"Why not?"

"Portals mess with the probability streams. Something about the spell dissipates spiritual energy, killing any living thing that passes through. Even inanimate objects have a fifty-fifty chance of quantum probability dissociation."

"Say what?" asked Simon.

"Complete breakdown of whatever probability matrix holds the atoms of an object together," said

Evarts. "Let's say she opened a Portal from here back to Headquarters. If you or I tried to walk through it, we'd be dead before our feet found the floor on the other side. But even if you tried to toss your sword through, there's an even chance that it would end up as a pile of metal shavings on the other side. That's why this type of casting has been a dead end for a hundred years, not even fit for bulk cargo transfer."

"So, this spell, whatever it was supposed to do, needed blood from a living animal to activate it, right?" Simon asked. Evarts nodded. "That explains why she kidnapped Swampwater. And when we stumbled into it, why she took Haldron instead."

"Blood Magic is dark business," said Evarts. "It's not a reputable branch of Magic Theory. I wonder why she was willing to sacrifice a sentient to power the spell? That implies a lot of power behind the casting."

Simon looked over to where the CSA mages were beginning to examine and image the dead Elf. "What in the hells were you trying to do here?" he asked.

The corpse made no answer.

CHAPTER THREE

It was almost the seventh hour of the day before Simon and his team could clear the scene and load their gear into the armored cargo sledge that was their utility transportation for armed raids. The CSA mages had removed Hightower's body and gathered the remains of the golems in carefully labeled evidence bags. They had imaged the room where Gripple and Hal had almost become sacrificial offerings from a dozen different angles and had taken aural readings from the still faintly visible glyphs on the floor. Liam had been assigned to escort Gripple back to Wycliffe House for debriefing by Lt. Gulbrandsen and the on-duty King's Prosecutor. Simon and Hal watched Liam and Gripple climb into a nondescript black government sled.

"He did a decent job," admitted Hal, as the sled left the farmhouse. "Kept his head and didn't lose focus when things went a bit sideways."

Simon grinned. "I told you he'd be fine. He scored in the top of his class at the academy and has a degree in advanced pyrotechnics from Caledonia."

Hal grunted. "Book learning and academy scores don't tell you how a man will perform in the field. He's acceptable. That's all."

They joined Jack and Hamish at the sledge. Hal shucked off his tactical vest and bolt thrower and stowed them in the rack along the left side of the cargo bed.

Simon shook his head as he slid the tactical vest off and stowed it on the rack next to Hal's. It took Dwarves a long time to warm up to new people, but once you gained their trust, they were fierce in their loyalty. Friendship came even harder for them, and Simon treasured Hal's. He clapped his friend on the shoulder and they settled themselves into the bench seat on the right side of the sledge's cargo box. Jack sat in the driver's seat and Hamish sat next to him in the guard position.

Jack muttered the incantation and pulled back on the steering yoke. The sledge rose smoothly on the cushion of compressed air created by the spell embedded in the cinnabar rods that lined the undercarriage. Jack swung the sledge around and started toward the main road, only stopping briefly as Hamish jumped out and picked up the last Veil emitter from the edge of the farmyard. They headed south, with the sun just poking above the roofs of the tract homes that surrounded the farmhouse. The winding neighborhood street fed them onto King's Route 34, a four-lane divided highway that was the main artery into Cymbeline, the capitol city.

Forty minutes later, Jack guided the sledge smoothly into the entrance that sloped down from Tanner Street into the underground stables beneath Wycliffe House. Known to the Peacekeeper squads that were headquartered there simply as "the House," the huge building covered a square block on the edge of the Government District in the center of Cymbeline, just south of the High Street.

Even in the bright sunshine of a cold winter morning, Wycliffe House looked forbidding. During its five-hundred-year history, it had been a fortress, a royal palace, an armory, and—most notably—a prison. During the Magisterium, Wycliffe House had been synonymous with despair, torture, and dark magic. The Restoration and establishment of the Commonwealth Accords under King Otto, one hundred and seventy years ago, had emptied Wycliffe's dungeons and torn down the thick walls and the bailey that had surrounded it. On the north side, the old moat and forecourt had been filled and turned into a greenbelt. Holes had been cut in the north face of the old fortress and huge glass windows installed to symbolize the enlightenment of the new order. On the south side, however—what Simon thought of as the working entrance to Wycliffe House—the gray granite walls rose sheer from the street level, broken only by narrow arrow slit windows and barred postern doors. Here, the House retained its dark face and promised no mercy to the King's enemies.

Jack parked the sledge and it settled to the flagstone floor. The squad moved quickly to remove and stow gear, clean their weapons and check them in to the armory. They began the mundane task of filling out the multiple forms that inevitably accompanied police work.

Simon gathered the individual reports and ammunition inventories from each squad member and bound them together in a heavy paper folder. He made sure to include the search warrant from Justice Severna and Hal's report on the connection between his snitch and the Azeri clans. He added his own endorsement, hoping that Gulbrandsen would pass over his flimsy reasonable cause statement and look at the events of the raid itself. By the time the cleanup was done and the reports finished, it was nearly tenth hour.

Jack and Hamish had showered and changed into civilian clothes in the team locker room when Simon met with them, checked their reports, and then dismissed them.

"Get some sleep," he said. "We'll muster in the squad room at seventh hour tomorrow morning. You both did good work last night."

"Thanks, Sarge," said Hamish. "Any idea what the LT will do about the Elf Lady?"

"Not a clue," Simon answered. "I wouldn't want to be the one to tell the Steward that his sister was killed in a Peacekeeper raid, though. The LT can have that duty. I don't need to tell you to keep quiet about who was in that farmhouse, do I?"

"Not me or Jack," Hamish said. "What about Liam? How well do you know him?"

"I'll deal with Liam. Just keep a low profile until we know how Gulbrandsen is going to play this."

"Aye, Sarge. Understood. Good parting. See you tomorrow."

"Good parting, Ham."

Simon tucked the bundle of reports under his arm and climbed the stairs to the squad room. The day watch was already at work, busy with FS calls, scribbling notes, and checking updates on their mirrors. The room smelled of burned coffee, stale smoke, and a century of foot traffic. On the far wall, a large magic mirror was tuned to a twenty-four-hour news network.

Simon crossed the room to his own cubicle. As a team leader, he rated a desk in an eight-by-four-foot enclosure with frosted glass walls that gave the illusion of privacy. Hal was already there, slouched on the ragged couch across from Simon's battered desk, his boots propped on the arm.

"Those boots clean?" Simon asked as he dropped the package of reports on the desk and fell into his own chair. The desktop was already cluttered with warrant forms, perpetrator updates, and arrest reports. A magic mirror, showing the King's Peacekeeper Force emblem on its inactive surface, perched precariously on the edge opposite Hal's oversized combat boots.

"Aye, aside from the odd bit of golem snot. Molly shined them up herself just yesterday, I'll have you know." Hal grinned as he lowered his feet to the floor. "Gulbrandsen told me to fetch you up to his office as soon as you showed your ugly mug."

Simon made a face. "Don't tell me. The Haven Consul is here."

Hal shrugged. "I'm just a lowly King's Agent. That information is way above my pay grade."

"Where's Liam?" Simon asked.

"Feeding your pet Orc tea and holding his hand until the duty King's Prosecutor can get around to taking his statement," said Hal. "Why? The LT didn't want to see him."

Simon sighed rather than revive the old argument with Hal over Orcish rights. He was far too tired to stand on principle.

"I wanted to talk with him for a second, before seeing Gulbrandsen."

Hal just grunted.

"What?"

"I said he was adequate," said Hal. "There's no need to coddle the lad."

"No, but he needs to feel part of this team. And if the manure starts to fly over this dead Elf noblewoman, I need to be able to count on his loyalty."

"That should be a given," grumbled Hal. "He's a Keeper. He took the oath."

Simon shrugged. "Times change. One thing I've learned since making Sergeant is that this job is as much about politics, as it is about police work."

"Trust granite over shale," said Hal, quoting an old Dwarfish proverb. "Don't let Gulbrandsen and this job geld you. He lost his balls years ago. Mark my words, he'll do nothing but grovel to Tintagel and then throw this whole team under the proverbial rock pile."

"All the more reason to make sure Liam is on board."

"If he ain't, he'll find my boot so far up his arse, he'll be chewing shoe leather."

Simon smiled. That was the simple calculus of Hal's life: absolute loyalty to his family, his team, and his friends. That and all the ale he could drink.

They found Liam near the stairs to the detention level. He stood leaning against the wall with his eyes closed. He started slightly when Simon reached out and touched his arm.

"Sergeant Buckley," said Liam, shaking his head. "Sorry, I must have dozed. Swampwater is with the KP now. I didn't know what other orders you would have and no one seemed to know where you were, so . . ." He trailed off as he noticed Hal standing just behind Simon. He nodded, swallowing hard. "Stonebender," he said, stiffly.

"Aster," said Hal.

"Liam," said Simon sharply. The Fire mage started slightly and looked from Hal to Simon. "I need you to focus here. Did Swampwater say anything else about Professor Hightower? Anything that wasn't in his initial statement?"

Liam continued to look from Simon to Hal. "No. No, nothing that mattered. I mean, he wouldn't stop talking about being chained up in that farmhouse, and about his own farm and his mother and such. But nothing about the Elf."

"That's fine, Liam. Just get your after-action report done before you go home. Leave it on my desk and I'll put it in the package for Lt. Gulbrandsen."

"Yes, sir." Liam started to walk toward his desk in the squad room, but Simon stopped him.

"You did good work last night, Liam," said Simon in a low voice. "But I need you to do one more thing. Write up everything you can remember of what Swampwater said to you in the van. Put it in a separate file. Not part of your report to Gulbrandsen." He searched Aster's face. "Can you do that for me?'

Liam nodded. "But—"

"Just for now, Liam," Simon squeezed the young mage's shoulder. "Just for now, we keep this inside the team."

Liam glanced at Hal, and then nodded. He turned away and walked across the busy squad room.

Hal watched the Fire mage leave. "I'm thinking you don't trust Gulbrandsen any more than I do," he said. "What do you think the kid may have heard the Orc say, that you don't want in the official report?"

Simon rubbed his eyes as if to wipe away the fatigue he suddenly felt. "I don't know. Maybe nothing. But Swampwater wasn't picked at random, and the why of it may be lost if the LT takes this investigation away from us. I don't want it buried on the word of some Tintagel flunkey."

"How do you figure the Orc was a specific target? That crazy Elf-bitch was just as ready to spit me, as him."

"Think about what Gripple said, Hal. His farm is down by Fernhill, on the south side of the Reservation. Bowater is north of there, almost halfway to the capitol. And the University is here in Cymbeline. You can bet that a noble like Hightower didn't live in some Bowater tract house that far from her job. More likely, she has an expensive flat in a high-rise on King's Road or on the High Street itself. Why go all the way to Fernhill to take some Orc at random when she could have her pick down in the Hollows just a few blocks west off Tanner Street? She went after Swampwater for a reason, and I want to know why."

Hal grunted the way he always did when Simon made an observation that he himself had missed. "Well then, lad, let's go see what our fearless leader wants with you."

CHAPTER FOUR

They climbed the ancient granite stairs to the upper level. Back in the days of the Magisterium, the floor above the squad room had once been divided into apartments for the King's closest courtiers. Now, those same rooms served as offices and meeting spaces for the bureaucracy that ran the King's Peacekeeper Force. Gulbrandsen's office was small by Command standards, but palatial compared to Simon's tiny cubicle. It included a small antechamber where his secretary, an ancient Dwarf woman with iron gray hair and a similarly iron will, cast a suspicious eye on anyone who entered.

"Good meeting, Mistress Cairn," Simon said with a slight bow. "I believe the Lieutenant is expecting us."

“Aye, Sergeant, he is,” she said, giving Hal a sour look. “But he said nothing about Stonebender.”

“Ah, now, Elvira,” said Hal. “You know I can’t leave this one on his own. Somebody needs to make sure the lad doesn’t embarrass himself in front of your boss.”

“He said nothing about Stonebender,” repeated Elvira, ignoring Hal’s comment. “He has that Elf in there with him already, and it isn’t worth my job to let anyone else in.” She finally looked Hal in the eye. “You can take yourself out into the hall and wait, Haldron Stonebender, or I’ll have words with your Molly about your lack of manners.”

The invocation of his wife deflated Hal’s air of breezy confidence. Simon hid a smile as he touched Hal on the shoulder and nodded. “Full report once I’m done, I promise.”

Gulbrandsen’s main office faced Tanner Street. Rather than the large glass windows of a more desirable space on the King’s Road side of the House, the windows here were glazed arrow slits that let in only a wan winters daylight. Glowglobes hovered in the four corners of the room, making up for the lack of natural illumination, but the bluish light cast by the Fire spells at their hearts was harsh and seemed to wash the color out of the room.

The office itself was richly furnished. The ancient wooden floor had been refinished recently and polished to a high sheen. Expensive bookshelves had been built into two of the walls and filled with leather-bound law books, atlases, and a full first edition set of the *Encyclopedia Magisteria.* Heavy tapestries draped artistically across the shelves concealed a weapons locker and a wet bar. Simon knew Gulbrandsen came from wealth, and although promotion in the Peacekeepers was supposed to be strictly on merit, he couldn't help wondering if family influence at Court might be just as important.

Gulbrandsen was a short man, broad in the shoulders and broader in the waist, with a full head of carefully coiffed black hair and a pencil-thin mustache. Gulbrandsen's business suit was cut to emphasize his shoulders and disguise his paunch, making him look something of a fop, more at home at a dinner party than in a Keeper squad room. He sat behind an antique walnut desk, its legs carved into the intertwined dragon and gryphon of the royal house. On the wall behind him, between the two narrow windows, hung the requisite portrait of King Thorston, constitutional monarch of the Commonwealth of Centralia. Two ornate chairs faced the desk, their high backs obscuring any occupants.

Gulbrandsen looked up as Simon stood in the doorway. The Lieutenant waved him forward.

"Come in Sergeant. We've been waiting for you." He indicated the chair on the left with a graceful sweep of his hand. "Allow me to present His Excellency, Syr Galen Flandyrs, Assistant Undersecretary of Foreign Affairs for the Grey Havens."

A tall Elf rose from the left-hand chair and turned to regard Simon through cold, violet-colored eyes. He had the elegant features and icy bearing of a Highborn Elf. His platinum blond hair was straight, parted in the middle, and fell loosely below his shoulders, his pointed ears framed by two long braids at his temples. He wore a silken green and gold gown rather than a modern suit, which in Simon's experience marked him as a Traditionalist.

The Elf held his hands together just above his waist and executed a perfect greeting bow, just deep enough to avoid insult, but shallow enough to convey superiority.

Simon instantly disliked him.

"Good meeting, Sergeant Buckley," the Elf said with a slight Tintagel accent.

Simon returned the bow. "Good meeting, Mr. Flandyrs," he answered, deliberately omitting the 'my Lord' that the title of *Syr* would merit in polite conversation. The only sign that the Tintagel envoy noticed the insult was a slight downward tic of his lower lip.

"*Lord* Flandyrs is here to discuss the Hightower case," Gulbrandsen said. "I asked you up here to share your preliminary findings with him."

Simon turned to face his Lieutenant. "I don't have all the after-action statements together yet, LT. It's an ongoing investigation. I don't think it would be appropriate for me to say anything until the official reports are filed."

Gulbrandsen waved his hand. "Never mind all that. I just want you to brief His Lordship on the preliminary findings. To keep the Havens in the loop, so to speak. Nothing will be regarded as official until the reports are finalized and signed."

"So, we're having an off-the-record conversation with a civilian about an open investigation?" asked Simon.

Gulbrandsen reddened. "I am asking you to perform a service for our friends from the Havens, Sergeant."

"Yes, sir. Has Captain Axhart approved this, sir?"

"Perhaps we could all sit down and discuss this rationally," said Flandyrs as Gulbrandsen opened his mouth to speak. The Lieutenant closed his mouth again at a wave from the Elf. Simon looked back at Flandyrs who was smiling, but the smile didn't reach his eyes.

"Sit down, Sergeant," ordered Gulbrandsen.

Simon sat, but it was already clear to him where the real power in the office lay.

"You will answer Lord Flandyrs' questions to the best of your ability," Gulbrandsen continued. "That is no longer a request, but an order. You will leave questions of protocol and propriety to me. I'll decide what we say to Captain Axhart, not you. Is that clear?"

"Aye, LT," said Simon. He turned to Flandyrs. "What do you wish to know, sir?"

Flandyrs pulled an ornately decorated handheld mirror from the folds of his robes and muttered the incantation to access its information store. Simon glimpsed a few lines of Elvish script crawling across the mirror's surface before Flandyrs waved a hand and it darkened.

"First, I'd like to commend you and your team on the good work they do enforcing the King's law. Unauthorized magic is a modern plague with wide-ranging consequences, even for those who live outside the Commonwealth jurisdiction."

Simon let slide this veiled reference to the Havens' special status. He didn't need to get into a political discussion with this Elf.

"I'd like to know how the team came to focus on that particular house in Bowater. I assume you obtained a warrant for the armed intrusion?"

"Yes. Justice Severna issued it about eight hours prior to the raid."

"I see," Flandyrs made a show of looking at his mirror again. "But my information suggests that the warrant was for a *search* of the premises, not an armed raid."

"When there is reasonable cause to suspect potential resistance to the search, the team leader has the authority to mount an armed entry." Simon kept his voice calm and deliberate. "I had a reasonable expectation that we were raiding an Azeri bomb-making facility. Past experience with the Azeri Liberation Brigade made me believe we would meet armed resistance."

"Indeed," Flandyrs nodded. "And was Professor Hightower engaged in making bombs?"

"No."

"Then the premise for the search warrant was in error, making the entire operation invalid."

"The fact that we had erroneous information doesn't invalidate the good faith of the warrant." Simon bristled. "And we found Hightower involved in several illegal and dangerous magical activities, fully justifying the raid."

"Do you know these activities were illegal? She was a Professor of Earth Magic at a respected university. As such, she may have had special authorization to conduct experimental conjuring that would otherwise be against the law."

"She had raised golems without a containment fence," said Simon, struggling to remain calm. "She was holding a Commonwealth citizen in chains and was preparing to sacrifice him in a Blood Magic ritual. She attempted to do the same thing to my partner just before my team stopped her."

"With a Fire bolt to the chest," said Flandyrs gravely. "A violation of the Accords. Could your shooter not have used a cold iron bolt? Perhaps Lady Hightower would then still be alive to give her version of events."

"The fact remains that she was resisting our entry with golems under her control. She was holding a citizen against his will, and she threatened immediate harm to one of my team."

"This citizen you mention," Flandyrs consulted his mirror again. "Gripple Swampwater. Is he an Orc?"

"Yes. So what?" Simon felt his patience wearing thin with this nonsense.

"His testimony would be inadmissible in a Haven court without Elven or Human corroboration, so I'm afraid we would have only your word that he was there against his will. Did you actually see Lady Hightower place the chains on the Orc?"

"Haven Court?" Simon's voice rose. "Bowater is on Commonwealth territory, last I looked. This is a King's case."

"But you must know that as a member of the Steward's family, Lady Hightower had diplomatic immunity. She could only be tried in a Haven jurisdiction, whatever her alleged crime."

Simon snorted. "Well, she's dead, so I guess the jurisdiction question is moot."

"Not so," said Flandyrs. "Her immunity extends to issues of slander against the Steward or his family. Any investigation into her actions must be conducted with full disclosure to, and involvement of, the Steward or his designated official." His genuine smile left no doubt as to whom that official would be.

"Slander? Hightower kidnaps and nearly kills a Commonwealth citizen and all you talk about is slander?" Simon shouted. "You sit there playing with your fancy mirror and think you can dictate terms to my team. The guts of that pretty toy of yours are just a tricked-up Ferguson Astral 4. It was probably made in a South Dundaria, Dwarf-owned spell factory and assembled about half a mile from here by Orcs in some Tanner Street sweatshop. Orcs work the land on the estates that let you call yourself Syr. They build the roads and do most of the hard labor all over both the Commonwealth and the Havens. Yeah,

Swampwater was 'just an Orc.' Not worth a second thought to you, much less the protection of the King's Justice. Shit, I'd rather protect one Gripple Swampwater than a hundred self-righteous, pointy-eared prigs like you."

He took a deep breath, seeking calm, and then turned to Gulbrandsen. "You'll have my reports before the fourteenth hour today. Am I dismissed, sir?"

"Damn right you are!" Gulbrandsen snarled. "Turn your reports and any other leads over to Sergeant Killian. You are off this case, as of now. And I'll expect a formal letter of apology to the Undersecretary on my desk by end of watch."

Flandyrs held up a hand. "That won't be necessary, Lieutenant. I deserved Sergeant Buckley's scolding. I would request that he continue as lead investigator. I will, however, require regular updates, and would ask to be able to station an observer here at Wycliffe House to follow the investigation in—what is the modern term? Real time?"

Gulbrandsen looked as if he had bitten an unripe persimmon, but he nodded. "As you wish, Lord Flandyrs." He scowled at Simon. "Get out of here, Sergeant. You must have something else to do."

Simon saluted and turned to leave. He saw the smug smile on Flandyrs' face and it filled him with a mixture of rage and fear. He felt as if he had fallen into very deep water, far from any friendly shore.

CHAPTER FIVE

Simon found Hal pacing the hallway outside Gulbrandsen's office. To the Dwarf's questioning look, he just said, "Not here."

Hal nodded and fell in beside him. Halfway down the stairway to the squad room, Simon stopped and glanced around. They were alone.

"We're going to be side-tunneled on this one," he said quietly. "We'll need to move fast if we're going to get ahead of Gulbrandsen and that snake from Tintagel."

"What happened in there?" asked Hal. "I heard shouting. You—and LT."

"Gulbrandsen was already sucking up to an Elf Lord from the Havens, Syr Galen Flandyrs something or other. Hightower had diplomatic immunity through her connection to the Steward, so this is now an international incident. Flandyrs is going to saddle us with an Elf overseer who will muck up every move we try to make. He says he's an Undersecretary for Foreign Affairs, but I know a Gray Ranger when I meet one."

Hal whistled softly. "Special Enforcement Division? Hightower must have been into some serious shit, if they're involved. You sure he's with the Rangers?"

Simon shrugged. "He didn't come out and say so, but I got a glimpse of the password image on his handheld. I can read Elfscript as well as the next man. It was an SED protocol, I'm certain of that. I saw that image enough when I was seconded to Border Security a few years ago. The Rangers ran things on the Havens side and we had joint briefings once a week. If Flandyrs isn't SED, he's getting his marching orders from them."

"So, why do we care?" Hal asked. "Look, lad, I know you hate leaving cases open, but if the Rangers want this buried, or if they want to take care of it themselves, why should we fight it?"

"A few minutes ago, you were ranting about some 'crazy Elf bitch' trying to spit you with a dagger. Now, you want to let it go?" Simon shook his head. "We have an obligation to make sure this gets done right. She tried to kill Swampwater; she tried to kill you. She had unrestrained golems running around a suburban neighborhood, for Providence sake. What if one of those things had wandered into another house?"

Hal held up a hand. "Not saying you're wrong, just asking why we don't let the Elves handle it."

"Because it's our case. It's our country, not theirs. I'm sick of the Havens ignoring the law whenever it suits their purposes. The SED has no jurisdiction in the Commonwealth, whatever they might think."

A door opened and footsteps sounded a flight beneath them. Simon raised a hand in caution, and Hal nodded.

For centuries before King Otto's Restoration and the establishment of the Commonwealth, the Gray Rangers had been a secret society of assassins, quietly and ruthlessly enforcing the will of the Gray Havens and the Steward of Tintagel. Under the Restoration Accords establishing the Havens as an independent and neutral Elf Homeland, the Rangers were supposedly disbanded, but many of the former assassins became the nucleus of the Special Enforcement Division. The SED was officially a law enforcement arm of the Gray Havens Foreign Service, charged with investigating Elf-related crimes in the Commonwealth and operating under strict Peacekeeper supervision. Unofficially, they were still known as Gray Rangers and were rumored to be active in espionage and political manipulation. No outright assassinations had been traced back to them, but enemies of Tintagel had a way of disappearing with disturbing frequency.

The footsteps faded, and far below, a door opened and closed.

"If you want to dig this tunnel, I'm with you," Hal said quietly. "Just be sure it's not old ghosts you're chasing."

"Alira has been dead for three years," said Simon. "That's history. This is about an illegal conjuring that almost got my best friend killed."

"Right, then," said Hal, grinning. "How do we stick it to Gulbrandsen and his pointy-headed boss?"

"It's his ears that are pointed, not his head. Don't underestimate Flandyrs, Hal. He's too smug by half, like he knows something we don't."

"Have you ever known an Elf who wasn't?" asked Hal. "What's the plan, partner?"

"I'll file Liam's official report, but for now we'll hang on to whatever he learned from Swampwater. I need to get to Caledonia University and have a look at Hightower's office and lab before Flandyrs can have them sterilized. I'd like you to talk to your Orc snitch again. Find out whatever else you can about this delivery Orc and the Azeri. I don't think this is about them, but if they are involved, we need to find out how. Also, ask if there have been any unusual disappearances down in the Hollows; Orcs who have gone missing or not shown up in their usual hangouts over the past few months. I have a feeling this wasn't the first time Hightower performed this ritual."

"Still thinking Swampwater was a special case?"

Simon nodded. "I'll have Liam get the transcript of Gripple's interview with the King's Prosecutor, before it's officially certified. There's more to that story than meets the eye. I sent Jack and Hamish home to get some rest, but we'll fill them in before muster tomorrow morning. They can go down to Fernhill tomorrow and see what they can learn about Swampwater's background." Simon paused and scratched at day-old stubble on his chin. "Maybe I can get the medics to admit him to Charity Hospital for observation on some pretense. That way Jack and Ham can get a look at his place for any connection to the Azeri or to Hightower."

"No warrant?" asked Hal. "Could be a problem if they find anything."

"We can always find a reason to follow any lead that comes of it. I don't want to risk showing our hand to Flandyrs by making this official."

Hal shook his head. "I hope you know what you're doing. Molly won't take kindly to me losing my job over this."

Simon laughed. "I'm not afraid of much, but Molly in a rage would be enough to send me looking for a deep hole to hide in."

Hal laughed as well, but quickly sobered. "Seriously, lad. This could get us both bagged and tagged if we don't mind our bracings."

"I know that, Hal. Watch yourself, and don't hesitate to throw me under the rock pile if it all caves in on us. You have a name and a family to worry about. I'm the team leader and it's my neck, not yours, that should be chopped if I'm wrong."

"Molly can protect the family," said Hal. "And as for the name, the Stonebenders may have noble blood, but we're all just citizens now, don't you know."

Simon gripped his friend's shoulder for a moment, then Hal headed down to the lower level and the stables. Simon continued down the stairs, nodding to a pair of agents coming up, and crossed the squad room to his own office.

Liam sat on thc edge of the couch reading through a sheaf of papers, and looked up as Simon entered. "All done, sir," Liam said, quickly ordering the papers in his hand.

"Thanks, Liam," said Simon as he sat down behind the desk. "And drop the sir. My name is Simon, or Sarge, if you must. You're a member of this team now. We don't stand on formality."

Liam blushed and nodded. He was a tall, slim young man, probably no more than twenty-three. He had light blond hair and pale skin, and his snub nose was covered in freckles, making him look even younger. Simon wondered if the lad had any Elven blood. If he and Alira had ever had a child, he might have grown up to look much like such a one.

Simon shook his head. Hal's comment had unnerved him. He hadn't thought about Alira for some time now.

Not for three days, at least.

"So, what have you learned from our friend Gripple?" Simon asked.

"Not much," Liam said. "He wouldn't stop talking on the way here, but it didn't make much sense. He was most concerned about his mother, but when I asked if she lived with him, he just said, no. He talked about his farm and his livestock. He apparently has no wife, only a woman he pays to cook and clean for him. By the way, I assured him that someone would get in touch with her and tell her he wasn't dead or hiding and that she'd be paid on time. Was that all right?" He paused and Simon nodded. Liam glanced at his notes. "Anyway, he didn't say anything directly about Professor Hightower, but he seems genuinely puzzled as to why she'd want to kill him. He seems to think it was personal, but again won't say why."

"Did he say anything about how he was taken?" asked Simon.

Liam nodded. "It's in his statement to the King's Prosecutor as well. He answered a knock at the door. An Orc he didn't know was there, standing a few steps back from the doorway with both hands held out, the traditional Orc peace greeting. He told Swampwater that there had been an accident on the road and one of his cows may have been hurt. As soon as Swampwater exited his house, some sort of sleep spell hit him, or maybe it was a dart, he doesn't know. He woke up in chains on that stone table. He'd only been there a few hours before we launched our raid."

Simon scratched at his chin. "When I first spoke to him, Gripple said he didn't know anything. Why would he say that? Did Hightower question him? And who was the Orc who lured him out of his house? We didn't encounter anyone on the raid other than Hightower and her golems."

"He didn't say anything about Hightower at all," said Liam, leafing through his notes. "At least not when I was with him, which is strange, since she must have been the one to chain him to the slab. I suppose he might still have been unconscious, but it's odd that he doesn't even ask who she was or why he was taken. He just went on and on about wanting to talk to his mother and worrying about his animals."

"And the Orc who knocked on his door was a stranger to him?" asked Simon.

"So he says."

"Is Gripple still with the KP?"

Liam nodded. "Yes, but they're arranging to have him admitted to Charity for a complete exam. He suffered some cuts and bruises but they want to watch him for any serious head injury."

"That's fortunate," Simon said. "All right, Liam. Thank you. And we'll keep this close inside the team for now. Go and get some rest. We'll muster at seventh hour in the squad room.

"Yes, sir—er, Sarge." He turned to go, but stopped. "What's going on here, Sergeant Buckley? That wasn't a bomb factory and it seems to me that if this Professor just wanted an Orc to work a Blood spell, she could have had her pick down in the Hollows. Why go all the way to Fernhill and lure Swampwater into a trap if she was just going to kill him? Why is he important?"

Simon smiled. The kid was smart. Hopefully, smart enough to keep quiet. "I don't know, Liam. Not yet, anyway. We need to get out fast on this before the diplomats get in our way. I'll have more for you to do tomorrow. Meanwhile, get some sleep and keep your thoughts to yourself."

CHAPTER SIX

By the time Simon got downstairs to the stables, Hal was gone, probably already south of Tanner Street, down in the Orc neighborhood known as the Hollows. It had been over seventy years since the laws restricting Orcs to specific areas of the city had been repealed, but few of them chose to live outside of the Orc-dominated enclaves that had once been their only legal residences.

Simon went first to the armory and checked out his personal sidearm—a Czech and Hawley spring-powered needle thrower—and a spare magazine of sleeper darts. He muttered an incantation and activated the Earth spell that powered the throwing spring in the weapon's amber and oak grip. He tucked the needler into his back pocket and walked to where his flyer was parked.

He climbed aboard the saddle, unlocked the steering vane, and spoke the words to activate the Air spell. The flyer rose on its column of compressed air and the steering vanes unfolded. The canopy slid forward, the clear bubble of glass that covered the saddle protecting him from the elements.

He turned the flyer toward the ramp and pushed the power stick forward with his thumb. The flyer accelerated rapidly as it climbed the ramp and sped into the bright winter sunlight.

Simon slid in and out through the Tanner Street traffic. He turned north on a side street until he reached King's Road and crossed the green belt marking the edge of the Government district. Once out of the official no-fly zone, he pushed the flyer into the air. At one hundred feet, he soared above the city, bypassing the crowded, twisting streets of North Anna, the traditional Guild district. Floating spell-powered mirrors illuminated the streets with continuous advertisements for everything from toothpaste, to the latest fashions, to personal security services. Foot traffic below him was heavy this afternoon. The weather was fine for midwinter and people seemed to be taking advantage of it to get some shopping done.

Caledonia University occupied a compact campus on the north side of the capitol. The main buildings dated back to the beginning of the Magisterium, nearly 900 years past. Newer construction mimicked the dome-and-spire Elven style of the earlier buildings but with modern methods and materials. Thick foliage grew around the base of the cold iron fence that encircled the campus. Neatly manicured lawns and fanciful topiary, crisscrossed by gravel paths, filled the spaces between the college buildings.

No air or ground vehicles were permitted inside the campus fence, so Simon landed the flyer on the top floor of a public stable about two blocks from the main gate. He paid the attendant the required fee, even though the Peacekeeper emblem on the canopy of his flyer could have ensured free parking anywhere in the Commonwealth. Simon was glad to spare the few coins. The attendant was an Orc and his pay was likely a meager percentage of the parking fees he collected.

Simon inquired at the concierge kiosk next to the gate as to the location of Professor Hightower's office. A pretty young woman with pink and green highlights in her blond hair that shifted and rippled whenever she moved, consulted a small mirror mounted next to the door and pointed to a path on Simon's right.

"Just along there, sir," she said. "Third building, which would be Noyes Lab, second floor."

Simon thanked her and complimented her on her hair.

She smiled. "It's a spell I designed for my Marketing 202 class. It was originally for a paper business card, but I adapted it for hair coloring. I'm trying to sell it to one of the big cosmetic companies, but so far no luck."

"Well, I like it," said Simon, a little dismayed at an attractive young woman calling him 'sir.' Did he look that old?

She nodded politely and returned to studying her handheld. Simon sighed inwardly and set off down the path.

The young woman's directions were good. In less than two minutes, he stood in front of a squat stone building that looked more Dwarfish than Elven. A brass plate next to the double door read, *Noyes Laboratory, Department of Experimental Earth Magic.*

Simon pushed open the glass and steel door and entered a wide, high-ceilinged hall. A broad staircase directly in front of him led to the upper floors while corridors opened to the right and the left. A low dais in the middle of the hall held a directory and map. Simon found the name *Hightower, Glendowyn* on the directory. The map informed him that office 246 was one flight up and midway down the right-hand corridor.

He found the right door easily enough. It was an old-fashioned oak affair with a large frosted glass window occupying its upper half and the words *Glendowyn Hightower, Professor of Earth Magic* etched into the glass in black letters. To the right, attached to the doorframe, was a slate on which were etched the Professor's office hours. A line was drawn through the times and the words "On Sabbatical" had been hand-written across the slate.

Simon tried the brass doorknob, but it was locked, not that he expected anything else. He had a set of fine steel lock picks in the inner pocket of his jacket, but hesitated to use them. His marginal sword skill was better than his lock-picking ability. Even if he could get in, it would likely take more time than he had, before someone noticed his efforts. He heard the scrape of wood on stone behind him and turned to see a balding Orc opening a door at the far end of the corridor. He wore a one-piece brown coverall and held a mop in one hand. A ring of keys dangled from his belt.

"Professor's not here," the Orc said as he dragged a wheeled bucket from the other side of the door. "Gone 'til Midsummer's Eve."

"Yes," said Simon. "So I see. Do you have the key to her office?"

"Might." The Orc eyed him suspiciously. "Who's asking?"

"I'm Sergeant Simon Buckley, King's Agent." Simon produced his badge and held it out for the Orc to see. "Are you the custodian here?"

"Aye." The Orc abandoned his mop and bucket and approached Simon. He was tall for an Orc; his head even with Simon's shoulder, and his arms and shoulders almost as broad as a Human. His black hair grew in random tufts scattered about his scalp, but was cropped so close that he appeared bald. His hooked nose and small narrow chin were typical for his race, and his black eyes glittered with cunning. He examined Simon's badge carefully.

"Name's Blackpool. Joby Blackpool. Janitor for the second floor. Professor's not here. Ain't been, for near two months, leastways, not official-like."

"Has she been in the office recently?" Simon asked.

"Oh, off and on." Blackpool nodded. "She pops in 'bout once a week to get her mail and do some work."

"When did you last see her?"

"Night before last," said Blackpool, folding his arms. "Why do you want to know? Professor Hightower's a Lady, right and proper. Why would the Keepers be sniffing around her?"

"Professor Hightower was killed last night under suspicious circumstances," said Simon. He didn't say that she was the one under suspicion. Blackpool jerked as if struck but recovered quickly.

"Dead, you say," he said. "How? Who done for her?"

"That's what I'm looking into," answered Simon. "I need to check her office for contact information, anyone who might know where she spent her time and what she has been doing for the past few weeks. Can you help me?"

Blackpool rubbed his scalp. "Don't see how. I mean, she were nice enough for an Elf; never acted all high-and-mighty the way some do, but she never said mor'n a dozen words to me, ever."

"I mean, would you unlock this door for me." Simon jiggled the doorknob for emphasis. "I could get a Peacekeeper locksmith in to do it, but that would take time and my LT wants results right now."

"I dunnow," Blackpool fingered his key ring. "Maybe I should check with the Dean."

"You probably should. I went to his office first, but his secretary said he'd gone home for the day," Simon lied. "Why don't we mirror him and ask him to come back." He pulled out his handheld and made a show of activating the image spell.

"Now hold on," said Blackpool, rattling his keys. "No need to bother the man at home. You're a proper Peacekeeper with a badge and all. Can't be no harm in helping out. I better stay and watch over things, though. The Professor is real particular about any of her stuff being moved."

Simon was about to point out that Hightower was well beyond caring if any of her things were moved, but the suspicious look in Blackpool's eye made him stop.

In a few seconds, Blackpool had unlocked the door and opened it. Simon fingered his badge and spoke the incantation to suppress any Warding spells Hightower may have had on the door. He didn't want to alert campus security and have to explain himself to someone with more authority than the janitor. He entered the office and felt a slight pinging sensation in his scalp as the counterspell removed the wards.

It was a large space made cramped by piles of crates, stacks of books, and mounds of parchment and paper all over the floor. Shelves lined the walls, all overflowing with books and scrolls, bottles of colored stones, bundles of sticks representing all of the Noble woods used in spell casting, and various strange figurines from a dozen cultures and magical traditions. Hightower's desk occupied the center of the room, almost hidden behind a stack of books and an inactive widescreen magic mirror. The desktop itself was surprisingly neat and clear, holding only a blotter, pen and ink, and a stack of spell parchments.

Simon checked the desk first. The top drawer was unlocked; it contained an address book, several candles, a small vial of quicksilver, tightly stoppered, and a few pencils. The bottom drawer was locked. Simon glanced up, but Blackpool was still watching him. He didn't try to force the lock, but concentrated instead on the desktop.

He spoke a startup incantation to the mirror but it flashed a request for a password and he shut it down. He'd have to get the tech mages to work on it once it was officially logged into evidence.

The desk blotter was spotted and stained, but held no discernible writing. He lifted it, but there was nothing under it. He rifled through the stack of spell parchments, but they were blank. He was about to set them down when he noticed some faint impressions on the top sheet. He opened the drawer and extracted a pencil. A light rubbing of the pencil across the sheet of parchment revealed several symbols etched into it, probably impressions from writing on another sheet on top of the one he was holding. He recognized one of the symbols from the floor of the farmhouse. Ignoring Blackpool's accusing stare, he folded the parchment and put it in his pocket.

He got up and surveyed the rest of the room. He took out his handheld and used the imaging feature to capture pictures of the office and its contents from several perspectives.

He turned to the shelves. Most of the books and scrolls dealt with arcane aspects of Earth magic, but there was a copy of McHenry's *Peerage of the Gray Havens* and Johnstone's *Evolution of the Races,* both recent editions. Here and there were small artifacts and figurines, most of which Simon recognized as fetishes from early Human tribes and a few from Orc lore. Next to an onyx statue of the Orc god Durlash, he noticed a small box covered with strange writing printed on its top and sides.

It was obviously a commercial product, made of cheap cardboard with a folded top that had a tab for opening and closing it. But the writing, block letters printed in red ink, was unlike anything Simon had ever seen. The alphabet vaguely resembled Dwarfish runes but Simon did not recognize it or the language. The printing and format suggested a sales package, mass-produced and intended to advertise whatever was inside. Whatever that might be.

Simon opened the lid. Inside were neat rows of round metal discs separated by cardboard partitions. In the center of each brass-colored disc was a small circle of silver-colored metal with a slight dimple in its center. He took out one of the discs and found that it was actually the end of a short brass cylinder about the same diameter and length as the middle joint of his little finger. It was tipped with a rounded piece of gray-colored metal that looked like lead. The cylinder reminded him of something familiar. He held it in his palm, thinking for a moment until it came to him. It looked like a miniature version of the copper-tipped Fire bolts that they used in their D'Stangs. But this thing was less than a quarter the size of that ammunition, and seemed to be made of brass and lead, the two most magically inert metals known to man. Lead inhibited any spell at all, and brass was the specific counter to Air or Fire casting. Who would make ammunition guaranteed to be totally inert?

Simon dropped the small cylinder into his pocket along with the parchment. He lifted the statue of Durlash. It was cheap glass, not the solid onyx that it initially appeared to be, and he turned it over. Etched on the bottom was a logo that read *Clearwater Glass*, probably the company that had made it. A crudely scratched series of numbers ran across the bottom of the statue below the logo. They weren't as well defined as the company name and appeared to have been etched by hand after the glass had been polished. Simon recognized the numbers as a mirror locus and used the pencil he had taken from the desk to write it on the back of the parchment.

He returned the statue to the shelf, placing it as close to its original position as he could. He took one last look around and then started for the door. Blackpool, still and silent while Simon searched, leaned against the doorjamb, his eyes on Simon. The look was far shrewder than it had been earlier, filled with an intelligence Simon had not noticed before.

"Find anything?" the Orc asked.

"Maybe," said Simon. "I'll have to check a few things back at Wycliffe House. You can lock up now, Mr. Blackpool. And don't let anyone else in here until an official Crime Scene Analysis squad gets here, understood?"

Blackpool's eyes blazed for a second, then a veil seemed to drop over them. "O'course Sergeant. I ain't stupid. I seen plenty of Keeper shows on the mirror."

Simon nodded and turned back toward the main stairway. He felt Blackpool's gaze boring into his back the whole time.

CHAPTER SEVEN

It was nearly sixteenth hour by the time Simon returned to Wycliffe House and settled into the chair in his office. The official reports for Gulbrandsen were still on the corner of his desk. He flipped through them one last time, corrected a time notation in Hal's report, and then called for an office messenger to take the package up to Gulbrandsen's office. Tired as he was, Simon doubted he'd be able to control his temper if the Lieutenant decided to dress him down over the meeting with Flandyrs.

Hal wasn't in the squad room but had left a note for Simon that he'd talked with his sources down in the Hollows and would report his leads tomorrow. He'd apparently gone home for the day, because the note ended with the suggestion that Simon do the same.

Simon rubbed his eyes for the hundredth time that afternoon. Gods, he was tired. He shuffled the papers on his desk, arranging them in some semblance of a neat pile and rose to leave, intent on taking Hal's advice. He remembered the parchment and the strange cylinder in his pocket. He took them out and dropped them into the top drawer of his desk, locking it with the small key on the key ring from his pocket. He patted the back pocket of his breeches. He'd have to return the needler before he left Wycliffe House or the armorer would be sending him nasty missives in the morning.

"State secrets, Sergeant Buckley?" said a crystal-clear voice. Simon looked up and his heart stopped for a moment.

Alira? But this was impossible. Alira was three years dead. The Elf-woman at the entrance to his cubicle was very much alive.

"I didn't mean to startle you," she said. "I'm Sylvie Graystorm. I've been assigned to work with you on the situation with Glendowyn Hightower."

She was not tall for an Elf, just about Simon's height. She wore her platinum-blond hair in a short straight cut that framed her face and fell only to the nape of her neck. A single black onyx comb swept her hair back over her right ear. Her face had the typical sharp features of the High Elves, but softened by a ready smile and a blush of modern cosmetics. She wore a dark blue business suit of matching calf-length skirt and short jacket over a silky grey blouse. Her emerald eyes swept up and down Simon's frame.

"You are Simon Buckley, are you not?" she said. "I was told I'd find you here."

"I, uh, yes, I'm Buckley," Simon stammered. Get it together, lad, he admonished himself. She's not Alira, and you have to stay sharp here. He bowed. "Good meeting, Lady Graystorm."

She laughed and extended her hand. "You can forget the m'Lady crap. I'm the sixth daughter and no more likely to get the family title than to sprout wings and fly. My name is Sylvie."

Simon shook her hand. Her grip was firm and strong. Surprisingly, she had calluses around the thumb and first finger. Must spend a lot of time holding a sword. "Nevertheless, you are a Graystorm. Your father is cousin to the Steward, and this investigation involves a Hightower of some importance."

Sylvie frowned. "Look, Sergeant Buckley, we can do this the hard way, if you prefer. Yes, Glendowyn Hightower was my *ghir*-cousin, related by marriage, not by blood. And yes, I was chosen to be the official liaison on this case because of that relationship. But that was only to reassure the Steward and certain factions within the Haven Council that the investigation would be thorough and discreet." She reached into an inner pocket of her jacket and produced a small red leather case. She flipped it open and displayed a silver badge. "I'm a Ranger with the SED. My job is to provide support for your investigation and assist wherever Haven resources might be useful."

"And report to Galen Flandyrs on our progress," said Simon, in the same official tone.

Her eyes flashed. “I’m no puppet for that self-important jackass.” She sighed. “He expects me to make regular reports, yes. But that doesn’t mean I won’t do my job.”

“And what is your job, Lady Graystorm?” Simon asked.

“I’m a Ranger,” she snapped. “Despite what you may believe, we want to find out what Hightower was doing, as much as you do. There have been disturbing rumors of meetings between Elves living in the Commonwealth and highly-placed Orcs from the Southern Reservation as well as with Overseers from the Hollows with ties to the Azeri.”

Simon leaned on the corner of his desk and rubbed his chin. “Was Hightower one of those Elves?”

She smiled in a disarming way. “Why, Sergeant Buckley, are you asking for information?”

Simon nodded. “All right, Ranger Graystorm—Sylvie. We’ll see how this works out. We share information, but I’m in charge of the investigation. I’ll decide what leads we follow. Are we clear?”

She offered her hand again. “Agreed. And really, Simon, I’m not here to mess up your investigation. I’ll keep my reports to Flandyrs vague and brief. If you like, I’ll even let you review them first.”

Simon took her hand and held it for a bit longer this time. Why, he was not sure. “As you say. Was Hightower involved with the Reservation leadership? Or with the Azeri?”

Gently but firmly, Silvie disengaged her hand. “I’m not sure about the Azeri. I understand there was some hint of a plot to make Fire bombs at that farmhouse you raided, but we have no information linking Hightower to the Brigades. She was a frequent visitor to the Southern Reservation, though. She published a paper recently on ancient Earth magic practices among the Orc shamans. It didn't generate much interest at the Academy, although I gather it was well received by her Human colleagues at Caledonia."

"The Orc she had set up for the Blood magic ritual has a small holding just outside the Reservation boundary down by Fernhill," said Simon. "His name is Gripple Swampwater."

"Swampwater?" Sylvie cocked her head. "I wonder if he's kin to old Gran Swampwater? She was one of the shamans that Hightower cited in her paper."

"That's one of the leads we'll need to follow. I have my partner asking around the Hollows through his informants about this Azeri connection, as well as any rumors about Orcs going missing from their usual neighborhoods. It's possible Swampwater wasn't the first Orc to end up on that slab."

"What was Hightower doing in a suburban wasteland like Bowater?" Sylvie asked. "Her family maintains a penthouse suite for her on the High Street not five blocks from the University."

"That's where you might be able to help," said Simon. "Can you get access to Haven property records? The farmhouse is owned by someone from there but under the Accords, I can't access the records without a court order."

She nodded. "That I can do. What about the forensic reports? Has there been any word from the Crime Scene Analysis unit or the coroner?"

"Nothing official," Simon replied. "What specifically did you want? I was there, you know. Hightower was killed by a single shot from a D'Stang bolt thrower loaded with Fire bolts. We were fighting golems under her control."

"Rein in, Simon," she said, holding up a hand. "No need to get defensive. I think the shooting was justified. I meant, did the CSA mages find any evidence of Fire magic? Any sign of any other presence in the farmhouse? Was she also making bombs for the Azeri, or just killing the random Orc?"

Simon smiled. "No word from CSA, but my team didn't find anyone else in the house. And I don't believe Swampwater was taken at random."

"Nor do I," Sylvie said, nodding. "Why go all the way to Fernhill when there are plenty of down-on-their-luck Orcs right here in Cymbeline?"

In spite of himself, Simon found himself liking this Elf-woman. Her resemblance to Alira was disturbing, but she was definitely a different person. Alira had been smart and strong-willed, but softer-spoken and gentler of spirit. Sylvie Graystorm was all business, and obviously very good at what she did.

He caught himself staring at the slim Ranger, only half-aware that she was speaking to him. He rubbed his eyes. "Sorry, could you say that again? I'm really tired. Not enough sleep in the last day or two."

"I was just saying that you looked exhausted and perhaps we could continue in the morning," she said, smiling. "And whoever she was, she left her mark on you."

"Say what?"

"The Elf-woman who loved you. The signs are all over you." She smiled again and turned her back, walking away with the smooth grace that only an Elf could manage.

"We muster in the squad room at seventh hour," he called after her.

She acknowledged with an elegant wave of her hand, but did not look back.

CHAPTER EIGHT

Simon slept soundly that night, more soundly than he had in months. As always, he dreamed of Alira, but the dreams were filled with peace and comfort, not terror and despair. He left his flat early and was at his tiny office before sixth hour, feeling refreshed. He found the preliminary report from the coroner already on his desk. He sipped a mug of hot coffee as he read.

The report affirmed that Glendowyn Hightower had been killed by the explosive force of a #3 Fire bolt that had detonated approximately three finger breadths beneath her sternum, exploding her heart and major blood vessels. Death had been instantaneous. The curious finding in the report was that Hightower was likely already dying before the bolt hit her. She was profoundly anemic. Her bone marrow was heavily scarred and was no longer producing the blood cells her body needed to sustain life or fight infection. The coroner stated the condition was similar to White Blood Disease found in Humans, but unknown in Elves or Dwarves. He offered no explanation for it.

Hal arrived next. He dropped a bundle wrapped in a checkered cloth on Simon's desk before assuming his usual slump on the couch. He slurped loudly at a steaming mug of tea.

"The package is from Molly," Hal said. "She's worried you aren't eating enough."

Simon opened the bundle and the smell of fresh-baked oatcakes filled the office. He loved Molly Stonebender's oatcakes. They were thick and chewy, packed with raisins and dried cherries and glazed with butter and brown sugar. He bit into one and found it still warm.

"My thanks to Molly," he mumbled around a mouthful.

"Hold on," said Hal, standing up to pluck a cake out of the bundle. "Don't hog all of them."

For a few minutes they didn't talk, only ate and sipped from their mugs. Finally, Simon swallowed the last bite of his oatcake and said, "I met our minder from the Gray Havens last night before I went home."

"Oh?" Hal took another bite of oatcake. "What's he like? Typical self-righteous Elven prig?"

"Not exactly," Simon said with a smile. "She's an SED Ranger, and a lot smarter than Flandyrs."

"She, is it? And a pretty one from the look on your face. Have a care, lad. Remember what I said about old ghosts."

"I'm solid, Hal," said Simon. "She's a Ranger, SED; and Flandyrs is too. I don't trust her, but she may be useful."

Hal just grunted and sipped his tea.

Hamish and Jack came in together, a study in contrasts. Hamish was tall, lean, and fair; red hair, clean-shaven, corded muscles showing through the black shirt, breeches and hose of his working uniform. Jack Ironhand stomped along beside him, dark, heavily bearded and broad-shouldered, even for a Dwarf. Hamish had a wife and three children, and house in a suburb not that different from Bowater. Jack was a bachelor, still living in the Darrowdowns with his mother and younger sisters. And yet the two were inseparable on the job, such that other teams would half-jokingly ask for Jack-n-Ham, as if they were one person.

Liam followed them in, a couple of steps behind, reading something on his handheld. He was in blacks like the rest of the team, with the red crossbelt that identified him as a Fire mage. A small pouch of aquamarine dust and two sticks of rowan wood hung from his belt in place of the baton and sidearm holster the others wore.

Hal moved over and Jack sat down next to him on the couch. Hamish helped himself to one of Simon's last two oatcakes, earning him a glare from Hal and a shrug of the shoulders from Jack. He leaned against the wall, munching on the cake. Liam stood in the doorway, not quite at attention, but not completely relaxed.

Simon checked his timepiece; ten minutes before the seventh hour.

"Good meeting, everyone," he said. "I hope you all slept well. We have a lot to do and may not have much time to do it." The team muttered their greetings. "Here's what we have so far: the raid was a bust as far as any Azeri connection was concerned. The Elf Ham shot was a Highborn named Glendowyn Hightower, yes, *that* Hightower, which is why this is now an international incident. The LT has already had a visit from the Tintagel Foreign Office and for now we have to assume he's giving them access to everything we send his way. They may even be calling the shots where he's concerned, so from now on, any order he gives you, any task he assigns you, you bring to me first. Understood?" That brought a pair of 'aye's' from Jack and Ham, a grunt from Hal and a brisk 'yes Sarge' from Liam.

"Does that include me, too?" Sylvie Graystorm appeared at Liam's elbow, and the young Fire mage jumped. Simon looked up and stopped talking, stopped breathing for a half-second. She was dressed in an SED uniform, charcoal gray breeches and hose with short black boots, a silver-gray shirt with black cross braces that offset her trim breasts. On her left side hung a scabbard and slim rapier with a finely wrought silver hilt, a Gallinberg Whirlwind. A serious dueling weapon, notoriously light and strong, very expensive, and well-used if the wear on the leather grip was any indication. From her right shoulder hung a black leather pouch, also finely made and worn smooth with heavy use. A short gray jacket was draped casually over her shoulders.

"Everyone, this is Ranger Sylvie Graystorm, Special Enforcement Division," said Simon, recovering his composure. "She's been assigned by the Gray Havens Consul, *Syr* Galen Flandyrs, as liaison to our investigation. And to answer your question, Ranger Graystorm, I have no authority to order you to do anything, but there's an old Dwarven proverb that says, 'Pick and shovel should work together.'"

Sylvie smiled. "Still the hard-ass attitude? As you say, Sergeant Buckley. My job is to help wherever I can."

An uncomfortable silence fell over the rest of the team as Simon and Sylvie regarded each other. Finally, Simon nodded. "My apologies. I was ungracious. Your help is welcome."

Sylvie smiled again. "I have the information you asked for last night."

"Good. Let me make some assignments for the team and then we'll hear what you've found." Sylvie nodded and Simon went on. "Hal, what did you find out from your contact down in the Hollows?"

Hal took a sip of his tea and gave Sylvie a hard look until Simon gave him a small nod.

"Snick still swears his cousin delivered the makings of Fire bombs to that particular farm house. The cousin isn't in the Brigade, but is close to some old boyos from the neighborhood who moved up from smash and grab robbery to collections for the Azeri mob rackets. They're known to freelance as muscle for hire and have done a bit of kneecap bashing for a Brigade Overseer who runs a protection racket on the side."

"Names?" Simon asked.

Hal consulted a small notebook. "Blackpool and Gorski. Snick didn't know if those are family names or aliases. No other info, but I've got the records fellas looking for priors."

"Blackpool is the name of the janitor over at the University who let me into Hightower's office," mused Simon. "I wonder if there's any connection." He turned to Liam. "That's one of your jobs, Liam. The CSA teams will be going through Hightower's office and lab. I want you there observing. I know she worked in Earth magic, not Fire, but you'll be better able than any of the rest of us to recognize something in her stuff that isn't level and square." Aster nodded. "See if you can talk to the janitor on the second floor, an Orc named Joby Blackpool. Find out if he's from the Southern Rez, or if he has family there or down Fernhill way. But be careful. He's smarter than he seems and we don't want to tip off Gorski and Blackpool if there is some relationship."

"What about us, Sarge?" asked Jack.

"I want you and Ham to go down to Fernhill. Search Swampwater's house. Talk to his cleaning lady. Find out who he spends time with, which tavern he frequents, whether he has any dealings with the Rez. Also, see what you can find out about his mother. He's been awfully keen to talk to her. Is he just a dutiful son, or is she into something that got him snatched by Hightower?"

"Aye, Sarge," they said in unison.

Simon turned to Sylvie. "Ranger Graystorm—Sylvie, what did you find out about the farmhouse?"

She didn't quite smirk at his stumble over using her first name. "You were right about it being owned by someone in the Havens. The property is registered to Farele Sindarin, an Elf from a minor house, who lives in Portalis near the Borderlands."

"Any connection to Hightower, or to the Steward?" asked Simon.

"Not directly. But the name tickled a branch with me so I asked my sister about it. She's the family gossip and would know why I recognized the name Sindarin. It turns out old Farele's grandson married a *ghir*-sister of an old family friend, then ran off with a Human and emigrated to the Commonwealth. Old Farele suffered some sort of brain seizure when he learned about it and has been living in the Green Dream most of the time ever since."

Simon knew what she meant, but the rest of the team looked puzzled. High Elves aged only over geologic timeframes and were immune to most diseases. They could be killed by the same violence that killed Humans, but if injured seriously enough, they could go into a kind of coma or deep sleep, the Green Dream. Some recovered, but many became lost in the dream and didn't awaken, nor did they die.

"He hasn't managed his own affairs for a good five years." Sylvie concluded

"So the house is a dead end," said Simon.

"Not exactly, but I'm not sure how it connects to Hightower," said Sylvie. "Inside the Gray Havens, his family manages his estate, but a Cymbeline legal firm, Greenleaf and Handfield, sees to his

Commonwealth holdings. Up until he was appointed to the Foreign Service, the head of security for that firm was none other than Galen Flandyrs."

"What does the law firm have to do with Hightower? And does Flandyrs know anything about the house?" asked Liam. Simon nodded, having thought of the same questions.

"I don't know," replied Sylvie. "The firm represents a number of Families from the Havens. It has both Elven and Human partners. Flandyrs left the security job before Sindarin became incapacitated. In fact, Farele's affairs in the Commonwealth are being handled by a Human advocate in the firm, not even a junior partner."

"So, interesting, but still a dead end as far as Hightower is concerned," said Simon.

"Maybe not," said Liam. He seemed to shrink when the rest of the team turned eyes on him. "I, uh, well, just because we don't see a direct connection, doesn't anybody else think it's odd that the same Elf who's trying to hijack this investigation, used to work for the people who manage things for the old Elf who owns the crime scene?" He blushed and turned to Sylvie. "No offense intended, m'Lady," he stammered.

"None taken." She favored him with a smile. "And just what I was thinking. I don't like coincidences either."

"Do you think you can get any information out of the advocate who manages Sindarin's affairs?" Simon asked Sylvie.

"Oh, I can be very persuasive," she said. "My family does a lot of business in the Commonwealth. If I drop a hint that the Graystorms may be looking for new representation, I'll probably get an invitation to lunch."

"Later," said Simon. "I want you with Hal and me."

"Doing what?" Sylvie and Hal said at the same time. Hal glared and Sylvie laughed. Simon ignored both reactions.

"First, I want another look at that farmhouse before the CSA mages issue their reports, in the daylight this time. Then I want to follow up on Blackpool and Gorski, find out where they are now and see if there's any link to either Hightower or the Bowater house."

"Why bring the Elf?" asked Hal.

"Her name is Ranger Graystorm, Hal," Simon said levelly. "I'm ranking Keeper here, and I say so. That's why."

Hal grunted and folded his arms, but said nothing more. A flicker of anger and maybe something darker colored Sylvie's face, and then was quickly replaced by what Simon thought of as the resting Elf face; bored, indifferent, and slightly haughty.

"You all have your assignments," said Simon. "Stay in touch on the team FS net and we'll muster back here at seventeenth hour." The rest of the team stood and filed out of the office.

"I'll get us a sled," said Hal. Simon nodded and Hal walked out, staring daggers at Sylvie the entire time.

CHAPTER NINE

Simon unlocked his desk drawer and took out the spell parchment he had found in Hightower's office. Sylvie stood at the doorway to his cubicle, still expressionless, but fell in beside him as he set off after Hal.

"I understand you have no reason to trust me," she said quietly as they started down the stairs to the stables. "But I hoped I'd buy at least a little good will by finding out who owns the farmhouse. Why not follow that lead? What purpose does it serve to keep me under your eye all the time? Even if I were spying for Flandyrs, what could I tell him?"

Simon stopped halfway down the stairs and she did as well. "First, I want to go over that farmhouse in the daylight. As good as the CSA mages are, they don't see things as part of an investigation, or make connections to other information. The more eyes on the scene the better, and a fresh pair of eyes may see something Hal and I would pass over." She smiled at the implied confidence. "Second, I want free rein in that house for as long as possible. If you start poking around Sindarin's affairs here in the Commonwealth, and Flandyrs *is* involved, he'll know we're looking at him and shut down any new veins we might uncover. And finally, no, I don't trust you. Not yet, anyway."

"So there's hope for the future?" she asked.

Simon wasn't sure if she was being sincere or sarcastic, but just said, "We'll see."

By the time they reached the stable level, Hal had commandeered a four-passenger sled and was waiting for them near the exit ramp. Simon stopped at the armorer and checked out his sidearm and the Bonecleaver. He holstered the needler on his belt and stowed the sword next to the front passenger seat. Sylvie climbed into the rear seat behind Simon and laid her Whirlwind across her lap. Hal had decided to forgo a hand weapon and had his short-hafted, double-bladed ax strapped to his back.

Hal glanced at Simon and at his nod muttered the incantation to activate the spell. The sled rose on its column of compressed air and glided up the exit ramp.

Street traffic was heavy on Tanner with all manner of lorry sledges, flyers, and passenger sleds crowding the ancient cobblestone street. A mix of bicycles, tricycles, and the odd steam-powered wheeled vehicle added to the confusion. The city had been laid out two hundred years before the Magical Revolution made the mass production of spell-powered vehicles possible. Tanner Street was a horse and wagon boulevard hopelessly inadequate to the modern crush of traffic. Hal reached out to activate the Keeper siren, which might have allowed them to force a path through the snarl, but Simon stopped him.

"No hurry, we can wait it out. Sirens just attract attention and we don't need that," he said.

It took almost twenty minutes to cover the half-mile to the entrance to the KR34, the main southbound King's Highway out of Cymbeline. Traffic on the controlled-access highway was still heavy, but at least it was moving. Hal shifted into the high-speed lane and opened the sled up. In less than an hour, he was guiding it through the wide suburban streets of Bowater.

Just beyond the faux-Elven gatehouse and fence of yet another tract of look-alike single-family homes, Hal turned down a narrow hedge-lined road that bordered a community greenbelt. The road ended in a half-acre plot surrounded by tall old oak trees, their bare midwinter branches still thick enough to obscure the view of the surrounding subdivision.

The farmhouse looked less sinister and more dilapidated in the daylight. Simon, Hal, and Sylvie climbed out of the sled and walked slowly around the perimeter of the clearing. The foundations of an old barn poked up through brown, ankle-high grass about ten yards from the back of the house. The wood and stone of the barn had long since rotted away or been scavenged for other purposes, leaving only a rubble-filled ring of flagstone and a few scrubby bushes.

The farmhouse itself was sturdy enough, built of dark flagstone and heavy oak. The roof rose to a sharp peak and was shingled with split cedar shakes. The eaves sagged a bit along one side, as if the wall had bowed outward there. The exposed wood of the eaves and window frames was gray and weathered with only occasional forlorn flakes of some ill-defined green paint clinging to them here and there. The few windowpanes that remained unbroken were covered with grime. Most had been boarded up so long ago that the weathering of the boards matched that of the window frames.

The front door hung open, its lock shattered by Liam's Fire spell. Orange rope crisscrossed the doorway and a sign tacked to the remnants of the doorjamb read: CRIME SCENE. NO ENTRY WITHOUT PEACEKEEPER AUTHORIZATION.

Simon rubbed his badge and spoke the release incantation, then waited as the Warding spells deactivated with a slight pinging sensation that he felt down his spine. He unhooked the rope and let it drop to the ground.

"I want a quick survey, starting with the front hallway and ending in the back room. We'll each look at the rooms independently, then compare notes, agreed?" Hal and Sylvie nodded. "Hal, take the sitting room I cleared first; Sylvie, start in the room to the left; I'll cover the door and the hallway."

Over the next twenty minutes, they each went through the rooms, checking the corners, examining the floors, checking the few items of furniture that remained. Simon paid close attention to the corner where he had surprised the first golem, but other than a dark stain on the floor where the thing had melted, he found nothing. Neither Hal nor Sylvie found anything of interest either.

The door to the back room stood open. Simon entered first and immediately noticed the smell. The rank odor of death and burned flesh still filled the space around them.

The room looked different in the daylight, larger and brighter than it had two nights earlier. During the raid, Simon had not noticed the row of narrow windows set high near the ceiling. They let in the diffuse light of the overcast winter day outside. Orange evidence tags were scattered about the floor, attached to places where the CSA team had taken images or collected samples. Simon cautioned Hal and Sylvie not to disturb them. Sylvie nodded and Hal gave him a sour look for pointing out the obvious.

The area had been a combination kitchen and living area when the house had been inhabited. A squat, wood-fired iron stove stood opposite the door, its flue vented through the thick stone wall. To its right stood a tall set of pantry shelves and to its left was a back door, presumably leading to the yard and the barn.

The floor was planked with worn oak boards, skillfully fitted but now splintered and warped in some places. The stone slab where Gripple had been chained was still up, held by the windlass and the iron locking bars bolted to its surface. The strange symbols were still there. Simon bent close to examine them. Sylvie leaned over his shoulder and gasped softly. Simon looked up at her.

"What?" he asked.

"These symbols," she said. "They're ancient."

Simon ran a finger around one of the symbols carved into the granite of the slab. The edge was smooth, either intentionally polished or worn smooth by countless years of exposure. From the looks of the slab, he doubted anyone had polished the surface.

"How ancient? Can you read them?"

Sylvie shook her head. "I wouldn't speak them even if I could read them. They're in the language of the ancient Orcs, from before the time of the Havens."

"How do you know that?" Simon asked, rising to his feet.

"There are copies of similar inscriptions in the library at the Academy in Tintagel. They're Blood magic runes, used by the old order Orc shamans, but what they mean is beyond me."

Simon nodded. "Right. We knew they were used in Blood rituals. The CSA guys imaged them as part of the crime scene documentation. When we get back to the House, I want you to get copies from them and see if anyone at your Academy can read them."

Hal meanwhile had made a circuit of the room and called out to Simon from the far-left corner. "I think I found another door over here. Don't know if those geniuses from Crime Scene noticed it." He pointed to the floor. "No tag. There's a seam along the edge of the foundation stone and this depression in the stone has been carved, it's not natural."

Hal reached out and hooked his fingers into a cup-shaped depression in the lowest tier of the flagstone that formed the back wall of the room.

Simon felt a faint tingling burn along his spine. "Hal!" he shouted. "Don't—"

Time seemed to slow. Simon saw Hal turn and dive to the side, away from the section of wall that was dissolving into blue flame and fragmenting stone. He grabbed Sylvie around the shoulders and dragged her to the floor as he dove to the side himself. Fire roared overhead and singed his hair. The sound punched him in the chest, roared in his ears, filling his head with pain and scattering his thoughts. The high windows exploded outward, then seemed to suck back inward as cold winter air rushed in to feed the greedy flames.

Simon tried to lift his head but the room spun around him. He could see Hal sprawled just to the right of the opening that had been the secret door. Hot blue fire gushed from it, rising to merge with the inferno that had once been the ceiling. He tried again to get up, succeeding only in rolling to his knees.

Sylvie pushed past him, crawling beneath the flame to Hal. She got hold of the haft of his ax, still strapped to his back, and began dragging him away from the wall. Simon shook his head, clearing it enough to get his knees moving and crawl forward. He got a grip on Hal's wrist and together he and

Sylvie dragged him across the stone slab and toward the front hallway.

Outside the room it was cooler, but smoke poured from the open door, filling the rest of the house. Simon waved Sylvie on, then pulled Hal into a sitting position. He ducked his head under Hal's arm, took a deep breath of relatively clean air and then stood, sweeping his friend into an over-shoulder carry as he did so. Holding his breath, he squinted through the smoke and ran for the outer door.

He tumbled through the open door into cool clean air. He fell to his knees, laying Hal on the ground as gently as he could. Sylvie was doubled over a few yards away, coughing and retching. Simon managed to stand. He lifted his head to take deep breaths of smoke-free air and felt the sharp pain in the back of his neck where the blisters were already rising. Hal moaned and stirred at his feet.

Sylvie staggered over and rested a hand on Simon's shoulder for support. Her breathing was slower, although she still wheezed as she exhaled.

"So," she said, her voice a coarse rasp. "Is this standard Peacekeeper operating procedure, or just your team?"

CHAPTER TEN

By the time the fire brigade arrived, the house was almost completely consumed. The flagstone walls held in the heat and acted like a giant flue, the flames quickly consuming the dry wooden floors and roof.

The Water mages did their best, and the proximity of an artificial lake on the suburban greenbelt gave them plenty of water to work with, but little remained once the fire was out. Hal was awake by the time the medics arrived. He protested, albeit weakly, as they loaded him onto a pallet and then into the ambulance sled. Simon promised to call Molly as the canopy of the sled closed and it sped away toward Queen Eleanor Hospital on the suburban ring road.

Sylvie had recovered remarkably by the time the medics arrived. Simon still felt like he'd been pole-axed, but she was up, striding briskly around the burning building, surveying it from all sides and picking up fragments of debris. The medics had wanted to take Simon in as well, but he refused, finally taking out his badge and pulling rank when they became insistent. He did accept a couple of Air spell treatments to increase the oxygen in his lungs, and was surprised at how much better he felt afterward.

He called Ham and Jack on the team FS net and filled them in. After reassuring them that Hal didn't seem to be in immediate danger, he asked what they had found out.

"We haven't found much at Gripple's farm. It looks pretty ordinary," said Ham. "But we did learn some interesting things about his mother. She's supposed to be some high-powered shaman over on the Rez. Most of Swampwater's neighbors are scared of her and so leave friend Gripple alone. They don't quite shun him, but we get the feeling that no one wants to be too close to him, either."

"Find out what you can, then meet us back at the House at sixteenth hour," said Simon. "Buckley clear."

He took out his handheld mirror and activated the image spell. Sylvie approached him, a couple of pieces of blackened debris in her hands. He held up a finger, indicating she should wait, and spoke the locus code for Molly Stonebender's personal mirror.

Molly's face swam into view in his mirror as she answered the summons. She saw him and frowned. Not even other Dwarves would call Molly Stonebender beautiful. Her round face was pleasant when she smiled, which was often, but her nose would have fit a woman twice her size. Her upper lip was thick and covered with a fine down of black mustache that clashed with the red-blond hair on her head. A dark wart on her left cheek gave her face character but did nothing to enhance her beauty.

"Simon, what's wrong?" she demanded.

"We had some trouble with what should have been a routine search," said Simon. "Hal's been hurt. It doesn't look bad but the medics are taking him to Queen Eleanor, out on the ring road near Bowater."

"Bowater?" she said. "What in Seven Hells were you doing down in Bowater?"

She waved a hand. "Never mind. I'm on my way. But you better have a good explanation, Simon. You're supposed to watch out for that fool husband of mine."

The mirror went blank as Molly cut the connection. Simon looked up to find Sylvie smiling at him.

"It sounds like you and Hal are in a bit of trouble," she said.

Simon nodded. "You don't want to cross that woman. What did you find?"

"Proof that your tip about this place being a bomb factory was right." She held up a pair of rounded objects, blackened by the fire. They were half spheres made of cold iron, the rims grooved with threads, as if they were meant to screw together. Both of the fragments Sylvie held had raised grooves, but the intent was clear.

"Pieces of Fire grenades," said Simon, taking one and examining it closely. "The iron has been stressed to fragment when the Fire spell goes off."

Sylvie nodded. "There are smaller fragments all around the back side of the house. If you hadn't shouted that warning to Hal, he'd have been shredded by the blast." She shivered slightly. "Thank you, by the way, for pulling me down to the floor. The fragment pattern was designed to blow at mid-chest level."

"So this was a turkey trap, set to take out anyone who found that hidden door," said Simon. "Hal's informant was telling the truth about the materials, but does that mean Hightower was actually making the bombs? So far, nothing I've seen links her to the Azeri. Besides, she specialized in Earth magic. She wasn't a Fire mage."

"Making Fire bombs with rowan and aquamarine is fairly simple," Sylvie pointed out. "Any apprentice mage, no matter what Discipline, could do it."

Simon rubbed his chin. "True. I just don't see how Hightower fits in. She wasn't a Traditionalist, but I don't see an academic with her family connections getting involved in radical politics."

"Family connections aren't that strong outside the Havens," said Sylvie. "Maybe she was, or maybe she wasn't, making bombs. She was certainly doing something illegal here. Something she couldn't have done in the Havens. Just a hint of unconventionality back home in Tintagel would get her shunned at the least, maybe locked up in some tower at the High Keep, if her brother decided that's how it should be." She sighed. "Why do you think so many Elves leave the Havens to live out here in the Commonwealth? Out here we can be what we wish to be. We aren't bound by Family, or by conventions that are thousands of years out of date."

She surprised Simon with the passion in her voice and the slight choke of emotion as she finished. She turned away from him.

Simon reached into his pocket and drew out the spell parchment he'd found in Hightower's office.

"Sylvie," he said, and she turned back, her face composed. "Look at this. Is this the same symbol as the one we saw on the slab in there?"

She studied the parchment. "Yes. This was up near the top of the slab, where the Orc's head would have rested. What are these numbers down here?" She indicated the mirror locus he'd copied from the bottom of the statue.

"Maybe a link between Hightower and the Azeri, or at least a lead." At her puzzled look, he explained, "There was a small statue of the Orc god Durlash in Hightower's office. It caught my attention because it looked out of place. I thought it was onyx, but it was a cheap glass imitation. These numbers were etched into the bottom next to the manufacturer's imprint. I don't know if they have any significance, but now I think we should follow up on it."

"How? Just summon that locus?"

"Not just yet," Simon said shaking his head. "The statue was made by a company called Clearwater Glass. I'm thinking we should look into them first."

Sylvie nodded. "Are they local?"

"Don't know." Simon checked his timepiece. "It's almost ten. I think we should get back to Wycliffe House, get cleaned up, and check the local business listings for this outfit. I want to see how Hal is doing after the Healers check him out, then follow up on this if there's time before meeting with Ham and Jack at sixteen."

Sylvie glanced down at her soot-stained blouse and singed breeches. "If you wouldn't mind dropping me at my flat, I'll change and meet you at the House."

"I'll wait while you change," said Simon. "I have a spare uniform in my locker back at the House. It'll save time if I drive you there."

Sylvie nodded with a faint smile and started toward the sled. Simon looked around. The regular Bowater Peacekeepers had the situation in hand, the fire brigade was packing up their gear and the farmhouse was a silent smoking wreck. Simon checked with the local incident commander, a Dwarf sergeant named Robert Steelhelm that Simon knew vaguely from the monthly regional antiterrorism briefings.

"Anything else you need from us, Rob?" Simon asked.

"Nay, I don't think so. I've enough shyte here to keep me busy until nigh midnight. Just file your reports with your LT and slide some copies my way when you're done. May need you back down Bowater way for the inquest, whenever my boss gets one scheduled."

Simon nodded and shook Steelhelm's hand. *Looks like I can't do much more damage*, he thought wryly and followed Sylvie to the sled.

They rode back to Cymbeline in silence, Simon alternating between worrying about Hal and wondering what possible connection there could be between Hightower and the turkey trap that had almost killed them.

Sylvie directed him to a quiet cul-de-sac just off of King Street, not far from the Gray Havens Consulate building. He parked in front of an old inn that had been converted into condominiums and followed her inside.

An elderly concierge with close-cropped steel gray hair and a military bearing sat at a desk next to the door. He stood as they entered.

"Good meeting, Lester," said Sylvie with a casual wave as she swept through the small lobby to the stairs. "Sergeant Buckley is with me."

Simon nodded to the man but got only a suspicious glare in return before the concierge made a purposeful show of replacing a thick-barreled bolt thrower into the rack under the desk.

Simon caught up with Sylvie as she was unlocking the door to a second-floor flat.

"Serious security you have here," he said, as casually as he could manage.

"Lester is a retired royal marine. We have several mid-level diplomats living here and he's contracted with the Consulate as armed security," she said. "I think he believes he's protecting my honor."

She led him into a small but elegant room with wide windows that looked over the cul-de-sac. Simon felt a tingle in his scalp as a security spell scanned him. A faint blue mist formed in the air near the shoulder holster that held his needler. It dissipated at a word from Sylvie.

"Take a seat," she said as she slipped the cross belts from her shoulders. She hung the Gallinberg rapier from a peg near the door and dropped the leather pouch onto a side table. "I'll only be a few minutes."

She started to unbutton her blouse as she crossed the room and entered a short hallway. A few seconds later, Simon heard a door close and a rush of running water. He went to the window and looked down on the street. He noticed a slight distortion in the air and tentatively touched the pane. He felt a jolt of energy and withdrew his hand quickly. A Warded window, expensive to maintain but proof against Fire and Air spells. It would likely repel all but the heaviest bolts, as well. Serious security, indeed.

He sat down in a comfortable leather chair near the window. The room was simply but expensively furnished with a couch and two more matching chairs made of fine wood and dark brocade. The floor was ashwood, lightly stained and highly polished. An Orcish folk art rug covered the space in front of the couch. Next to his chair stood a low bookcase. Most of the titles were in Qetchwa, the ancient language of the Elves, which was still spoken in the Havens. Simon understood it well enough, but read its characters poorly. Here and there were books in the Common speech. The titles surprised him: a well-worn copy of Watson's *Histories of the Dwarves* and a first edition of Golgan's epic *The Path to Wisdom.* Hardly light reading, and not what a Highborn Elf would be expected to take an interest in.

Sylvie stepped out of the hallway, toweling her hair. Her slim body was wrapped in a second towel that left her arms and shoulders bare. She went into the small kitchen area to the right of the front door.

"Would you like something to drink?" she asked. "I think there's some small beer in the chiller." She took out a bottle of water for herself and uncapped it.

As she tilted her head and drank deeply, Simon saw Alira, in the same pose, a towel wrapped around her in the same way. He averted his eyes and said, "No, thank you. We should get going."

She laughed. "Why, Sergeant, are you shy?"

Simon reddened, but said nothing, looking carefully out the window. She must have noticed the pain in his face, because she stopped her laughter and said, "I'm sorry, that was cruel of me."

She finished the water, set the bottle in the sink, and disappeared into the rear of the flat. A few minutes later she reappeared in a fresh uniform, wearing a black skirt this time instead of trousers. She switched the rapier scabbard to a dark belt and buckled it around her waist, then slung the pouch from her shoulder.

"All ready," she said.

CHAPTER ELEVEN

Twenty minutes later, Simon sat on the bench in front of his locker at Wycliffe house. His neck burned where the flames had blistered it and, in the shower, he'd discovered several bald spots on the back of his head where the hair had been burned away. He still smelled faintly of smoke, but at least the soot had washed off.

He pulled on clean breeches and hose from his locker and stuffed the dirty ones into a net laundry bag. He was buttoning a clean shirt when his mirror vibrated on the bench next to his leg. He answered the summons and the stern face of Elvira Cairns appeared.

"Sergeant Buckley," she said. "Lieutenant Gulbrandsen wants to see you and Ranger Graystorm in his office immediately."

"Yes, Mistress Cairns," said Simon with a sigh.

The secretary's face softened. "How is Agent Stonebender? Have you heard anything from the hospital?"

"No, ma'am. But he was awake and talking when they took him away. Hopefully that was a good sign. I plan to go down there as soon as I get off watch."

She nodded. "See that you do. And give my best to Molly." She broke the connection.

Simon winced as he buttoned the collar of his uniform shirt. He'd have left it open in his office or the squad room, but for a meeting with Gulbrandsen, nothing short of regulation appearance would do. After a second, he unbuttoned it again, easing the pain in his blistered skin. What the hells. After blowing up a crime scene, he wasn't going to worry about an unbuttoned collar.

Sylvie met him at the top of the stairs. He shrugged, then winced again. "You're not in Gulbrandsen's chain of command," he observed. "He can't order you to his office. You could wait here until I come back. Then we'll either go check out the glass company, or I'll turn in my badge and sidearm and clean out my desk."

"Doesn't work that way, Sergeant, "she said. "Team spirit and all that. Besides, my boss summoned me and as much as ordered me to go with you."

"Flandyrs?"

She shook her head. “I told you I don’t work for that ass. He’s SED, but in the political operations unit.” She smiled at Simon’s raised eyebrows. “Don’t pretend you didn’t know the Rangers had spies and political operatives in the Commonwealth. You’re too smart for that.”

“Oh, I knew. But I never heard a Ranger admit it.”

“Well, you didn’t hear it from me, either. Understand? I report to the law enforcement arm, Senior Ranger Summerfield.”

Simon had never met Summerfield, but knew of him from his time in the Borderlands. He had a reputation for integrity and little tolerance for political games. Some said he could have been Steward, but wouldn’t engage in the type of political maneuvering needed to take and hold the scepter.

They climbed the stairs to Gulbrandsen’s office. Elvira ushered them in and closed the door.

Simon stood before Gulbrandsen’s desk, not quite at attention. Sylvie took a seat in one of the high back chairs without waiting for an invitation. Gulbrandsen frowned.

“So, it’s not enough to kill a High Elf, a member of the royal family for the Mother’s sake, you have to go and blow up the crime scene where it occurred?” Gulbrandsen’s voice rose to a shout. “If there was any, ANY, mitigating evidence that might have smoothed this over with the Havens, you have just destroyed it. What the hells were you thinking?”

“I—” Simon started to say.

"Sergeant Buckley was attempting to secure that evidence when the explosion occurred," Sylvie interrupted, her voice at once silky smooth and deadly cold. "The scene was turkey-trapped and one of your agents was badly injured in the blast. I myself might have been killed if not for Sergeant Buckley's quick action. Had it gone differently, you might be explaining to *Syr* Galen how your department managed to kill two High Elves in as many days."

Gulbrandsen reddened, then sighed as if deflated. "How is Hal?" he asked Simon. "Any word from the Healers? And for the gods' sake, sit down."

Simon sat in the chair next to Sylvie, catching a glimpse of her mischievous smile. *Well played, Ranger Graystorm.*

"No word yet, sir," said Simon. "I plan to go by Queen Eleanor's at the end of watch."

Gulbrandsen nodded. "What have you learned so far?"

Simon considered what to reveal. Sylvie spoke up before he could answer. "The farmhouse was definitely being used to make Fire bombs, whatever else Lady Hightower was doing there." She placed a piece of the bomb casing on Gulbrandsen's desk. "Several of these fragments were found in the wreckage after the fire burned itself out. Sergeant Buckley tells me the iron has been pre-stressed to fragment when the bomb explodes—a nasty antipersonnel weapon of the type the Azeri seem to prefer." Simon noticed that she didn't mention the ownership of the house, or the possible link to Flandyrs.

"Also," Simon took up the narrative, "Hal traced the delivery of the materials for the bombs to an Orc from the Hollows who gave up a couple of names. Both are low-level criminals who are known associates of an Azeri Overseer and loan leech. The Azeri has ties to the Brigades, although nothing that we've been able to use to justify an arrest."

"How is Hightower linked to the Azeri?" asked Gulbrandsen.

"We don't know," admitted Simon. "Other than the farmhouse being used for both making bombs and for whatever Portal magic she was trying to perform there, I don't have any direct evidence."

"Hightower does have links to the Southern Reservation," said Sylvie. "She spent quite a lot of time there doing research. She knew old Gran Swampwater, a respected shaman down on the Rez. We don't know for sure, but we suspect Gran Swampwater is Gripple Swampwater's mother. That would suggest he was not taken at random, but was specifically targeted by Hightower."

"We?" asked Gulbrandsen, raising an eyebrow. "My understanding was that you were to be an observer only, not a participant in this investigation."

Sylvie went rigid and started to rise. Simon cut her off with a sharp wave of his hand. He was mildly surprised when she settled back into her chair, clearly unhappy but deferring to him.

"I've included Ranger Graystorm in all phases of the investigation, sir," he said. "She's an investigator with the Gray Rangers, reporting directly to Senior Ranger Summerfield. I thought it best to give her complete access. Did I misunderstand our meeting yesterday with Lord Flandyrs?" He managed to keep even a hint of sarcasm out of his voice.

Gulbrandsen gave him a sharp look, but only said, "I see."

"I sent Liam Aster to observe the CSA mages as they searched Professor Hightower's office." Simon continued. "I figured he'd recognize anything out of the ordinary that would pertain to the case."

Gulbrandsen sighed. "He's wasting his time. Lord Flandyrs exercised the Havens' right of diplomatic immunity and had the office sealed. He claims that as the private office of a member of the royal family, it has the same status as Hightower's domicile, which he has also sealed."

"That's horse crap," said Simon. "The office is University property. Hightower is granted use as a courtesy. That precedent was set years ago when the Azeri Empire tried the same ploy to protect the apartment their Ambassador had rented for his mistress."

"I understand your frustration," said Gulbrandsen. "I made a formal protest to the KP's office and to the Foreign Minister."

Simon doubted there had been much spirit behind those protests, but said nothing. He glanced at Sylvie, but saw only her resting Elf face.

"For now," Gulbrandsen continued, "you'll have to pursue other avenues of investigation. Hightower's office and personal life are strictly off limits until the diplomats can come to some agreement."

"Yes, sir," said Simon. He decided not to mention his own examination of Hightower's office.

"Do you have any leads aside from these names Hal has uncovered?" Gulbrandsen asked.

"No, sir," said Simon. "We'll check around down by the Rez as well. See if this Gran Swampwater has any history with Hightower and whether there was bad blood between them. Hopefully it will explain why Gripple was targeted. I'll also have Liam research the spells she was trying to use. Maybe if we can understand their purpose, it will lead us to her motive for trying to kill Swampwater. And Hal." He laid emphasis on that last to remind Gulbrandsen that this was personal.

Gulbrandsen stiffened but didn't respond. He looked at Sylvie.

"Was there anything else, sir?" Simon asked.

Gulbrandsen continued to stare at Sylvie who returned his gaze calmly, looking unperturbed. Gulbrandsen broke first.

"No, nothing. Get back to work and have the hospital send me regular updates on Stonebender."

"Yes, LT." Simon rose and turned toward the door. Sylvie stood and removed the bomb fragment from Gulbrandsen's desk and put it into her pouch. The Lieutenant opened his mouth as if to speak, then closed it, and made a shooing gesture in

Simon's direction. Sylvie grinned once her back was to Gulbrandsen and brushed past Simon on her way out. Simon followed her into the hallway.

"That went well," she said, as they reached the top of the staircase.

"If by that, you mean I'm still a King's Agent, then yes," said Simon. "I noticed you didn't say anything about Flandyrs and his connection to the farmhouse."

"And you think I should have?"

"No," Simon shook his head. "Especially now that Flandyrs has shut down any search of Hightower's office or apartment. It's pretty clear that we're being warned off of looking too closely at her. Flandyrs doesn't want a real investigation for some reason, and I don't think it's as simple as protecting the Steward's good name."

"You're right there," Sylvie agreed. "Flandyrs is a pompous ass, but he's a sharp political operator. He has his own agenda here. The Steward disavowed Glendowyn when she took an appointment at Caledonia rather than staying home at the Academy or letting herself be married off to a political ally of the royal house. I can't imagine he'd care very much what happened to her out here in the Commonwealth. If anything, it would reinforce the Traditionalists' propaganda that all things Human are debased, violent, and dangerous."

Simon regarded her thoughtfully. "Thank you for interrupting Gulbrandsen back there. I might have lost my temper and said something I'd later regret. That was skillfully done."

"Does this mean you've started to trust me? A little anyway?" Her look was pure innocence but her tone was playful.

Simon laughed. "Let's just say I don't think you're Flandyrs' spy anymore, and leave it at that."

Sylvie nodded. "Good enough for now. So, what's our next move?"

Simon checked his timepiece. "It's midday, near about. I want to check on Hal, then track down an address for that glass company. If there's time, we'll check them out before Jack and Ham get back from Fernhill."

"Let me help with that. You get in touch with the hospital and I'll check the business directory for the glass company."

Simon nodded and they descended the stairs to the squad room. Sylvie went to find the research office while Simon crossed to his office and sat at his desk. He used the large screen mirror on his desk to send a summons to the hospital. A polite receptionist asked his business, scrutinized his badge as he held it up to the mirror, and then connected him to the ward where Hal was being treated. To his surprise, it was Molly Stonebender's face that appeared.

"Molly! How is Hal? I thought they'd connect me with his nurse."

Molly scowled at him. "She stepped out to get Hal's medication. I saw the Wycliffe locus and knew who was calling. Hal's resting. He has some broken ribs, smoke in his lungs, and a concussion." Her expression softened. "They say he'll be all right and should be able to go home in the morning. Simon, what happened out there? All Hal told me was that you saved him."

Simon sighed, as much relieved that Hal was not in danger, as that Molly didn't blame him for her husband's injuries.

"Someone turkey-trapped the crime scene we were investigating. I felt the Fire spell trigger and shouted a warning to Hal. It was close; the blast almost got all of us."

"Jack and Ham were there, too?" Molly asked.

"No," said Simon. "Sylvie Graystorm, a Ranger with the SED, was with us. She's the one who got a grip on Hal's harness and dragged him away from the worst of the flames."

"An Elf?" Molly's eyes narrowed. "Simon, what have you gotten us into now?"

"I really can't talk about it, Molly. At least not on the mirror. I'll come by the hospital after I get off watch. Meanwhile, keep Hal from doing anything stupid like trying to come back to work."

"The fool has already tried. Twice. The Healer on his case had to threaten to put him in restraint if he didn't stay put."

Simon smiled. "Stubborn as stone," he said, quoting an old Dwarfish saying. "Tell him I'll be by this evening and update him on everything."

Molly nodded and broke the connection just as Sylvie walked into the cubicle.

"Hal?" she asked.

"Mending. Causing trouble for the Healers. Molly is there and will keep him on a straight line. What did you learn?"

"Clearwater Glass is located in the Hollows, just off Canal Street, six blocks south of Tanner. They make mostly household products – plates, drinking glasses and the like. A sideline is cheap reproductions of religious icons that are marketed at several temples and shrines around the city. Research gave me an address and a mirror locus. It's not the same as the locus you showed me, by the way."

"I'm not surprised," said Simon. He checked his desk mirror but there was no report yet from the CSA forensics team. "I don't want to attract attention to it by asking for a reverse look-up. There may be a trace detection spell on that mirror. Let's see if we find any answers at Clearwater Glass."

CHAPTER TWELVE

The Hollows hadn't changed much since Simon had patrolled a beat there ten years earlier. Run down tenements and liquor stores, derelict buildings and vacant lots were interspersed with the occasional block or two of relative prosperity. In those blocks, small neat houses and shops huddled together as if for protection. Most of the houses and all of the shops had heavy cold iron grillwork covering the windows and triple-locked security doors facing the street. On the streets, stripped and rusting sleds competed for space with the elaborately decorated flyers favored by pimps and loan leeches. Most doorways sheltered a resident derelict sleeping off his latest high.

Tanner Street marked the division between the Government district and the upscale neighborhoods of King's Road and the High Street to the north, and the down-and-out southern slums of the Orcs. Cymbeline had grown tenfold since the Magical Revolution transformed manufacturing in the Commonwealth from cottage industries and craftsman's guilds to mass production. New jobs in the burgeoning spell factories drew a huge migration from the Orc reservations. Immigrants from the Azeri Empire, driven by civil war and famine, swelled their ranks until the Orc population of Cymbeline nearly equaled that of Humans.

The Commonwealth Accords guaranteed equal rights to all races, including Orcs, but the old Magisterium segregation laws were slow to change. Only in the past seventy years had the legal restrictions on Orcs owning property outside of the Hollows been repealed. The social segregation of Orcs had yet to change. Few lived outside of their traditional neighborhoods.

Peacekeepers in the Hollows were virtually all Humans and Dwarves. Few Orcs sought careers as Keepers and fewer still rose above the clerical and support ranks. The Keepers policed the streets with a siege mentality; their encounters with the citizens they were supposed to protect often descending into a cycle of intimidation and violence. The real power in the streets lay with the Overseers and gangs who controlled the jobs, drugs, and money. Overseers recruited from the Rez and from the Azeri refugee camps, and marketed labor to the factories and sweatshops of the south side. No one worked down in the Hollows without an Overseer's blessing,

Organized gangs were a relatively recent development, mostly run by Azeri immigrants. Drug running, smuggling, intimidation, and prostitution were their primary enterprises, but ties to the Azeri Liberation Brigades were suspected. Much of the Brigades' funding and weapons moved through the Orc Gangs who operated out of the Hollows.

Simon knew the streets, but most of his old contacts were dead, in prison, or had been lucky enough to get out. Hal managed to maintain a network of informants and small time operators, but they were all deeply suspicious of anyone else and unlikely to talk to him without Hal at his side; even less likely with an Elf as his companion.

Hostile eyes tracked them as Simon glided the sled slowly down Canal Street, looking for the side street that the business directory had given as the address of Clearwater Glass. He noted Azeri clan tattoos on a number of the watchers and two of them spoke urgently into handheld mirrors as soon as they noticed Simon and Sylvie. Lookouts, Simon realized; probably spotting for some pimp or drug peddler and rightly identifying Simon as a Keeper. He smiled, imagining the scramble the false alarm was causing.

Sorry boys, he thought. *We're hunting other game today.*

Simon turned the sled down a narrow side street and let it settle to the cobblestones across from the Clearwater Glass factory. The building occupied about half of the short block. A pair of high roll-up doors, now closed, fronted on a loading dock in the center of the factory. To the left, a short concrete walk led from curbside to a glass door with the company logo etched into it. Two narrow windows looked out onto the street on either side of the door.

Simon got out and walked up to the door, only to find it was locked. He peered through the window to his right, but a black curtain covered it completely. Sylvie checked the loading dock, but the roll-up doors and the shipping window were secured with heavy locks.

"Looks like nobody's home," said Simon, returning to the curb to survey the building.

"Ain't nobody inside," said a voice from behind him.

He turned to see an older Orc approaching him. The newcomer's business suit was old and threadbare, but clean. He was clean-shaven and his hair was neatly trimmed and swept back from his low forehead.

"I see that," said Simon, taking out his badge. "I'm Sergeant Simon Buckley, King's Peacekeepers. This is Ranger Graystorm of the Special Enforcement Division. May I ask who you are?"

The Orc executed a deep bow. "I'm Durking Bogrunner. Used to be the Overseer for this and a couple of other factories south of Knacker Street." His voice was smooth and respectful, almost obsequious, but with an undertone that Simon found annoying.

"What can you tell us about Clearwater Glass?" asked Simon. "Did they close down or are they just on holiday?"

"Used to be a right prosperous operation, not too big, but steady," said Bogrunner. "All of a sudden, not two days past, these suits from north of Tanner show up with a bunch of papers and a couple of bully-boys from the Knacker Street Loblollies and toss everybody out on the street, even old Mr. Clearwater what owned the place. Them as tried to ask questions got knocked upside the head for their troubles. Twenty good Orcs, out of work with no job prospects. I done what I could, got some of them work at the other factories I supply, but not near all."

"Suits?" asked Sylvie.

Bogrunner cocked his head at her. "Men, m'Lady. Law types from some fancy office up on the King's Road. Said they had a court order to shut the factory. Poor Mr. C., he shouted at 'em, tried to summon his own advocate on the mirror, but the Loblolly boys busted it. Then he went over and talked to the Elf who was with them. The Elf said something to him that made him shut up. He told all the boys who worked for him to go home and he'd get things right by the morning. Never did, though."

"Elf," said Simon. "What Elf?"

"Don't know." Bogrunner shook his head. "Never got out of the big black sled they all came in. He were tall, though, even for an Elf, and he dressed all in green in one of them old-timey robes they sometimes wear."

Simon and Sylvie exchanged a look.

"Do you know what law firm the advocates were from?" Sylvie asked him.

"No, m'Lady. They was just Suits, like I said. Mr. Clearwater might know."

"Where can we find Mr. Clearwater?" Simon asked.

"Might be at home. He lives up on Tanner, just the other side of the Temple. Number eight-seventy-three, I think. "

"Do you know what the factory was making when they were shut down?" Simon asked.

"Not rightly," said Bogrunner. "Just glass stuff. Most of the boys who worked here did shoveling and pouring jobs. You know, shovel the sand into the furnace, move the big crucibles around and pour the hot glass into molds, that sort of thing. Mr. C. had a couple of mold makers and a really good glass blower here. They were easy to fix up on other jobs. The fellas who did grunt work, not so much."

"Well, thank you for your time, Mr. Bogrunner. You've been very helpful," said Simon.

"Not a'tall," said the Orc with another deep bow. "Always glad to help a King's officer. Hope you can help Mr. Clearwater get out of whatever bog he's stuck in. I liked working with him. He weren't a bad sort for an Azeri."

"Azeri?" asked Sylvie. "Clearwater isn't an Azeri name."

"Nah," said Bogrunner. "He changed it more'n twenty years ago when he first came to the city. Don't know what it used to be, but he's Azeri all right. Got the tattoos and all. Everyone knows the Azeri are the best glassmakers in the world. Weren't no secret that he came from the Empire."

"Thank you again, Mr. Bogrunner," said Simon.

The Orc bowed and walked off toward the south. He glanced back once as he reached the street corner, then turned to his left and walked out of sight.

"What do you want to do now?" asked Sylvie.

"I want to get inside that factory," said Simon. "But first I want to be prepared." He walked back to the sled and opened the rear storage compartment. He pulled out a tactical vest and put it on. Then he reached under the front seat and retrieved his Bonecleaver, strapping the scabbard to the back of his vest. He checked the magazine of his needler.

"I'll go in first," he said. "Once I clear the first room, you follow. I don't have a second vest, so stay behind me."

Sylvie loosened her rapier in its scabbard. "I can take care of myself," she said. "You know we don't have a warrant for this."

"If Flandyrs is behind this and was able to get a court order closing the factory, do you really think a Justice is going to issue a warrant? And if one does, do you think it won't get back to Flandyrs?"

"No on both counts," she said. "Just making sure we're on the same path here." She flashed him that mischievous smile. "Lead on."

Simon crossed to the front door. It was a sturdy steel and glass construction with a standard Simpson key and tumbler lock. He fished in the front pocket of the tactical vest and drew out a set of lock picks. Saying a quick prayer to the Smith, he set to work.

Two minutes later, he was rewarded with a satisfying click as the lock opened. He rubbed his badge to release any alarm Warding on the door and pushed it open.

“You’re pretty good with those picks,” said Sylvie.

“Not really,” said Simon. “Sometimes it’s better to be lucky than good.” He drew his needler and brought it up in a two-handed grip. “Ready?”

At her nod, he pushed the door farther open with his foot and stepped inside. He quickly checked the corners of the small reception room, sighting along the barrel of his needler. “Clear,” he called over his shoulder, stepping into the room to allow Sylvie to enter. She stepped in behind him, rapier at high ready, point forward.

Behind a wooden counter covered with brochures and product catalogs, an open doorway led to a cluttered office. On the other side of the office, Simon could see another door that opened onto the factory floor itself. He stepped around the counter and checked low but saw nothing. He turned to the doorway to the office.

Sylvie touched him on the shoulder to indicate she was ready behind him. He stepped through the second door, checking left then right.

“Clear,” he said again as he moved deeper into the office. Once again he checked the corners, high and low, but saw nothing. He heard Sylvie behind him as he stepped up to the entrance to the factory.

Through the door, he could see a much larger space that occupied the rest of the building. To his right, near the center were the huge roll-up doors, now closed. Just beyond the doors sat a half-dozen pallets filled with wooden boxes all bound together with coils of hemp rope, awaiting loading.

A huge caldron, nearly as tall as a man, occupied the center of the floor flanked by a pair of brick and ceramic furnaces. A large water tank hung from the wall above the furnaces with pipes leading down to four narrow troughs used for tempering and cooling the molds. Closer to the office, several long workbenches were covered with molds, half-finished castings, and rows of drinking glasses awaiting polishing.

He leaned through, checking right and left on either side of the door, then stepped back and closed it.

Sylvie lowered her blade. “Why close the door?” she asked. “Don’t we want to check out the factory?”

Simon nodded. “I want to search the office first. I don’t think there’s anyone here, but with the door closed, we won’t be surprised by someone hiding out in there until we’re ready to go in.”

For the next several minutes, they looked through the files and papers on the desk and the shelves in the office. Other than various orders, account statements and inventory lists, they found nothing of particular interest. Simon did find a duplicate of the Durlash figurine he’d seen in Hightower’s office, but there were no numbers etched on its bottom. At least it confirmed that the figurine had come from this factory. He was about to suggest that they move on to the factory floor, when Sylvie spoke up.

"Found something." She held up a square of paper. "A shipping order for two hundred-weights of powdered aquamarine. I don't suppose they make colored glass from that, do you?"

"Seems a bit lavish," agreed Simon. "But perfect for making Fire grenades. Does the order show where it went or who paid for it?"

"Clearwater ordered it from a mining company down in Dundaria province. Took delivery three weeks ago, paid in full. This doesn't say where it went after that."

"Not surprised," said Simon. "But it does suggest he's tied to whoever was making bombs at that farmhouse. After we check out the factory, we need to have a chat with Mr. Clearwater. Make a note of the mining company, too."

Simon set the Durlash figurine back on the desk and motioned toward the door. Sylvie nodded and got behind him. Simon pushed the door open and stepped into the factory. Immediately he felt a tingling burn down his spine.

"Warding spell," he said, sighting left and right over the barrel of his needler.

"No shit," muttered Sylvie as she stepped a little to the side to free her reach and have better room for her rapier.

They advanced slowly down the line of workbenches. Simon noticed small clues that the workplace had been abandoned unexpectedly; a partially closed mold, a drinking glass still under the polishing wheel, small personal items left on the benches, even an abandoned lunch pail with a desiccated half-loaf and some dried sausage. His sense of unease grew.

With a muted roar, the furnaces burst to life. Within seconds, Simon could feel the heat, even from twenty feet away.

Simon stepped closer. "I don't see anyone," he said to Sylvie. "Do you?"

"Fire spell," she said. "Triggered by the warding. I don't like this."

"Neither do I." Simon took a step backwards. "Out. Now. We need backup."

He took another step back, just as a ball of molten glass oozed out of the nearest furnace and rolled across the stone floor. It stopped and began to stretch upward, sprouting arms, legs and a flat sloping head. Two more globs of liquid fire oozed out of the second furnace.

Glass golems? What in the hells? Simon holstered the now useless needler and drew the Bonecleaver. He glanced back and saw that Sylvie had shifted her stance to a low guard. She nodded to him and he moved beside her.

The first three golems came at them in a group. They moved fluidly, their outer translucent skin flexible, the inner fire of the still molten glass inside them shining through. Simon stepped to his left to free Sylvie's right arm, then swung the Bonecleaver down on top of the first creature's head. Instead of dissolving as golems he'd fought before had done, the creature went rigid as the glass solidified. Then it shattered into thousands of fragments.

Sylvie dispatched the other two with quick thrusts to the head with her rapier as five more globs rolled out of the near furnace and three more emerged from the far one. Two of them rolled quickly past Sylvie and stopped between Simon and the door.

"Shit," he said softly and shifted his stance to face them. Sylvie pressed her back to his as she faced down the other golems. "Stay with me," he said over his shoulder. He started to edge toward the still coalescing golems to his front.

"To your right," Sylvie shouted as she thrust out and down with her rapier. Simon half-turned and brought his short sword down in a sweeping arc to cut through the neck and shoulder of the golem rushing in from the side. The shattering glass sprayed his arm, fragments biting into his skin.

With the recovery stroke, he swept left. The cut was awkward, but went between the eyes and upper jaw of another golem. He felt Sylvie leave his back as the creature shattered.

"What are you doing?" he shouted. "Stay with me!" Then the two golems by the door rushed him. He missed his first stroke as the nearest creature came in range, slicing through its shoulder and deep into its chest. The momentum of his stroke died as if he had struck one of the hay bales around the practice ring back at the House. He wrenched it free, converting his violent tug into a spin and slashing through the neck of the second one. He got a glimpse of Sylvie, her rapier sheathed, leaping from one of the workbenches to an overhead pipe as three golems reached for her.

Simon turned as the first golem came at him again, now inside his reach. He leapt back, bumping against one of the workbenches. The golem was still too close. He thrust at it with the point of his Bonecleaver but it was like pushing molasses. The thing reached for him. He could feel the heat it radiated through his tactical vest. He pivoted to his right and shoulder-rolled over the bench, shattering and scattering dozens of drinking glasses. The wooden top of the bench smoldered and started to burn as the golem levered itself up onto it.

Simon regained his feet, looked up and saw Sylvie hanging from the overhead pipe by her hands and one ankle, her skirt hiked up to her upper thigh, as she kicked with her other foot at the valve at the base of the big water tank. The golem reared above him. He thrust upward with the short sword, this time getting the point under the thing's guard and into its neck. He pushed the point of the Bonecleaver deep as the golems hands closed on his arms, burning through the wool serge of his uniform. The point of his sword finally bit deep enough and the golem shattered, bits of hot glass burning his face and hands. He backed up against the wall. By now ten more of the things had spawned from the two furnaces and were taking form all around him. The first three were starting to move.

Above him he could hear Sylvie breathing hard and grunting with each kick she threw at the valve. He heard a loud clang and a sudden hiss as water sprayed from the weld where the valve met the tank. Sylvie gave a loud cry and kicked once more. The valve flew off and water gushed under pressure from the tank.

The sudden cascade hit the furnaces with an explosion of steam. Sylvie swung back and dropped lightly to the floor, narrowly avoiding the scalding cloud. She drew her rapier and ran to Simon just as the nearest furnace burst open, the sudden change in temperature cracking the domed firebrick of its top. The second furnace burst with an even larger cloud of superheated steam. Simon and Sylvie ducked low and raced for the door.

Water and steam sprayed across the room, showering the golems. Their outer skins cooled instantly and hardened, freezing them in place. The first two exploded as Simon shoved Sylvie through the door into the business office and dove through after her. He kicked the door shut, temporarily halting the assault of the scalding air. Together they ran through the reception room and out into the street.

CHAPTER THIRTEEN

Simon bent over and tried to breathe, but his throat felt raw and scalded. His arms burned. The black serge fabric of his uniform was scorched, but had not burned through. It still hurt like hells.

Sylvie stood next to him, breathing hard. She stood easily but he noticed that the bare skin below her skirt was red and beginning to blister. He recalled her bare thighs as she had kicked at the valve and wondered how far up her legs the burns extended.

"We need to get out of here," he wheezed.

She glanced back and forth. Traffic was moving steadily on Canal, but this side street seemed deserted. Simon straightened up and winced. Sylvie started walking toward the sled, her gait slower and less graceful than usual. Simon followed her, careful not to move his arms too much.

They managed to get into the sled and Simon got it moving toward Canal. By the time he made the turn north toward Tanner, he was breathing easier. Lifting his arms still burned, but he didn't have to move the steering yoke very far to control the sled.

Sylvie shifted in her seat, winced and then began to laugh. Simon looked at her sitting awkwardly on the one hip that wasn't burned, her knees bent and splayed to keep the blistered skin away from her skirt and the seat. The rust from the pipes had stained her hair, her face was beefy red, but her eyes were bright with excitement.

"And here I thought this assignment was going to be dull and boring. You are a very dangerous man to follow around, Simon Buckley."

"Yes, m'Lady," said Simon with a grin. "Ow! Don't make me smile."

"How are we going to explain this to your Lieutenant?" she asked, sobering.

"We aren't. Unless someone else talks to Bogrunner, as far as the LT knows, we were never there. I doubt there's much more to be learned from the factory. We need to talk to Clearwater and see if he can confirm that it was Flandyrs who shut him down. And find out what he did with the aquamarine powder."

"I'm more interested in who set up the Fire and golem animation spells back there," Sylvie said. "That was some of the most sophisticated magic I've ever seen; and in two different Disciplines. The probability cascade for the trigger alone had to be at least three levels deep."

"The what?"

Sylvie sighed. "How much Magical Theory did you get in school?"

"Not much," admitted Simon. "We got the basics: the noble woods, the casting stones, the complimentary metals, some of the symbology. In Agent training we got more practical details about the mechanics of spell casting and especially the symbols and tools of restricted spells. But when you start talking about quantum magic or probability matrices, I'm totally lost."

"Right," said Sylvie. "So, magic is nothing more than the willful manipulation of probability. When a mage casts a spell, he's altering the local probability matrix, the background likelihood that a given event will occur spontaneously. The ingredients of the spell, the casting stone, the wood, the metal, help focus his will and channel it into a particular path that produces the desired outcome. With me so far?"

"Sure. The mage does his thing and the world around him obeys his will."

Sylvie grimaced. "Sort of. Quantum theory tells us that only certain actions are possible, and then in discrete all or none packets. It's why spells are limited in power and range."

"Got it," said Simon, less certainly.

"Right." Sylvie smiled. "A probability cascade happens when a mage sets a spell on an object to activate with a specific trigger. This was the big discovery that made the Magical Revolution possible. It's why the Traditionalists hate Humanity so. Because the Elves, who always used magic, who introduced it to the First Men, never really understood how or why it worked. It was Humans who figured that out.

"Anyway, a first order cascade is the simple Air, Water, Fire or Earth spell that is triggered by an action or incantation. The person activating it doesn't have to know how the spell works, he or she just uses it. A second level cascade is where the triggering of one spell increases the probability of a second spell activating. The second trigger may be automatic or may depend on certain conditions being met. But each level on the cascade is more improbable, so more skill, will, and energy is needed to make the spell work. Second level cascades are only cast by very experienced mages. Third level cascades have been accomplished by only a few Masters. To cast a third level trigger and then have it activate a powerful conjuring like an animation spell is ridiculously difficult. I've never known or heard of a mage with that level of skill."

"So this super mage, whoever he is, set up those spells to activate automatically? How do we know he wasn't watching from somewhere else, say on a hidden mirror or something?" asked Simon.

"Not likely unless he was very close by. Close enough that we'd have known. Quantum theory limits the range over which spells can be cast directly. The will and energy needed to create the spell increases by the square of the distance to the target."

"What do you mean, 'we'd have known'?" asked Simon.

She gave him an impatient look. "Don't pretend you can't sense spells as they're cast. I saw you at the farmhouse. You knew that door was trapped and managed to warn Hal before the spell fully activated. I felt it, too, but you reacted faster. How much Elf blood do you have?"

Simon shrugged, which made him wince again. "I don't know. Both of my parents were human, but I know my mother was a foundling. The family story is that she was left at the Temple of the Mother in Holdfast, out East by the Azeri Borderlands."

She looked him up and down. "Less than half Elf, I'd say, but at least a quarter, to judge by your eyes and chin."

Simon knew his eyes shaded to a darker blue than most, not quite the violet of some pure Elves, but dark for a Man. He thought little of it. His father had come from the Northwest Territory where such eyes were common.

"Does it matter?" he asked.

"No," she said. "I just wonder why you keep your ability a secret."

"I don't," he said. "Not really. Hal knows. I just don't talk about it. It doesn't seem to give me much of an advantage on the job." *And it didn't save Alira.*

Sylvie nodded thoughtfully. "And you didn't really figure out how to use it until you took an Elf as a lover."

Simon gripped the steering yoke, aware of her eyes on him. "That's something else I don't talk about." He managed to keep his voice level in spite of the pain. Sylvie sighed but said nothing more.

It was halfway through the fifteenth hour by the time Simon had parked the sled and cleaned and checked in his weapons. Sylvie spent some time in the women's locker room and seemed to be walking more comfortably when she emerged. Her hair was wet but no longer rust-stained.

They walked up the stairs and across the squad room in an uncomfortable silence that continued as Simon sat behind his desk and began checking through reports on his desk mirror.

"Look, Simon," Sylvie finally said. "I'm sorry. I shouldn't keep needling you about falling in love with an Elf. Relationships between Elves and Humans tend to end badly and I'm sorry if she hurt you. But we don't often stay for the long term, even with our own kind."

Simon didn't speak for a few seconds. Then he pushed away from the desk and stood facing her.

"Her name was Alira Autumnfall," he said in a quiet, carefully controlled tone. "And she didn't leave me. She died. Nearly three years ago now."

"Oh, Simon. I am genuinely sorry I tortured you so. I know the Autumnfalls of Talien. Were they her people?"

Simon nodded. "Alira managed some of the family businesses here in Cymbeline. We met one spring when the team investigated a series of thefts from one of her warehouses, which seemed to involve illegal entry spells. The case dragged on and we spent a lot of time together. One thing sort of led to another and by summer we were living together." Simon paused and looked at the ceiling, struggling to control himself. "We talked about getting married. I know, I know, Elf marriages are fifty-year contracts, not forever things. But at my age, another fifty years would be damn near a lifetime. And Alira wanted it, too. At least she said so."

"I'm sure she did," said Sylvie. "Elves take contracts very seriously." She paused and her voice softened. "How did she die?"

"She was on her way to meet me for lunch, walking across the greenbelt on the King's Road side of Wycliffe House, when an Azeri threw a Fire grenade at the King's Prosecutor who was walking beside her. I was standing by the Judiciary Gate. I sensed the spell and shouted her name. She saw me and waved and then just disappeared into the fireball." Simon didn't realize he was crying until he felt the tears dripping from the raw skin of his chin.

Sylvie didn't say anything more. She reached out and took his hand and just held it gently until he wiped his eyes and returned to his chair. Neither of them spoke until they heard Jack Ironhand's Dwarfish accent in the squad room.

"I'm telling you, Ham, Roister will take him down before two minutes into the second round. He's got the reach, he's got the power, and he's always been a snake with the short sword."

"Reach won't count for much, once Stonewarden gets inside his guard. Then that ax will start to take its toll. Blunted or not, getting whacked in the greaves and back-slashed in the fork will make Roister drop his shield. Then it's game over."

Simon smiled. Tourney Combat was Jack and Ham's favorite subject, even though they never agreed on anything. He wondered if they were talking about a real bout, or one of their frequent what-if scenarios.

Jack and Ham entered a moment later. They both paused, sensing the tension in the office. Ham noted the fresh burns on Simon's neck and face and the singed sleeves of his uniform. He raised an eyebrow. Jack took in the same sight and turned to glare at Sylvie.

Simon held up a hand. "Stand down, Jack. Sylvie saved us both this afternoon. It's been a difficult day, so let's just sit down, report what we've learned and set the watch. All good?"

Jack looked from Sylvie to Simon, then at Ham, who nodded. "All good," he said.

"Where's Liam?" Simon asked.

"He'll be along directly," said Hamish. "We saw him in the locker room. He was going to stop by the lab and check with the CSA guys before he came up."

Simon filled them in on the fight at the glass factory, the shipping order they'd found and his suspicions that Flandyrs had been behind the factory closure. The more he spoke of the investigation, of the job at hand, the more the pain of talking about Alira receded.

Sylvie nodded to him when he credited her with stopping the golems by breaking the valve on the water tank, and Jack's looks in her direction were now respectful rather than hostile. For some reason, Simon found that satisfying.

"So, tomorrow," he concluded, "we need to talk to Clearwater and find out who shut his factory down and who he bought the aquamarine for. What more did you two learn down in Fernhill?"

"Not much more than we already told you," said Hamish. "Gripple's mother is a high shaman on the Rez, but none of his neighbors are willing to talk about her. We did go to the Rez, but nobody outside the administrative center was willing to talk to us, either. The local Marshall was friendly enough and said he'd let the old lady know we wanted to interview her, but even he wouldn't tell us where she lived unless he got an order from the LT or from Captain Axhart making it an official investigation."

Simon shook his head. "Not yet. Maybe we can persuade Gripple to make an introduction."

"Already arranged," said Liam from the doorway.

"Good meeting to you, too, Liam," said Simon. "And what do you mean?"

Liam blushed at Simon's jab. "I spent some of the afternoon with Gripple at the hospital. They plan to release him tomorrow. Anyway, I spent several hours talking with him. He didn't add much to what he'd said before. I think he really is baffled as to why Hightower kidnapped him. He knows she spent time on the Rez talking to Gran Swampwater, and Gripple always thought the two of them were, if not friends, at least cordial toward each other. He's worried his mother may be in some sort of danger and wants me to arrange protection for her."

"We can offer," said Simon. "But our jurisdiction is limited. That's more the job of the Marshall service and the Reservation Council."

"I get the feeling she'd turn it down anyway," said Liam. "Gripple makes her sound stubborn and a bit peevish."

Simon nodded. "That'll likely be your job on the morrow. What happened at Hightower's office this morning?"

Liam grinned. "The quickest squirrel gathers the most acorns," he said. "After your briefing this morning, I had a feeling the CSA team would get officially shut out. So I made fast tracks over to the University before they did. I found a security patroller, nice old guy, and persuaded him to unlock the office before he went off shift so that it would be ready when the CSA team showed up. I managed to get a pretty good look around the office and her laboratory before the team arrived. Not ten minutes after they started their own work, Flandyrs marched in with a Cease and Desist order from the Foreign Affairs Minister, signed by Minister Alorton himself no less, and threw them out."

Simon and Sylvie exchanged a look. "I know about that," said Simon. "The LT told us earlier today."

"Well, Evarts wasn't happy, I can tell you," said Liam. "Pitched a holy fit until the LT called him on his personal mirror and ordered him to stand down.

Anyway, I just came from the Crime Lab and Evarts is still hot. He says he'll have his report on the farmhouse on your desk by morning, but wanted to know if you managed to salvage anything else from the fire."

Sylvie took the bomb fragments out of her pouch. "Only these," she said. "I doubt they'll reveal much. They were exposed to some intense heat, and both Simon and I have handled them."

"I'll take them down to the lab anyway," said Liam, taking the fragments from her with a nod. "You never know."

"Get on with it, Liam," said Simon impatiently. "What 'acorns' did you find?"

Liam produced the cardboard box of strange ammunition that Simon had seen in Hightower's office and set it on the desk. "These are totally inert, magically speaking. I cast several Reveals on them and there is no magical energy in them at all, none. I can't think of any complex manufactured object in the world that doesn't have at least some residual aura on it. Unless every component of these things was handmade—unlikely given how identical each one of these little cylinders is—then some process we don't understand made them. Completely mechanical manufacturing is possible, but why bother? The investment in time and resources alone would be exorbitant and these things were clearly made for sale. By whom? And why?"

"Any ideas?" asked Simon, passing over the fact that Liam had stolen evidence from a crime scene.

Once Flandyrs shut down access, Simon figured the scene would be sterilized by the SED anyway.

Liam shook his head. “Not a clue. I did find evidence the good Professor was working on some strange stuff. Most of the symbologic notations in her lab were beyond my understanding. It was clearly some sort of mix of Earth and Blood magic, but beyond a basic summoning spell, I couldn’t follow it. It’s either brilliant or complete gibberish.

“Also, she was doing some basic Fire magic. There was a bit of aquamarine dust on the underside of her reaction shield, and some splintered rowan wood in the trash. If she wasn’t making those bombs, she was showing someone else how to do it.”

“Did you get a chance to look over any of her files? Any names, mirror loci, addresses?” asked Simon.

“No,” said Liam. “Sorry, I didn’t have time. Like I said, I got a good look around but nothing like a thorough search. The only other odd thing was the scorch marks on the walls and ceiling of her lab. I assumed that they had something to do with her messing around with Fire spells. That can be tricky. But now that I think about it, they weren’t right for that. Too uniform. More like some sort of bright light had caused them rather than actual flame.”

“Good work, Liam,” said Simon. Liam grinned broadly and glanced at Sylvie.

“What next, boss?” asked Ham. “Should we make another run at the Rez?”

"Yes. I want you and Jack to go with Liam and Gripple, at least as far as the Reservation gate. If Gripple does manage to get Liam some time with Gran Swampwater, I want the two of you to talk with the Marshall again. Don't lean on him about the Swampwaters. See if he's had any visits from Elves other than Hightower. Also, I'd like you to check with the Fernhill Keepers. Get a line on the local Orc scene—frequent offenders, known troublemakers, any political unrest and the like. Someone knows who lured Gripple out of his house so he could be taken. That's the Orc we need to find."

CHAPTER FOURTEEN

The ride back down to Bowater was long and painful. Simon elected not to go home first and get out of his singed and stained uniform. Sylvie had insisted on accompanying him. He'd offered to stop at her flat and drop her off, or allow her to change first, but she'd refused. He wasn't sure why she'd wanted to come at all, but he didn't ask. He really didn't want to have a conversation with anyone.

They'd finished with the rest of the team and sent them home just after seventeen. The next day's assignments had been made and they would only check in by mirror or FS rather than meet again as a group.

By the time Simon pulled the sled out of the stables and onto Tanner, the local traffic was light. That changed as he swung south onto the KR34.

The highway was jammed with the usual evening crush of southbound commuters all heading home to their dinners.

Over an hour later, Simon exited onto the Ring Road at Bowater. He was exhausted, but traffic was lighter on the four-lane commercial shipping route and they made good time to the exit for Queen Eleanor Regional Hospital. Still, it took a major effort to let go of the steering yoke and climb out of the sled once he had it settled into the "Peacekeeper Only" slot in the parking area outside of Casualty Receiving.

Sylvie seemed to be moving easier, but stayed by his side as he walked slowly through the double doors and sought out the Control desk. A polite Orc receptionist scrutinized his badge, gave Sylvie a curious look, and then checked her directory for Hal's room.

"Yes, sir," she said. "Agent Stonebender is still here. He's in room three-twenty-four, just down this hallway and up to the third floor, turn left to Ward B."

They waited by the lift for a time, but when a pair of Healers pushing a patient on a wheeled litter shoved them aside and entered it, Simon decided the stairs would do.

Hal was sitting up in bed, frowning at a tray of food in front of him. Molly stood over him, also frowning.

"I don't care what it smells like," Molly said. "You're going to eat it and then you're going to sleep. The Healer said you could only go home if you could keep down a full meal and could walk to the door."

"I'll show you walking to the door," Hal said, kicking at the blankets across his legs. "Then I'll walk down to the nearest tavern for a proper supper. Sausages and some good ale, that's what I need. Not this slop."

Sylvie laughed and both Hal and Molly turned to look at them.

"About damn time, lad," said Hal. "They're trying to kill me here. Talk to that harpy of a nurse and get me out of here."

"Sorry, Hal," said Simon. "Healer's orders. Besides, while you've been loafing here, we've had a busy day. I'm too tired to keep you out of trouble right now."

"You keep me out of trouble? Ha! If I hadn't set off that turkey trap, you might have blundered into it yourself. It takes a Dwarf to stand up to a blast like that. Might have killed a Human like you."

"That's enough of that twaddle, Haldron Stonebender," said Molly. "You've Simon and this Elf Lady to thank for rescuing your sorry hide." She turned to Sylvie and gave her a long appraising look. "Simon tells me it was you who pulled my husband away from the fire. For that, I do thank you, m'Lady."

"It was Simon who saved us both, Mistress Stonebender. He shouted the warning to Hal and pushed me to the floor so that the blast went over me. If not for him, I wouldn't have been able to do anything for Hal. And my name is Sylvie. Sylvie

Graystorm. Forget the 'm'Lady' business." Sylvie held out her hand.

Molly looked at it for a moment, then smiled and shook it. "Well met, Sylvie Graystorm. You are always welcome in the Hall of House Stonebender."

Simon blinked in surprise. Molly was always polite when meeting Hal's teammates or other coworkers, but offering someone Rights of the Hall was usually reserved for close friends.

He looked at Hal who nodded. "Seriously, lad," he said. "Thank you. And you, Lady Graystorm. I affirm my wife's welcome. Meat and mead, hearth and home, safety and fellowship be yours."

For once, Sylvie look nonplussed. Her eyes went from Molly to Hal, to Simon. Then she stood back, placed her right hand on her heart and bowed deeply. "I am honored, Mistress Stonebender. Food and drink, fire and fellowship, I share, and pledge myself to the defense of the Hall," she said, reciting the proper formula. She straightened, looking a little unsure as to what to do next.

Molly stepped forward and embraced her. "Call me Molly, Sylvie. Now tell me what this fool has gotten us into this time," she said, pointing at Simon.

"Best come over here, lad," said Hal. "You'll not fare well at the hands of two women."

Simon watched as the women retreated to a corner of the room, talking in low tones. He turned to Hal. "How are you holding up?" he asked.

Hal grimaced. "Not worth shale," he said. "But don't let Molly know or she'll chain me to a bed for the next week. I'll be up and ready for the field by morning."

"The hells you will," said Simon. "You're on desk duty for at least the next two days. Sylvie and I were nearly parboiled this afternoon. I'm not sure I'm fit for field duty, myself. I don't want you out there until you're granite solid, understood?"

Hal started to protest, but then closed his mouth and sighed. "Right. Truth be told, I don't think I'd be much help in a fight right now. But you've got to get me out of this place. I'll do anything you say as long as I'm not stuck here or at home with Molly glaring at me every time I turn around."

Simon smiled. "She means well, Hal."

"Aye. She's a good woman. But she worries too much."

"Two days ago, I'd have agreed with you. Now, I'm not so sure," said Simon. "Every lead we've followed in this mess has tried to kill us. Someone is seriously covering their tracks."

"What happened this afternoon? You said something about boiling?"

Simon told him about the Durlash figurine and how it led to the glass factory. When Simon described the glass golems and Sylvie's maneuver with the water tank, he whistled softly.

"Tough and smart," Hal said, "Watch yourself with that one, lad."

"She's a Ranger, Hal. She may report to Summerfield, but she's here on Flandyrs' orders. I still don't know what she's reporting about us." He held up a hand when Hal started to protest. "I don't mean she'd intentionally sell us out or undermine the investigation, but Flandyrs has a lot more leverage than he should if he can get a crime scene analysis shut down or get a court order with a wave of his hand. The less he knows about our movements, the better I like it."

"So what do you want me doing?" asked Hal.

"The CSA lab reports should be in by morning. I'd like you to go over them with an eye toward anything that links Hightower to the Azeri. We know someone was making bombs at that farmhouse. Was it Hightower, or someone else?" Hal nodded understanding and Simon continued. "Also, get on the mirror to the Eastern Borderlands station. See what you can learn about recent Brigade activity there. Any big influx of suspected Brigade sympathizers, or known contacts? Any rumors of a big operation in the works? Find out if there is any word out of the Empire about the same sort of thing."

"I get the idea," said Hal. "I'll check with our own Foreign Ministry, too. I have a source in the Security Office. I'll see if there are any upcoming visits from the Empire that might be targets." He thought for a moment. "I can also check in with Will Tunnelsmith down in Warrants. He has the Hollows division. He may have a line on Gorski and Blackpool. Priors and descriptions, at least. I doubt Snick will talk to anyone but me, and that only face to face, so we're stuck midtunnel on finding them until I can get back in the field."

Simon scratched his chin and winced. It was still raw from the steam. "See if Tunnelsmith has anything on Joby Blackpool, either priors or any association with this enforcer that Snick gave up. I have a hunch that friend Joby is more than just a custodian."

Hal nodded and said, "It looks like Molly and your friend have finished their talk."

Simon half turned as Molly and Sylvie approached.

"So, Sergeant Buckley," said Molly. "Not only did you get my Hal involved in an international incident, but you managed to destroy two buildings in a single day and nearly got this brave woman scalded to death. What do you have to say for yourself?"

"It wasn't my fault," protested Simon.

"Dreck and tailings," scoffed Molly. "You're the team leader. It's your job to keep the rest of them digging the same tunnel and see to the shoring, not go running off chasing fool's ore. Next time, you get proper back-up and communications before going in. Didn't Hal teach you anything?"

Sylvie stood behind Molly, stifling a laugh. Simon smiled but said, "Yes, Molly," in his most contrite voice.

Molly glared at him for a second, then nodded and smiled as well. "Good. Now take Sylvie back to her flat and go home yourself. You both look terrible. And you're both to be in my kitchen by seventeenth hour tomorrow for a good meal. Real food, not that Dundari chicken take-away trash you eat almost every night."

"Yes, Molly," Simon and Sylvie said in unison.

They left Hal's room with promises to check in regularly during the day. Sylvie asked if she could bring anything for the meal the next evening and Molly scoffed again as if the idea was preposterous.

The ride back to Cymbeline was long and quiet, but less tense than the trip down had been. Sylvie sat with her eyes closed part of the time. Simon couldn't tell if she was asleep or simply resting. He said nothing until they approached her street.

"You must have made quite an impression on Molly Stonebender," he said. "She rarely invites anyone into her kitchen."

Sylvie smiled. "Molly loves you like a son. She's strong and smart and terribly afraid that you'll get hurt."

Simon shrugged. "Being a King's Agent is dangerous. She knows that. Hal's been a Keeper for longer than I've been alive. Molly knows the drill."

"It's not the job that she fears will hurt you," said Sylvie.

Simon wasn't sure what she meant, or so he told himself. He parked the sled at the curb a half block from Sylvie's building and they walked the rest of the way.

There was a different concierge by the door this time, but he looked just as formidable as Lester. He stood as Sylvie was unlocking the street door and watched them enter.

"Good evening, Hiram," said Sylvie as they walked toward the stairs. "Sergeant Buckley is with me."

Hiram nodded, looked Simon over carefully, and sat back down. He was subtler than Lester had been as he replaced the bolt thrower.

Sylvie unlocked the door to her flat and turned to face Simon. "Would you like to come in?" she asked, opening the door. "I think I have some leftover Azeri noodles from the take-away stand down the block."

Simon smiled. "You too? No wonder Molly insisted on feeding us both. She probably told you that you were too thin as well."

"She did say I was 'not much wider than a mop handle,'" Sylvie admitted.

Simon laughed. "Thanks for the offer, but I'd better go home. I'm barely keeping my feet as it is."

Sylvie nodded. "Good parting, Simon."

"Good parting, Sylvie." He touched her hand and suddenly she was in his arms. Her lips were soft and parted as they met his. Her lithe body pressed against him, strange and yet familiar, so like Alira's. For a second he felt lost. Then she pulled away from him and the spell was broken.

"I'm sorry," she said. "I shouldn't have done that." She looked away.

He touched her cheek. "No worries. We're both tired, and it's been a difficult day, that's all. Good parting, Sylvie. I'll see you at seventh hour." He turned and walked toward the stairs on legs that threatened to betray him and turn back to her, forcing himself to keep his eyes forward and head high, and heard the door to her flat close behind him.

CHAPTER FIFTEEN

Simon sat behind his desk at fifteen before seventh hour, looking over the forensics report from the Crime Lab. There was nothing new in the coroner's section, other than the curious notation about White Blood Disease. The Forensics team had indeed found traces of aquamarine and rowan on Hightower's clothing, making it virtually certain that she had been involved in the actual fabrication of the bombs.

There was a catalog of other items found in the room, mostly mundane tools and a few old kitchen implements. Two items caught Simon's eye. One was a pair of long gloves; elbow length at least, constructed of heavy leather but lined with lead. The other was an oak pole, about six feet long with a claw-like scoop on one end. Both the pole and the scoop were also sheathed in lead.

He puzzled over the gloves and the pole. Lead was magically inert, not susceptible to any type of spell. Its presence near an active casting could even cancel the spell. Why would any mage have items that could cancel out whatever spell they were trying to cast?

Simon shook his head and put the list aside. He took out the images the team had captured of the strange symbols on the floor. According to the report, they had actually been etched into the wood, not just drawn on the floor. The etching was only a fraction of an inch deep, but traces of Platinum were present in the grooves. When Simon thought about that, it made some sense. Platinum was a noble metal that augmented Earth spells, just as Gold augmented Fire, Silver augmented Water, and Aluminum, Air.

He thought about what Evarts had said about the nature of portals and wondered if somehow the lead allowed Hightower to overcome the limitations on living tissue passing through them. That thought was intriguing, but how could reaching through a portal be of any use? Robbery? She was already rich, so what would her motive be?

Finally, at the bottom of a list of contents removed from elsewhere in the farmhouse, he saw two highlighted notations: *37. Nickel-plated mechanical device, steel and unknown material (enamel?); use unknown. 38. Handheld mirror, possibly fire-damaged; attached rigid card of inlaid silver and gold; use unknown.* He sent Kyle Evarts a message that he would like to examine those two items in person.

Precisely at seventh hour, Sylvie stepped into the office, dressed once again in the charcoal breeches and gray shirt of her working Ranger uniform. She smiled politely but avoided his eyes as she sat on the end of the couch and settled her rapier and pouch on the floor next to her.

Simon looked at her for a long minute then sighed. "Look, Sylvie, about last night . . ."

"Nothing to be said," she interrupted. "We were both tired and I took advantage of it. My fault. I promise I won't let anything like that happen again. We have a job to do and getting emotionally entangled will only make that harder."

Simon sat back in his chair, a bit nonplussed. He had meant to say something similar, tell her that he shouldn't have taken advantage of the situation, and that he wouldn't presume any emotional involvement. But he knew that was a lie, Alira forgive him.

He simply nodded and said, "All good, then."

"Right. So, what's our plan for the day?"

"We need to stop down in the lab. I want to look at a couple of odd things the CSA team found in the farmhouse. We should hear from Jack and Ham soon, and Hal should be on his way home from Queen Eleanor. If Molly will let him, I'd like him to review the forensic reports for anything I might have missed. I'll have Evarts mirror copies to him." He paused, calculating times. "By then it should still be early enough to expect Clearwater to be at home, but not so early as to alarm him. We'll drop by for a quiet conversation."

"Good," said Sylvie. "I have a lunch date at midday with the associate from Greenleaf and Handfield who manages Farele Sindarin's affairs in the Commonwealth."

"When did you have time to set that up?"

"I didn't." Sylvie replied. "I had my older brother's secretary call and make the appointment. He's our family agent outside the Havens, so it looks legitimate and won't trace back to the investigation."

"Unless someone thinks to ask your brother about it." Simon pointed out.

"Maeve won't make a record of it, so he won't know. She's worked for him for so long that he never questions what she tells him."

Simon shrugged. "All good. I still don't think we'll find any evidence that Flandyrs knew who owned the farmhouse or had anything to do with Hightower using it."

"Perhaps not," agreed Sylvie. "But someone gave Hightower access to the house. She doesn't strike me as the type to scout suburban locations for illegal bomb-making and experimental conjuring."

"Don't forget Molly's orders to be in her kitchen by seventeenth hour. Best eat a light lunch. Molly sets a full table."

Sylvie groaned. "Dwarf food. Huge roasted joints of meat, potatoes five different ways and endless rounds of toasting with mead."

Simon smiled. “Molly may surprise you,” he said.

Evarts met them in the Crime Lab. He led them past rows of marble-topped workbenches where technicians examined, cataloged, and collated evidence from a dozen different crime scenes. Evarts stopped at the door to a locked evidence room, opened it and waved them inside.

A long counter separated the door from the remainder of the large room lined with warehouse-type shelves filled with evidence boxes. On the counter was an open box and next to it were the two items Simon had wanted to examine.

Evarts pointed to the first one. “This is clearly a weapon,” he said. “But I was reluctant to call it that, since I have no idea how it works. I’ve tried half a dozen Reveal spells on it, but there is simply no trace of any aura on the thing. It is precision made, and part of a larger group of similar weapons—what look like serial numbers are etched on the barrel and body, but I don’t recognize the numerical system.”

“May I?” asked Simon, reaching for the short-barreled weapon. Evarts nodded, and Simon picked it up. It was surprisingly heavy for such a small object. The grip was clearly designed for one hand. It fit comfortably into his. There was a trigger and guard assembly very much like that of his needler or a D’Stang bolt thrower. Just above the grip was a round cylinder perforated with six holes, each the width of his small finger. A surprisingly short barrel, only about as long as the width of his hand, extended from the front of the cylinder, while a small bit of metal that looked for all the world like a tiny claw hammer was positioned at the rear, just above his hand.

He pointed the barrel at the floor, well away from anyone nearby and squeezed the trigger. The hammer clicked back then slammed forward onto the rear of one of the holes as the cylinder rotated to bring it into alignment. Nothing other than the loud click occurred, but it made Simon very uneasy. He remembered the box of small objects in his locked drawer, so obviously designed to fit into this weapon. He had no doubt that once they were in the holes in the spinning cylinder, this thing would become deadly.

The weapon had the look of a well-designed, mass-produced object, not a hand-built, custom device. But who would manufacture such a thing, and how?

He replaced it on the counter and examined the handheld mirror next to it. This he thought he understood. It was slightly smaller than the Astral Silverline that he carried, but the black screen and frame were of the same sort of design—functional and rugged. The bottom right corner was bent and distorted, as if melted. When he turned it over, all familiarity disappeared. The backing was missing and instead of the aquamarine and ebony chips that made up the functional spell casting part of a magic mirror, he saw a thin flat plate of enamel embedded with silver and gold wires, what appeared to be bits of colored glass, and a square of black metal about the thickness of a half-penny coin. He looked at Evarts.

The CSA mage shrugged. “Don’t ask me. I’ve never seen anything like it. It’s magically inert, just like the weapon, and I have no idea what that wafer everything is stuck to could be made out of. It’s more like the chitin of a beetle shell than anything else.”

“Maybe Hightower pulled these things through portals that she had previously opened,” said Sylvie. “We suspected Swampwater wasn’t her first victim. Maybe she’s done that spell before, maybe a number of times.”

“Certainly possible,” agreed Simon. “But from where? I don’t know of anywhere in the world where stuff like this is made.”

“I don’t either,” she said. “Not in the Havens or the Commonwealth. But who knows what sort of secret projects the Azeri Empire may be working on. And then there’s the Ironlands, and the Free States to consider.”

“The Ironlander Dwarves do quality manufacturing, but always to Commonwealth designs. And always by conventional means,” Simon said. “They actively suppress magical theory and research within the Iron Fence. And the Azeri aren’t known for innovation or quality. That’s why they buy or steal technology from us. The Free States will gladly sell you one of these if they get their hands on it, but they manufacture next to nothing. Trading is their way, not making things.”

"All good," agreed Evarts. "But someone made these things, and I don't know who or why. And that frightens me."

Both Simon and Sylvie nodded in agreement, but had nothing more to offer. They left the evidence room and Evarts locked it behind them. Simon didn't mention the box of what was obviously ammunition for the weapon. He wasn't sure why, but had a feeling that he should keep that bit of information inside the team. He looked at Sylvie who seemed to sense what he was thinking and nodded, touching a finger to her lips.

Jack called on Simon's FS receiver as they were descending the stairs to the stables. He and Ham had picked up Liam and Gripple at Charity Hospital and were now on the S393 heading toward the Reservation. He promised to check in by midday whether Liam had met with Gran Swampwater or not.

Simon went to the armorer and picked up his needler and his Bonecleaver. The needler went into a concealed shoulder holster and he slid the short sword under the seat of the two-man sled he'd drawn for the day. Sylvie placed her rapier beside it and swung into the passenger seat. Simon pulled back on the yoke and guided the sled out into the morning traffic.

Clearwater's house was a tidy bungalow on a cul-de-sac near the All Gods Temple about three miles from Wycliffe House. Tanner Street ended at All Gods Square, which fronted the Temple grounds. Simon parked on the square and they walked the short block to the house. It looked like most of its neighbors, with a short iron fence at the sidewalk, a neat front garden and a narrow white porch. Hanging from the eaves was a small camel fetish, the only hint that an Orc, and indeed an Azeri, lived here.

Simon knocked at the door, then stepped back and stood with his hands by his sides, palms outward and slightly away from his body. Sylvie stayed behind him, off the porch but still in plain sight.

A small peephole opened in the door and a shrill voice asked, “Who are you and what do you want?”

“Mr. Clearwater?” said Simon. “I’m Sergeant Simon Buckley, a King’s Agent. I’d like a few words with you, please.”

“Show me some identification,” the voice demanded.

Simon reached slowly into his pocket and drew out his badge, which he held up toward the hole.

The peephole slammed shut and they heard a chain rattle, then the click of several deadbolts. Finally, the door opened a crack and a tall wiry Orc looked out.

He was almost as tall as a man, slight of build with narrow shoulders. His hair was thick and brown and seemed to sprout from his eyebrows. He had pale skin, a long hooked nose, narrow red eyes, and very large ears that twitched and moved as he peered at Simon and Sylvie. Intertwining black tattoos wrapped around the Orc’s neck and disappeared beneath the collar of a well-pressed blue shirt.

"May we come in, Mr. Clearwater?"

"Who's that?" Clearwater asked pointing at Sylvie.

She took a small step forward, mimicking Simon's pose. "My name is Sylvie Graystorm, Mr. Clearwater. I'm responsible for cracking your furnaces yesterday. My family will cover the cost of repairs and compensate you for your lost production. We'd really like to talk with you. It will only take a short time."

Simon didn't know if it was Sylvie's soothing tone or the promise of compensation that persuaded the Orc, but he nodded and opened the door wider, standing aside so they could enter.

The front room reflected Clearwater's Azeri heritage. The floor was covered with thick, multicolored carpets. There were no chairs, only a dozen or so fat pillows around a low central table. A wide-screen magic mirror hung from one wall and a small shrine to Durlash occupied another.

"Sit," ordered Clearwater as he arranged himself on a thick cushion at the head of the table.

Simon and Sylvie sat on opposite sides of the table, signaling in Azeri custom that this was a business meeting and not a social call, so that Clearwater wouldn't feel compelled to offer food or drink.

"Once again, I apologize for the damage to your factory," said Sylvie.

"Don't matter," said Clearwater. "Place was closed and the bank was going to take it, anyway." He shook a finger at Sylvie. "That doesn't mean you're not going to pay for the damages, though. I owned the contents, free and clear, and those furnaces were worth over a thousand crowns each."

Sylvie nodded. "Why was the bank going to take the factory?"

"Foreclosed on the property owner," said Clearwater. "I was just leasing the space from a management company. The real owner is some Elf off in the Havens who couldn't give two shits about what happens to a bunch of Orcs. They were happy enough to take my money, but they were six months in arrears on the mortgage. Now my boys are all out of work and I won't be able to reopen in new spaces for months."

"How do you know the owner was behind on the mortgage?" asked Simon.

"It was all in the papers those fancy advocates from up on the King's Road showed me. I understand foreclosures, Agent Buckley. The law says I have at least a month to vacate. I tried to tell them, but they had some Loblolly muscle with them and I didn't want anyone hurt. I even talked to that fancy Elf who was directing the whole show, for all the good that did."

"Did the Elf tell you his name?"

Clearwater snorted. "He gave me a name, but I knew he was lying. He sat there in his green and gold gown and said he was Glendower Serilene. But, I know the Serilenes. I sell high quality plate to their construction company. They'd have given me plenty of notice. And not a one of them would be caught dead dressing up in that Traditionalist silliness."

"The advocates, were they Human? Which law practice?" asked Sylvie.

"Aye, they were Human. Aren't they all? It was Greenleaf and Handfield. Those snakes do all the Elf dirty work in Cymbeline. "

"You have legal rights here, Mr. Clearwater," said Simon. "As you said, you have the right to a reasonable time to vacate once notice is served. Do you want to file a complaint?"

Clearwater reddened. "I tried to call Hervey Marshgrass, my own advocate, but that bully-boy smashed my mirror."

"But you've had two days since then to do something," said Sylvie "Why haven't you?"

Clearwater looked away, not meeting her eyes.

"Were you threatened in some way?" Sylvie asked gently. She glanced at Simon who nodded. "We can offer you protection."

"Ha!" the Orc said harshly. "Not from your own government." He sighed and rolled up his left sleeve. A complex tattoo of intertwining snakes covered his arm from wrist to elbow. "I'm Serpent clan. Never made any secret of the fact that I was Azeri. I came here over twenty years ago when it didn't matter who you were related to. Now, though, the Brigades have made life hells for any Azeri who shows his clan tattoos openly, but especially for Serpent clan. That Elf told me that if I as much as whined about losing my business he'd make sure the whole city knew I supported the Brigades."

Simon understood. The most recent wave of bombings and terror attacks originated with the Azeri Liberation Brigades, a splinter group of the larger Azeri Freedom Party which advocated overthrow of the current Azeri Emperor and institution of a representative government. The Empire was huge, and although technologically backward, maintained a large standing army. King Thorston voiced support for the idea of regime change, but often softened his rhetoric when a direct confrontation appeared imminent. The Brigades, led by Hargash Barsaka, Chieftain of the Serpent Clan, had renounced peaceful negotiation and declared war on the Empire and on the Commonwealth both.

"But you did support them, didn't you?" said Sylvie.

Clearwater stared at her. "What do you mean?" he asked cautiously.

"She means you purchased two hundred-weights of aquamarine from a south Dundaria mining company, and then passed it on to someone who was making Fire bombs for the Brigades," said Simon in a matter-of-fact tone. "Who got the aquamarine powder?"

"I don't know what you're talking about." Clearwater fidgeted on his cushion.

Sylvie produced the shipping order from her pouch and laid it on the table.

Clearwater reddened. "Look," he said. "I didn't have a choice. When your clan Chieftain comes to your house and tells you to do something, you do it. If you want to keep breathing, that is. I didn't ask who the stuff was for and I don't want to know. I stored it at the factory for a few days until a couple of cargo sledges came and carted it away. That's all I know."

"Who drove the sledges?" asked Simon. "Did you recognize any of them?"

Clearwater said nothing.

On a hunch, Simon asked, "Was it Gorski and Blackpool?"

The Orc jerked as if Simon had struck him. "How . . .? You didn't hear that from me," he said in a hoarse whisper. "You can't let them find out I talked to you."

"When did they pick up the powder?" asked Simon.

"Two weeks ago," said Clearwater.

"And you have no idea who they delivered it to?"

"I told you, I don't want to know," said Clearwater. "Chief Barsaka told me to get the stuff and pass it on to anyone who came with his sigil on their sword arms, tattooed right there." He pointed to the back of his own arm. "He said that in a fortnight, we'd all either be patriots or martyrs. I've got no desire to be either. I just wanted to run my business. I didn't ask questions when they picked the stuff up. I was relieved to have it out of my factory."

Simon took out his handheld mirror and activated it. With a brief search incantation, he found a public picture of Flandyrs in his official role with the Consulate. He turned the device so Clearwater could see it.

"Is this the Elf who was with the advocates who served the eviction on you?" he asked.

Clearwater glanced at the image and his eyes widened when he made a note of the name and source of the image. Then he turned away.

"I'm saying nothing more," he stated. "I'd like you to leave now, unless you're going to arrest me as a terrorist, in which case I want my advocate."

Simon looked at Sylvie, who shook her head. He blanked his mirror and put it back in his pocket.

"No, Mr. Clearwater," he said. "That's not necessary. Thank you for your time. Good parting."

He and Sylvie rose and left, the front door slamming behind them.

"Did you see his reaction to that image?" Sylvie asked, as they reached the sled.

"Yes," said Simon. "Any doubt that Flandyrs leaned on him to keep quiet?"

"None. It also makes a pretty convincing case for Flandyrs having serious influence at Greenleaf and Handfield." Sylvie smiled. "My lunch date just got a lot more interesting."

CHAPTER SIXTEEN

They returned to Wycliffe House just before tenth hour. Hal sent Simon a message over his mirror that he had the forensics files and was starting to review them. Jack and Ham checked in by FS from the road. They were with Liam and Gripple but had been delayed by traffic on the S393. They had cleared the worst of it and were making better time. They promised to call once they reached the Reservation.

Sylvie had left some clothes in the locker room and went in to change. Simon waited. She reappeared a few minutes later dressed in a deep green skirt and matching vest over a pale yellow blouse. Simon felt a visceral pang of desire but covered it with a casual nod of approval and she smiled.

"Can I give you a lift?" he asked.

"Better not. It would look odd if anyone saw me arrive in a Keeper sled. I'll hire a cab. I should be back before fourteenth hour. But . . ."

"What is it?" he asked.

"Flandyrs has demanded a meeting," she said, looking away. "What should I tell him?"

"Whatever you like. It's not up to me."

She frowned. "Don't be difficult, Simon. I'm committed to finding the truth here. There are too many troubling things going on around this case, not to mention someone trying to kill us. What do you want me to keep back?"

"Tell him everything, except the glass factory," said Simon with a sigh. "We weren't officially there and so the golems, Clearwater, and his information aren't on the record. We have to assume he has access to anything that Gulbrandsen or the Crime Lab have, so don't try to cover. It will make him suspicious."

"What about Sindarin owning the farmhouse?"

"What about it?" Simon shrugged. "He'll know what happened there and it's a legitimate lead for us to follow. If he's got as much pull with Greenleaf and Handfield as he seems to, he'll know about your lunch. Assume everything you talk about will get back to him."

"Maybe I should cancel it."

"No," Simon said with a shake of his head. "Then he'll really suspect something. I don't know how he's connected to all of this, but it's more than just protecting the Steward from political embarrassment. We can't afford let him find out we know about Clearwater or the aquamarine. What I don't understand is why Flandyrs would be mixed up with Barsaka and the Brigades."

"All good," Sylvie agreed. "What are you going to do?"

"Stay here and monitor progress. Jack and Ham promised to report in; Hal is cross-checking the forensics report, and looking into priors on Joby Blackpool. I'm going to write up some notes on this mess and try to outline what we know for sure, as well as what we suspect. Then I can make a plan to follow up on our suspicions." He paused and thought for a second. "Have you had a chance to check out those symbols with the Academy library?"

She shook her head. "Not yet. I imaged them to a librarian I know, but he hasn't responded yet."

She continued to look at him and he met her gaze. The conversation had turned superficial, unnecessary words just to have something to say, but he didn't want to see her go. She took a step closer and he felt his hand twitch with the desire to reach out and touch her. Her eyes seemed to bore into him, searching for something. He lifted his hand toward hers. A rattle of gear and footsteps on the stairs broke the spell, and three patrol Keepers heading out for traffic detail brushed past on their way to the stables.

"I should go," said Sylvie.

Simon nodded but didn't speak. She turned slowly and followed the patrol Keepers to the stables where she could call a sled for hire.

Simon climbed the stairs up to the squad room. He shook his head as if that would clear the confusion. It didn't help. In his head, Alira's voice spoke softly to him. He didn't understand the Qetchwa phrase, but her tone was sweet and soothing. He shook his head again. He was too busy for this crap right now. No more ghosts.

As he slumped into his office chair, his mirror pinged with a summons from Hal. He passed his hand over the screen and the Dwarf's face swam into view.

"You look like hells," Hal said.

"Good meeting to you too, partner," said Simon.

"I hope that Elf girlfriend of yours isn't keeping you up at night. Molly won't take it kindly if you fall asleep at her table."

"Would you shut up about Sylvie," snapped Simon. "She's a Ranger. She's going to be reporting to Flandyrs about the case this afternoon. Whatever passes between us is purely professional."

Hal laughed. "Just keep telling yourself that, lad. Maybe you'll believe it."

"Why did you call, Hal?" Simon asked.

"Ah, right. I checked into that Joby Blackpool like you asked me to. Turns out he has a record. Did three years up at the Bear for illegal conjuring. Seems he's some kind of shaman for the Serpent clan. His clan name is Barsaka, cousin to Hargash himself. He changed it to Blackpool when he emigrated here from the Empire a dozen years ago."

"Any known connection to the Brigades?" Simon asked.

"None," said Hal. "Since he got out of prison he's been clean as a mountain spring. Either he's on the straight, or he's very careful. He's on the antiterrorist watch list, but nothing has ever been reported."

"What was the conjuring charge?"

Hal frowned. "Blood magic, Earthquake spells. He tried to collapse a building for the insurance money."

"Pretty powerful casting," said Simon. "He's an Earth mage?"

Hal shrugged. "Orc shamans aren't Disciplined. They tend to be powerful Earth conjurers, but do a lot of healing and Blood curses as well. Orc magic is just different."

"Any connection to the Azeri enforcer your Orc informer named?"

"Likely," said Hal. "They're both Azeri, and it seems that Barsaka means 'dark water' in the Azeri tongue. I learned that from Will Tunnelsmith. He got me the offense summaries on Gorski and Blackpool." He paused and looked down as if reading from a file. "Murg Gorski, originally from the Eastern Reservation, Azeri but Commonwealth-born. Convictions for Strongarm Robbery, Extortion, three for Deadly Assault; served six years at Bruno Prison Farm. His bunkmate there was Wadelok Blackpool, Azeri immigrant, sent up for

Strongarm. They got out at about the same time and have been working as a pair ever since."

Simon told him about the interview with Clearwater. "I'm certain Gorski and Blackpool were the ones who picked up the aquamarine dust. I agree it's likely that Joby and Wadelok are connected. But why would Flandyrs be trying to cover up the connection between Clearwater and the Brigades?"

"You've got me there, lad," said Hal. "Oh, and I heard from my source in the Foreign Ministry. Nothing official as far as any Imperial visits go, but there's a trade show highlighting Azeri imports starting today down at King Olaf Hall."

"I'd put out an alert for the security detail there," said Simon. "It may be an overreaction, but we have to assume that the Brigades have a few hundred Fire bombs at their fingertips. They must be planning something."

Hal agreed to pass that on to his contact in the Ministry and signed off. Simon sat back in his chair, drumming his fingers on the armrest. He rubbed his chin, thinking about what Clearwater had said about patriots and martyrs. A fortnight. The aquamarine powder was picked up a fortnight ago, about the same time that Hal got the tip on the farmhouse.

He stood up and started for the stables. The trade show seemed an unlikely target, but he couldn't stand to sit around doing nothing any longer.

He sent a summons to Sylvie's mirror but she didn't respond. He checked with Jack and Ham. They were almost to the Reservation and would report if anything developed.

Simon had left his sword in the sled. He checked to see that it was still stowed under the seat, retrieved his tactical vest from his locker and tossed it in on the passenger side. His needler was still in the shoulder holster and he checked that a needle was chambered and the spring was fully charged.

The trip to King Olaf Hall took almost twenty minutes in midday traffic. The Hall had once been the premier exhibit center in Cymbeline, but twenty years of progress had left it behind. Larger, grander facilities had opened away from the crowding and congestion of the city center. King Olaf had become a secondary venue, fine for smaller functions or the occasional midlevel Arena Combat match, but too small for first level shows and conventions.

The building retained the neoclassical elegance of its early days. Despite being small by modern standards, it still conveyed a sense of respectability and style. For this event, the front entrance was hung with red and gold banners displaying the Azeri Imperial sigil of a spoked wheel and curving crossed swords.

The steps and sidewalk in front of the hall were crowded. Humans and Orcs in business suits mingled with Azeri in breeches, high boots, and sleeveless vests, their bare arms displaying the tattoos of a dozen clans. The crowd seemed to be waiting for something. Simon noticed that a purple carpet had been rolled out on the steps and sidewalk and a half dozen Foreign Ministry security officers were beginning to clear a path through the crowd. The situation made him uneasy.

He pulled to the curb in a no-parking zone, flipped down the King's Peacekeeper placard on the visor, and climbed out of the sled. He shrugged on the tactical vest and slid his Bonecleaver into the vest's rear sheath. He moved his needler to his front pocket and made sure his badge was visible on the lanyard around the vest's right shoulder.

The royal coach glided around the corner as he started walking toward the crowd. The security team moved into high gear, chivvying the crowd away from the curbside and clearing the path down the purple carpet. The coach halted precisely in front of the carpeted walkway and four liveried footmen jumped down.

Simon quickened his pace. Hal's source in the Foreign Ministry had said nothing about a royal visit to the trade show. Perhaps he hadn't known, or it was a spur of the moment decision by the King. Or maybe it was kept secret for security reasons. Simon was suddenly certain that this was a planned visit and that Barsaka and the Brigades had known about it for more than two weeks. He drew his needler and scanned the crowd, but it was too dense and shifting to really pick out any individual for scrutiny. He moved quickly around the periphery, looking for sudden movements, for someone who didn't belong.

One of the footmen stepped up to the coach door and opened it. Crown Prince Henrik stepped down and stood for a moment at the curb, his right hand raised in greeting, waving to the crowds. A man resplendent in the tall hat and sash of a Guild Master stepped forward and bowed, greeting the Prince. Simon quickened his pace around the crowd, now heading toward the coach, ready to shout a warning.

He almost missed the Orc in the heavy topcoat and furred hat. It was midwinter, but the sun was bright and the temperature unseasonably warm. Most people in the crowd wore at most a light jacket or cape. Simon edged closer. The Orc was sweating profusely and started edging his way forward, elbowing people out of his way. Simon brought the needler up in a two-handed grip.

"King's Agent!" he shouted. "Everyone get down! You in the coat—don't move!"

The Orc froze, looked back over his shoulder at Simon, and began reaching into his coat. Simon put two needles into his neck, drew the Bonecleaver, and rushed forward. People scattered to get out of his way. The Orc started to fall as the sleeper needles took effect, but continued to grope at the front of his coat. Simon shifted the sword to his left hand and managed to get a grip on the Orc's arm with his right, pulling it away from whatever he was reaching for. The front of the coat ripped open as the Orc fell, finally unconscious. Twelve Fire grenades, arranged in four rows of three, were strapped to his chest.

"Get back," Simon shouted, waving the Bonecleaver over his head. "Everyone back."

He looked around to see the security team and the footmen bundling the Crown Prince back into the coach. Three more security officers had heavy bolt throwers out and were pointing them at him.

"King's Agent!" he shouted lowering the sword and holding his badge over his head with his free hand.

One of them stepped forward, bolt thrower leveled at Simon's head. "Identify yourself," he said.

"Simon Buckley, Sergeant, King's Peacekeeper Force, Magic Enforcement Squad," Simon answered, lowering the Bonecleaver to the ground. "I'd appreciate it if you'd lower that weapon. This Orc is strapped with enough Fire grenades to take out half the block."

The security officer looked down at the unconscious Orc and paled. He lowered the bolt thrower. "Lieutenant!" he shouted over his shoulder. "We've got a situation here. Bomb Protocol."

The rest of the team sprang into action, moving the crowd back with shouts and physical force when needed. A tall Half-Elf in a security uniform strode over to Simon. He stood a head taller than Simon, but walked with a slight stoop to his left shoulder and a decided limp on his right leg. His left ear was missing and faint crisscrossed scars marred his left cheek.

"I'm Lieutenant Harold, Royal Security detail," he said. "What have you got, Sergeant?"

"Orc with a bomb vest, LT," said Simon, indicating the form at his feet. "Likely Azeri Liberation Brigade, or at least working for them."

Harold knelt carefully next to the Orc, taking in the rows of grenades, the two needles in his neck and the Serpent clan tattoos winding around the exposed skin of his arm.

"Gering," he said, addressing the officer with the bolt thrower. "Has the crowd been cleared yet?"

"Almost, LT," the man answered. "Everyone is back at least a hundred feet; all except the Trade Minister. He's yelling at Sergeant Hammerforge."

"Hammerforge will handle it," Harold said. He stood and regarded Simon. "I want to know what you're doing here, Sergeant. And why you didn't alert me and my detail if you knew there was a threat on the Crown Prince's life."

"I didn't, sir," answered Simon. "I'm investigating a case of illegal conjuring and bomb making and something one of my witnesses said made me suspect there was a threat to the trade show. I had no idea Prince Henrik was going to be here."

"No one was supposed to know," Harold said. "This was supposed to be a surprise informal visit."

"One that was planned more than two weeks ago," said Simon. "Hardly a surprise."

Harold looked at him sharply. "How did you know that?"

"Two weeks ago, Hargash Barsaka arranged for a shipment of two hundred-weights of aquamarine powder to be delivered to a farmhouse in Bowater. It was used to make Fire grenades. My team raided the farmhouse and during the assault killed the mage who made the bombs. One of my team was almost killed by a turkey trap filled with these things when we were searching the place. I had a hunch that the Brigades were planning something big with the rest of the bombs. This was the only event that fit the time frame my witness mentioned. They obviously knew someone important would be here."

"Who is this witness?" asked Harold.

"Sorry," said Simon. "That's confidential. He's under my protection."

"And he has material information about an assassination attempt on a member of the royal family," retorted Harold. "That trumps your investigation."

"No, sir, it does not," said Simon. "My investigation is ongoing and has Foreign Ministry sanction. I can't reveal my source without authorization from the Minister himself."

Simon hoped Harold wouldn't call that bluff. He doubted Gulbrandsen would back him in it, but he wasn't about to give Clearwater up without a direct order, and then only if the Orc could be protected.

Harold glared at Simon for a long second then muttered something about 'gods-damned diplomats', and said, "As you say. Clearly the Minister didn't see the need to involve his own team. Is there anything else I should know?"

"Nothing specific, unfortunately," Simon answered. "But we suspect there are several hundred Fire bombs out there. Barsaka didn't make them for nothing."

Harold nodded and turned to Gering. "Get this Orc restrained before he comes too. Gag him in case he can trigger this thing with an incantation. Then get the bomb team in here to get this vest off of him." He gave Simon a hard look. "I appreciate your help here. You may have saved the Crown Prince's life, but I'm not satisfied with your explanation. I'll be checking this out with the Minister once I have a chance to question this Orc." He turned and strode away, shouting orders to the approaching bomb team.

Simon made it all the way back to the sled before his hands started to shake.

CHAPTER SEVENTEEN

He'd been in combat before, at least the street level kind that came with the job. But he'd never come so close to death this many times in only two days. He gripped the steering yoke, gasping as he struggled to control his breathing, then it dawned on him. The stakes in this case were far beyond the possibility of just his own death. Had today's attack succeeded, it could have caused open warfare between the Commonwealth and the Empire. Tensions were already high in the East. Who knew what spark might ignite a shooting war?

He breathed deeply, forcing himself to calm down. He got out of the sled and paced back and forth until his heart rate slowed and his shaking subsided. Then he replaced the Bonecleaver under his seat, removed the tactical vest, and holstered his needler.

The trip back to the House took nearly an hour. Security forces had locked down much of the city center in the typical mode of a day-late-and-a-shilling-short ass-covering. He had to show his badge at several intersection checkpoints in order to get back to Tanner Street and the entrance to the stables.

It was well past the fourteenth hour by the time he parked the sled and stowed the vest in his locker. Only then did he realize that Jack and Ham had not checked in. He summoned Jack's mirror, then Hamish's, but neither one replied. He tried the FS net as he climbed the stairs to the squad room, his unease growing as repeated FS calls and summonses to Ham's mirror went unanswered.

He sat behind his desk, wondering if he should try Liam. If the young mage had succeeded in getting to see Gran Swampwater, a mirror summons might come as an unwelcome intrusion. After a moment's thought, he put the summons through anyway. It wasn't like Hamish to miss a check-in call. Simon was certain something was wrong.

At first he thought that the summoning had failed. It seemed to go through but the screen of his mirror remained black. After a second the image shifted as something in front of the mirror was moved. The black was replaced with a tilted image of the sky and a bare tree.

"Sarge?" Liam's voice was faint and rasping. "Is 'at you?"

"Liam," said Simon. "What's wrong? What happened?"

Liam's face appeared. Blood ran from his nose. The mage's face was swollen and his left cheek bled from a deep gash. Scorch marks blackened his collar.

"Ambush," croaked Liam. "Hit us on the road. Send help. Oh, Mother, Simon. Gripple's dead, Jack's down, still alive, I think. I can't find Ham. He was watching Gripple, but I can't find him."

Simon jumped to his feet and started toward the squad room. "Where are you, Liam?"

"Don't know for sure," said Liam, his voice becoming clearer as he got control of himself. "About three miles north of the Rez, I think. On the main road, just past the turnoff for Fernhill."

"How badly are you hurt?"

"I'll live. Feels like cuts and bruises." Liam looked around. "Jack's sitting up, now. I think he's all good, too." In the background, the whooping sounds of emergency sirens could be heard. "Help's coming. Should I leave this connection open?"

"Are you sure Swampwater is dead?" Simon asked.

Liam nodded. "There was a sledge grounded in the middle of the road. It looked deserted, but we stopped and Jack and I got out to investigate. They hit us with Fire grenades as soon as we did. I managed to get a containment spell activated but it only enveloped Jack and me. Our sled went up in the fireball from the grenades. We were blown clear but not burned. What's left of Gripple is still strapped in the back seat. I can't see Ham anywhere, but—" Liam stopped and choked a sob. "Oh shit, Simon, he couldn't have gotten out."

Simon stood still in the middle of the squad room, the entire day watch looking at him, knowing something was very wrong. He pushed down a sudden rush of despair and grief. No time.

"Don't dwell on that now," he managed to say calmly. "Close this connection and do what you can for Jack. Help the local Keepers to secure the scene. I'll have a team down there in two hours."

"Yes, Sarge," Liam said. "What are you going to tell the LT?"

"Never mind that. This is bigger than we thought. Let the locals deal with the scene and the recovery, but don't say any more than you have to about this case. Got it?"

Liam nodded. "Yes, Sarge," he repeated. "Aster out."

Simon looked around the squad room and found Servi Lillihammer, team leader for the Civil Enforcement squad. She hurried over to him.

"What is it, Simon?" She pointed at the squad room mirror on the far wall. "We heard about the attack at King Olaf Hall. It's all over the news. Were you there?"

"I was, but that's not the problem. Jack and Ham were with Liam Aster, taking a witness down to the Southern Rez, near Fernhill. They were ambushed on the road, possibly by Azeri from the same bunch who were at the Hall earlier today." Simon paused, controlling himself. "Servi, Ham may be dead. Our witness certainly is. Jack and Liam are hurt. I'm going to talk to the LT now, but I want a team mobilized to go down to Fernhill, coordinate with the local Keepers, and do the forensics. Can you talk to Kyle Evarts and ask him to get his people on it?"

"Sure, Simon," Servi said. "But Ham? Are you sure?"

"No," said Simon. "I don't know anything for sure. I just got off the mirror with Liam and he's pretty shaken. Just get down to the lab and tell Evarts to start for Fernhill. Tell him it's related to the Bowater case. He'll understand."

"On it," she said. "Keep us posted about Ham. He has a lot of friends in this House."

Simon nodded and turned to climb the stairs to Gulbrandsen's office. He opened the door to the outer office and Elvira Cairns looked at him in surprise.

"How did you know the Lieutenant wanted to see you?" she asked. "He only told me to summon you a few seconds ago."

"Instinct, Mistress Cairns," said Simon. "The mark of a good Keeper."

She gave him a sour look. "Well, go on in. He didn't sound too happy."

Simon bowed to her and opened the door to the inner office.

Gulbrandsen sat behind his ornate desk, scowling at Simon. "That was fast," he said. "Guilty conscience? Or did you think you could control the damage by talking to me first?"

"I only just found out. I got through to Liam Aster when agents Ironhand and McPhee didn't answer my mirror. How did you know about the ambush?"

"What in the hells are you talking about, Buckley?" demanded Gulbrandsen. "What ambush?"

"The ambush down by Fernhill," said Simon. "Liam and Jack seem to be all good, but Swampwater was killed and we fear Hamish McPhee may be dead also."

Gulbrandsen rocked back in his chair as if Simon had smacked him. "What? When did this happen?"

"Just a short time ago," answered Simon, perplexed at the Lieutenant's reaction. "I got through to Liam and he was still pretty shaken. I gathered it was only a few minutes after the fireball hit the sled."

"What in the hells are you talking about? What was your team doing down in Fernhill?"

Shit, thought Simon. This wasn't about the ambush. LT hadn't known.

He proceeded cautiously.

"They were transporting Swampwater back to his home and planned to question potential witnesses to his abduction. Meanwhile, we hoped Liam would be able to talk to Gran Swampwater about her connection to Professor Hightower." Simon paused to consider what to say next. "This was in my report, sir. Ranger Graystorm was able to identify some of the runes from the farmhouse as ancient Orc symbols. Gripple Swampwater's mother is an Orc shaman. We hoped she'd be able to explain the symbols to us."

"That's no longer your concern, Buckley," said Gulbrandsen, regaining his composure and swelling with new anger. "You are relieved of duty as of now. I'm placing you on administrative leave pending a full hearing."

"Relieved?" said Simon. "Why? I'm in the middle of an investigation. What am I supposed to have done?"

"You withheld critical information about investigative leads," answered Gulbrandsen. He ticked each point off on a finger. "Concealed material evidence, recklessly exposed an unofficial observer to potential harm, and lied to a sworn security officer about the nature of your investigation. I should be placing you in irons, not just suspending you."

"If this is about the attack at King Olaf Hall, I may have misled Lieutenant Harold, but I prevented a potential assassination." Simon held on to his temper—just.

"And failed to inform the proper security officers of the threat once you knew of it. Are you stupid, or did you just want the glory for yourself?"

His temper got away from him. "I didn't know for sure there even was a threat," shouted Simon. "I was following a hunch."

"Based on information you failed to report, even to your own team," sneered Gulbrandsen. "Did you think you could destroy another building and no one would notice? You're lucky Clearwater isn't suing this department for the damage to his property."

"How do you know about that?" asked Simon warily.

"So you admit you withheld that from your reports," Gulbrandsen said with a satisfied smile. "What other information are you sitting on?"

"I promised Clearwater his information would be kept off the record," persisted Simon. "His life could be in danger if Barsaka and the Brigades suspect he talked."

"I'm heartily sick and tired of your Azeri Liberation Brigades nonsense," said Gulbrandsen with a dismissive flick of his hand. "You and Stonebender cooked up a wild conspiracy to justify your botched raid on that farmhouse—with a warrant that was for a search *only*, I might add—and then pushed it again and again to cover your incompetence."

Simon struggled to control his rage. "It isn't nonsense. Hightower made Fire grenades for the Brigades. I don't know why, but based on the amount of aquamarine dust in that shipment, there are probably several hundred of the things out there right now. The Orc who tried to kill the Crown Prince is an Azeri. He had a dozen grenades strapped to his chest. Fire grenades have injured three of my team members. Hamish may be dead from a Fire grenade attack. Look at the evidence,

LT. This is more important than your political career, or making points with the Steward's lackey."

"Watch your damned tongue, Buckley," roared Gulbrandsen. "One more word and I'll have you in irons for obstruction of justice. Turn your notes over to Sergeant Killian. He'll head this investigation from now on. You are relieved and your team is on ninety-six hour stand down until a new ranking Keeper can be assigned."

Simon opened his mouth to protest, then stopped as the truth hit him. Gulbrandsen could only have found out about Clearwater from Flandyrs. And the only way Flandyrs would know about Simon's conversation with the glassmaker was if Sylvie had told him.

Gulbrandsen saw the defeat in Simon's eyes and tapped his desk with a forefinger. "Your badge and your sidearm, right here. Then get the hells out of my sight."

Simon tossed his badge on the desk. Then he cleared the chamber of his needler, canceled the arming spell, and dropped the weapon next to his badge. He took some petty satisfaction when the barrel gouged a small chip out of the polished finish. He turned smartly on his heel and marched out of the office.

He nodded brusquely to Mistress Cairns as he passed and resisted the impulse to slam the outer door. He managed to get down the stairs, across the squad room and into his office before the rage broke through his control.

"Damn her to all the Seven Hells," he roared, slamming his fists onto his desk top. He knew the rest of the day watch could hear him through the thin partition that made up the wall, but he didn't care. They would make a point of ignoring anything that went on in his office, at least for as long as it was still his.

He slumped in his chair. Stupid! Stupid! Stupid! She knew just what would get to him. How much of an idiot was he, for falling for it? Just because she reminded him of Alira?

Oh, 'Lir, forgive me, he thought. *I fell for her act and betrayed you.*

He pounded the desk until his hands hurt and the worst of his rage was spent. Then, for the first time in his life, he broke the law.

He activated his desk mirror and muttered the search incantation. He called up all the reports from his team, the Crime Lab, the coroner, and any other source related to Hightower and her death. He created a new heading containing all the information, then made two copies. As the pages scrolled off the printing press in his office, he checked his timepiece. Nearly sixteenth hour.

The last pages drifted to the floor. He gathered them up, neatly arranged one copy in a cardboard folder and sealed the folder into a heavy envelope. He labeled the envelope with Killian's name and set it in the center of the desk.

He opened the leather bag he kept in the office for nights when work prevented him from going home and pulled out the fresh shirt and hose he kept inside it. He stuffed the papers, along with the box of strange ammunition into the bottom of the bag, repacked the shirt on top, and closed the bag.

He stood up and slung the bag over his shoulder, just as Killian appeared at the office door. The man at least had the decency to knock before he entered.

"Sorry it came to this, Buckley," said Killian. "I always thought you were a good Keeper."

"I'm sure," said Simon without allowing a hint of sarcasm into his tone. "All the files are in the envelope on the desk. Good luck, Killian."

Without waiting for a reply, Simon brushed past him and crossed the squad room toward the stairs. He paused for a moment to raise an eyebrow at Servi Lillihammer, who nodded in reply.

He stopped at the Crime Lab rather than going directly to the stable and his personal flyer. He confirmed with the duty clerk that Evarts had personally led the team to Fernhill. Then he asked, as matter-of-factly as he could, to examine the evidence from the farmhouse again. The clerk nodded, had him sign the logbook and then retrieved the box containing the strange devices Evarts had shown him earlier.

"Just let me know when you're done, Sergeant," said the clerk. "I'll log the stuff back in myself."

"No need," said Simon. "I just want to confirm something. I'll shelve the box when I'm done. You look busy enough that you don't need another interruption."

"Thanks," said the clerk.

Simon waited until the clerk returned to his desk before he lifted the lid of the box. The strange weapon was on the top, and Simon quickly put it into his bag. The clerk was busy, but Simon made a show of rummaging through the box for a minute or so, examining objects at random. Then he replaced the lid and returned the box to the proper shelf.

He thanked the clerk on his way out and resisted the impulse to run down the stairs to the stable level.

CHAPTER EIGHTEEN

Simon flew slowly westward across the broad Finnegan River estuary, breathing deeply of the salt air. The docks of Westport, Cymbeline's waterfront, spread out below him, stretching up and down the river as far as he could see. Great ocean-going ships, their Water-impelling outriggers hauled in close to their hulls, were pushed and pulled into the cargo docks by steam and Air-powered tugs. Smaller barges from the upriver countryside glided slowly down the channel, their impellers rigged fore and aft in order to navigate the narrower canals that branched from either side of the river. The estuary, the river, and the canals were the arteries that kept the great city alive. They had given birth to it, had grown with it and were now so deeply engrained in it that few of its citizens even gave the waterways much thought. They just were there, like the sun and the rain. Just a part of life.

Westport was the Cymbeline of Simon's youth; the narrow streets and alleys, the quayside shops and chandleries, had been his whole world for the first ten years of his life. Even now, he would often walk the old neighborhoods or fly low over the broad flat water when he needed to think. He was an outsider here these days, a Keeper, a Bluebelly to the locals; and still the odors of salt water and wet hemp and rotting fish smelled like home.

He thought of his father. Chester Buckley had been a ship chandler, one of many who sold salt beef and provisions for ship captains to feed their crews; garnet dust and willow wood to power the Water spells that drove their ships; and traded stories and information about the City and the Commonwealth for news about the wider world. Simon's mother had died when he was an infant. He'd never known her and his father had said little about her other than she had been a foundling and that Simon had no other relatives.

Simon had loved working in his father's chandlery, listening to the sea captains' tales of storms and treacherous currents, strange cities with even stranger customs, and the daily pressures of commanding a crew. He'd dreamt of having his own ship one day.

But that world had ended when he was ten. Chandlery was a volatile business and his father had fallen deeply in debt. That was common enough on the banks of the Finnegan. They had managed before, and Chester Buckley expected to manage again. It also was common for the local loan leeches, mostly expatriate Free Traders from Lithuria or one of the other Free States, to offer to bail the troubled business out at ruinously high interest. They would then settle the mounting debt for a controlling share of the chandlery.

Chester had said no to the first two who approached him. It was business as usual: no blood, no harm. The Azeri hadn't been willing to take no for an answer, or maybe hadn't understood the rules of the game. Chester had thrown him bodily into the Finnegan the third time he'd shown up and threatened to foreclose on some short-term debt he'd bought from one of Chester's suppliers. Three days later, Chester's body had washed up on the banks of the estuary a mile from his own dock.

The murder had spawned a backlash of rage against the loan leeches that threatened to become violent. The Bluebellies came out in force and broke up the mobs, arrested several of the most usurious moneylenders, and surprisingly, got enough witness testimony to hang the Azeri for the murder of Chester Buckley. All well and good for the citizens of Westport; the King's justice was served. But Simon was still an orphan.

One of the Peacekeepers who had worked the case had seen something in Simon and had petitioned the King's Juvenile Advocate to become his foster parent. Hal and Molly Stonebender had taken him in and given him a home and a new family. He'd repaid them by becoming a Keeper. Hal had never pressured him, but his example had taken root in Simon's heart, and he couldn't imagine doing anything else.

By the time Simon flew across the estuary to Westbank and the low hills of Glenharrow, his rage had been replaced with a cold anger. Whatever Sylvie had done to him mattered less than what she might have done to kill the investigation. He would see what she had to say in front of Hal and Molly, before doing anything rash. Maybe he could control the damage and somehow protect Hal, Jack, and Liam from Gulbrandsen's anger with him.

Hal and Molly lived in an older neighborhood in the Glenharrow district. Many of the homes there were built Dwarf-fashion as tunnels and halls dug directly into the low hillsides. The area had fallen on hard times a half-century ago when many Dwarves followed Timon Halfhelm back to recolonize the ancient halls of the Darrowdowns. The great migration had drained the population of several Dwarven districts, but the promise of ancient glory had faltered when it encountered the reality of making a vast underground city habitable after centuries of neglect. More recently an influx of younger Dwarf and Human professionals had rehabilitated and gentrified the area, driving up property values.

Stonebender Hall was modest by ancient standards, but large for a Glenharrow hill house. Molly had raised seven children there, and although they were all grown and had families of their own, the Hall was often filled with visiting grandchildren, nieces and nephews, and various other family and friends.

Simon parked his flyer in the detached stable next to Hal's battered yellow Oxley sports sled and walked up to the big oak door. Before he could touch the latch, Molly flung it open and shook a wooden spoon in his face.

"You're nearly a half hour late, Simon Buckley," she said severely. "And you haven't answered your mirror. Hal has sent three summons in the last hour. Where have you been?"

"Flying," said Simon. "Out over Westport. I needed to clear my head."

Molly's annoyance changed to concern. "Simon, what's wrong?"

"Why would something be wrong?"

"Because you always go to Westport when something vexes you," said Molly. "Now come inside to the kitchen. Sylvie is already here."

Simon clenched his fists, controlling his anger, and followed Molly through the entry hall, across the huge open common room and into the kitchen. The air was warm and filled with the aroma of baking bread and stewing meat. Two massive iron stoves stood along the back wall. The other walls were lined with shelves and cupboards. A huge worktable, hewn from a solid piece of pine, stood in the center of the room. It was covered with bowls, cups, and pots as well as food in various stages of preparation.

Off to the right, a smaller table was set with four place settings. Hal sat at the head, drinking from a tankard. Sylvie stood at the worktable, chopping carrots with a long knife, laughing at something Hal had said. She saw Simon and her face changed. There was a flash of anger that was rapidly replaced by her resting Elf face. Simon glared back at her.

Molly noticed the sudden tension in the room. "Well, right then," she said.

Hal frowned and drank deeply from his tankard. "What's all this, then, lad?" he asked.

"Why don't you ask Sylvie?" Simon answered. "How about it, Sylvie? How was your meeting with Flandyrs? Did anything happen?"

Sylvie's eyes narrowed. "Don't mock me, you son of a gnome. You know damned well what happened. I don't know who you got to, or what favor it cost you to get me reassigned, but you could at least accept that you won without gloating."

Simon shook his head. "I don't know what the hells you're talking about. You're the one who sold us out. You're the one who told Flandyrs about the glass factory and about Clearwater. Now I've been suspended, the whole team is on a Ninety-Six, and Killian is all set to whitewash the case so Gulbrandsen can cover Flandyrs' ass."

"Suspended?" said Hal, setting down his tankard. "What's all this about?"

"Gulbrandsen found out we'd investigated the glass factory and talked to Clearwater. I didn't get a warrant for the factory and chose not to mention any of it in my report. Flandyrs is up to his neck in this and I didn't want Gulbrandsen to know that we knew it. The only person who could have told him about Clearwater was Flandyrs, and the only way Flandyrs would know, was if Sylvie told him." Simon pointed at Sylvie, shaking now with rage. "I asked you not to mention Clearwater. By now, Barsaka knows that Clearwater talked. The poor sod will be lucky to survive the night."

Sylvie's face paled as she set down the knife and shook her head.

"No," she said. "That's not true. I didn't even get a chance to say anything about the investigation to Flandyrs. He was waiting in his office with a Senior Ranger from Summerfield's staff. He started in on me as soon as I walked through the door about how I was supposed to observe and report, not participate, not get emotionally involved with the case. The Ranger didn't say anything, just stood there. Flandyrs told me I was relieved of duty and would be transferred to the Borderlands Division. The Ranger handed me orders to report to East Watch within a week for reassignment." She paused, her anger flaring again. "How could you think I'd betray the team? I thought we'd moved past all that. After yesterday, you still don't trust me?"

"I could say the same thing about you," said Simon. "You think I have the kind of steel it would take to get you transferred? If I did, you wouldn't have been assigned in the first place." He saw the hurt in her eyes and despite his anger, immediately regretted his words.

"Rein in, both of you," said Hal. "Sylvie, what Simon meant was that he wasn't keen on having any observer watching the team." He looked at Simon and held out a hand toward Sylvie. "I know how it may look, lad, but I trust Sylvie. You know me; I don't say that often. Now both of you sit down and figure this out. You're tunneling crosswise with each other."

"Sit. Listen to Haldron," said Molly, nodding to her husband. "I'll not have discord at my table. We'll sort this out over food."

Sylvie stood looking down at her hands, then reached out and grasped Hal's. "Thank you for that," she said softly. She allowed him to pull her toward the table where she sat in the chair to his left.

Simon rubbed his chin. Molly gave him a look and gestured toward the table. He crossed the kitchen and sat opposite Sylvie. Molly brought over a breadboard, knife, and a crock of butter. The warm smell of the fresh loaf seemed to lighten the air.

"I'm sorry I put it that way," said Simon. "I didn't mean that personally."

Sylvie nodded. "I know. I should have thought this through before I said anything."

"So," said Hal, taking up his tankard again. "Start from the beginning."

Simon shook his head. "Not yet. Molly, come sit down. You need to hear this too." She sat opposite Hal, wringing her hands on her apron. Simon gripped the table to steady himself. Still, his voice shook as he continued. "Earlier this afternoon, Jack, Ham, Liam, and Gripple Swampwater were on their way to the Southern Rez. They were going to question some witnesses and Gripple was going to try to set up a meeting between Liam and Gran Swampwater, Gripple's mother. Just outside Fernhill, a couple of miles from the Rez, they were ambushed. It looks like the Azeri; at least the attack was with Fire grenades like the ones we found in the farmhouse." He stopped and took a deep breath. "Jack and Liam are all good, but Swampwater was killed and, oh hells, it looks like Hamish was too. Liam couldn't find any trace of him after the explosion."

Molly gasped and said, "Oh, poor Reba. Has anyone told her yet?"

Sylvie sat silent, her face blank. Hal took a long pull from his drink and muttered something under his breath.

"Not yet, Molly," said Simon. "I made sure Kyle Evarts took a forensics team down there. Liam promised to contact me once they looked at the scene. I don't want to talk to Reba unless I'm sure her husband is dead."

"I'll go with you when the time comes," said Hal.

"As will I," said Molly. "She'll be needing a woman to help her."

"But why?" asked Sylvie. "Why attack them there?"

"I don't know," said Simon miserably. "I've mucked up this case from the start; almost got Hal killed, got myself suspended, put the whole team at risk, and now Ham." He leaned on the table, head in his hands.

"Enough," said Hal, thumping his palm on the table. "You're a better Keeper than this. We all know the risks when we take the King's shilling and put on the badge. Ham was a good man and we'll grieve him at the proper time. Our job right now is the find the bastards who did this and bring a rock pile down on them."

"But how, Hal?" Simon rubbed his eyes and straightened up. "I'm on suspension."

"I'm not, and I've been a Keeper for longer that Frank Killian has been wiping his own ass."

"Haldron," said Molly in a warning tone.

"None of that, Molly," he retorted. "I'm healthy enough, there are gods know how many more Fire grenades out there, and one of our friends has been killed. I'll not let that pass."

To Simon's surprise, Molly only lowered her eyes and nodded. "I'll bring the rest of the dinner," she said. She got up and began bustling about the kitchen.

Hal looked from Simon, to Sylvie. "First, the two of you make nice. Someone pulled the bracings out on you and we need to be digging together. Now, who would have the steel to get you reassigned, Sylvie?"

She glanced at Simon before saying, "Flandyrs, for sure. Maybe Summerfield, but I doubt he would." She looked at Simon again. "He specifically told me to get to know the lead investigator on this case. He said the Steward wanted the Rangers to do whatever it took, to make sure it was it was done right. Beyond Flandyrs and Summerfield, no one short of the Steward himself."

Hal grunted and poured more ale from a flagon on the table. He offered some to Simon who nodded. Sylvie declined.

"So, why would Flandyrs want you off this case?" Hal asked.

"If he knew we had found out that he was behind the Clearwater eviction, and if he found out that my lunch meeting at Greenleaf and Handfield confirmed it, I can see how he'd want to get me out of the way." She looked at Simon. "But I didn't tell him about Clearwater."

Simon nodded. "I believe you," he said. "But how could he know about our meeting with Clearwater?"

"Never underestimate an Elf when it comes to subterfuge," said Hal. "Apologies, Sylvie."

"None needed when you're talking about Flandyrs."

"Who knew the two of you were at the factory?" asked Hal.

"Just Simon and me," said Sylvie. "And Clearwater, of course."

"Would he talk to Flandyrs?"

Sylvie shook her head. "I doubt it. He didn't know who he was until Simon showed him an image. Flandyrs gave him a false name when he confronted him during the foreclosure, and Clearwater was frightened into keeping quiet when Flandyrs threatened to expose him as a Brigade sympathizer."

"Wait," said Simon. "There was one other person. Bogrunner."

"Who?" asked Hal.

"An Orc overseer who supplied labor to Clearwater. He's the one who told us about the factory being shut down."

"But why would he talk to Flandyrs, assuming he even knew who he was?" asked Sylvie.

"For money." Simon shrugged. "Down in the Hollows, information is a trade commodity. He could have found out from Clearwater who Flandyrs really was—the picture I showed Clearwater was an official Consular image. He might have thought Flandyrs would pay to know that a King's Agent was snooping around the factory."

"Makes sense," said Hal. "This Bogrunner sells the information to Flandyrs who adds one and three and gets four. He realizes the two of you know he's involved in covering up the aquamarine shipment and decides to get you off into a side tunnel until he can bury the truth."

"Enough talk," Molly interrupted. "We need to eat this stew while it's hot."

She carried a tray of bowls filled with a venison stew along with a plate of fresh greens to the table. She set a bowl in front of each of them and put the greens in the center of the table along with bottles of oil and blood orange vinegar.

Simon and Hal tore chunks of bread from the still warm loaf and began eating. Sylvie picked up a spoon and took a small bite of the stew. She tasted it and smiled, then followed Simon's lead.

For several minutes no one spoke. The flagon of ale was passed around and this time Sylvie poured herself a small mugful. The greens made a light counterpoint to the stew and Sylvie helped herself to them with obvious relish.

The meal was interrupted by a summons tone from Simon's mirror. He took it out and passed his hand over the screen. Kyle Evarts' face appeared, looking grim.

"What have you found, Kyle?" asked Simon. "Hal Stonebender is here with me."

"I'm sorry, Simon, but Hamish McPhee is dead," said Evarts. "We found his body in the burned-out sled. I identified him from his badge. Aster and Ironhand are at the Fernhill Clinic being checked out. Your Fire mage has quick reflexes. His containment spell saved the both of them."

"Were the grenades a match for the sample Sylvie Graystorm gave you earlier?" asked Simon.

"Yes. The aural patterns match. They were created by the same mage."

"Thank you, Kyle," said Simon. "I appreciate the call. Give your official report to Frank Killian."

Evarts looked surprised. "Why Killian?"

"I'm off the investigation. A severe case of insubordination."

Evarts smile was grim. "I hear that's going around. I might have caught a touch of it myself. I'll keep you informed. Evarts out." The mirror went black.

"I'll get cleaned up and we can go see Reba McPhee together," said Molly quietly. Simon nodded, his appetite gone. He'd thought he'd accepted Hamish's death, but hearing Evarts confirm it had suddenly made it more real.

"We'll get them, lad," said Hal, seeing his face.

"How?" asked Simon. "This case is a jumble. Too much information and too few links. How can we figure out who to go after?"

"We work the case," said Hal. "Step by step, like we always have. First, start with the who. Who is involved and what do we know for sure about them?"

"Hightower," said Simon. "We know she made the Fire grenades at the farmhouse. Forensics found traces of aquamarine dust and rowan wood on her clothes. The same grenades that almost killed you at the farm were used to kill Ham. Hightower was also doing some kind of strange Blood magic there, some sort of Portal spell, but why is still unknown. She was an Earth mage, she knew a lot about Orc magic and shamans and she definitely knew the Swampwater family."

"Good so far," said Hal. "Who else?"

"Flandyrs. He's been trying to cover up Hightower's connection to the grenades from the start. He knew the aquamarine powder was funneled through Clearwater and tried to shut him down by closing his factory and threatening him. He got Sylvie assigned to us, hoping that she'd spy on us and keep him informed so he could manage the investigation. He has deep influence in the law firm that manages the farmhouse where the whole thing started, and he's tried to cover that up as well."

"He didn't count on my orders to work with Simon rather than spy on him," said Sylvie. "That's why he had me relieved and Simon suspended. He couldn't control the investigation through us, so he pushed us aside."

"All good," said Hal. "What about Clearwater?"

"He's a pawn, near as I can tell," said Simon. "He was coerced into ordering the aquamarine by Hargash Barsaka because he's Snake clan, and Barsaka could compel him through his clan connection. He's genuinely scared that Barsaka will kill him if he talks."

"Who else?" asked Hal.

"There's Gripple Swampwater and his mother," said Simon. "Gran Swampwater spent a lot of time with Hightower, and someone intentionally lured Gripple out to be taken captive. I don't think Hightower picked him at random for her spell. There was something special about him that she wanted."

"And Gorski and Blackpool fit in—how?" asked Hal.

"Muscle," said Simon with a shrug. "They worked for Barsaka. I suspect Blackpool is a relative of Barsaka's, possibly close. We know the janitor, Joby Blackpool, is Barsaka's cousin, but other than working in Hightower's building at the University, I don't see any other connection."

"And the Azeri?"

"Barsaka's clearly behind the Fire grenades, but why Hightower would work for him and why Flandyrs would be covering for him is a mystery to me. She didn't seem political—quite the opposite. And while the Havens aren't exactly our allies, I can't see any official tilt toward the Empire. Flandyrs is a Gray Ranger in their political division. Is he running some operation to use the Brigades to destabilize the Empire? Or the Commonwealth? That doesn't make much sense."

"Maybe more sense than you think," said Sylvie thoughtfully. "Flandyrs is a Traditionalist, as is the current Steward. Who would benefit if the Commonwealth and the Empire got into a shooting war? Maybe they think they could work it to the Havens' advantage."

Simon shook his head. "I still don't see it. It would take more than a war to bring down the Commonwealth. Fighting the Azeri Empire would bleed us, sure, but not to the point that the Havens could benefit. Besides, what would they gain that they don't already get through trade?"

"You don't really understand the Traditional Party, Simon," Sylvie said. "They hate Humanity for what you've achieved that they could not. They hate your culture, your consumer economy, and your freedom from tradition. And they see younger or more liberal Elves embracing that way of life. Worse, emigration to the Commonwealth is increasing every year. They're afraid of losing their own culture."

"Maybe they should rethink the way they treat everyone except High Elves," said Simon. "Alira left the Havens because the patriarch of one of your Noble Houses was pressuring her father to marry her to his son. It would have meant a valuable alliance for her House, but she'd have been forced to be a Traditional wife. She loved running her family business and wouldn't give it up."

"I know," said Sylvie. "And that's my point. Our best and brightest are leaving to find a life in the Commonwealth. The Steward and Elves like Flandyrs resent it and they hate your country because of it. They'd applaud a war between the Commonwealth and the Empire, if only because it would hurt you."

Simon didn't answer her. He'd seen enough of the attitude she was talking about in his time on the Borderlands. But he also knew that Elves like Summerfield, and Alira and her father, didn't think that way. He didn't want to believe that the Traditionalists held all the power in the Havens.

"What leads do we have?" asked Hal, after an uncomfortable pause.

"Slim to none," said Simon. "There are the symbols from the farmhouse. Sylvie thinks they're some sort of ancient Orc runes, but what they mean is still unknown. Maybe if we knew what kind of Portal spell Hightower was attempting, it would lead to the reason she was working with the Azeri."

"This Gran Hightower is something of a shaman," observed Hal. "Could she tell us what they mean?"

"Maybe," said Simon. "But we got her son killed, or at least had him in custody when that happened. I doubt she'll talk to us."

"There's that mirror locus," said Sylvie. "The one Simon found on the bottom of that Orcish figurine. We could track that."

"We could, but it might tip off Gulbrandsen that we were still working the case," said Simon.

"So, we need to know why Flandyrs was covering for Hightower and why both of them would help the Azeri," said Hal. "We need to find out why Swampwater was specifically targeted, and whether the attack on our team was aimed at him or at the team itself."

That hadn't occurred to Simon. He'd assumed the attack was on his team. "Why would they want Gripple dead?" he asked.

Hal shrugged. "Why would they want to kill a Peacekeeper team? Did anyone outside the team know they were going down that way?"

"Only Gripple . . . Oh, I see."

Hal nodded. "And finally, we need to know what the hells Hightower was doing with that Portal spell. Any leads there?"

Simon shook his head. "We do have these," he said, reaching under the table and pulling out the strange weapon and its box of ammunition.

Hal stared at them for a moment before laughing. "In for a shilling, in for a crown," he said. "Lad, when you break the rules, you don't play small, do you?'

"What is that thing?" Sylvie asked.

"I don't know," said Simon. "A weapon, but I'm not sure how it works."

"No time like now to find out," said Hal.

"Here?" asked Simon.

"Why not? There's no one else around. The walls are thick and that worktable is near a foot of solid pine. Point it at that and see what happens."

Simon picked up the weapon and looked at it closely. There was a small latch just above the trigger guard. He pushed it and the cylinder rolled out sideways, giving easy access to the holes around its circumference. Simon picked up one of the small pieces of ammunition and slid it into a hole. He closed the cylinder and it clicked into position smoothly. He pointed it at the thick tabletop and squeezed the trigger. The cylinder rotated and the hammer clicked, but nothing else happened. Simon noticed that the hole containing what he presumed to be a projectile had moved closer to the top. He squeezed the trigger again, another click. He gripped the weapon with two hands, like he would his needler, aimed and squeezed the trigger.

A loud bang accompanied by a short flash of flame and a scant amount of smoke erupted from the barrel of the weapon. It bucked sharply in his hand and he almost dropped it. Through the thin haze of smoke he could see a splintered hole in the tabletop.

Molly ran in. "What was that?" she asked. "What in the name of Stone are you doing to my kitchen?"

Hal was bent over slightly, examining the hole. “No real harm done, Molly,” he said. “Just some noise, and less smoke than you make toasting bread.”

Simon stared at the thing in his hand as if it might bite him. He was used to handling deadly weapons. His needler could kill with the right ammunition. A D’Stang bolt thrower could penetrate an inch of solid oak and still be deadly if the cold iron bolt hit you. But he’d detected no magic when this thing made the noise, only violent recoil and a sense of dreadful purpose. Looking at the hole in the table, he had no illusions about what would happen if it had been a person in front of the weapon.

He thumbed the small latch and was surprised to see the end of the brass ammunition still in the little hole. It was slightly blackened. He tipped it out into his palm and noticed it was uncomfortably warm. It looked different. Where before it had ended in a smooth dome of lead, it was now an empty shell, like a tiny cup, blackened on the inside.

Hal grunted as he used a narrow blade to dig the tiny projectile out of the tabletop. He held it up between his thumb and forefinger, a misshapen lump of lead. He whistled. “Wouldn’t want to be hit by one of these,” he said.

CHAPTER NINETEEN

Hamish had a home in West Wray, a suburb near the Darrowdowns, west of Cymbeline. It was a twenty-minute drive from Stonebender Hall. Sylvie elected to return to her flat. She hadn't known Ham well and wasn't sure how an outsider would be received.

Molly had the strength of granite. Simon broke the news to Reba McPhee, but Molly immediately stepped in with comfort and practicality. Family was called; care was arranged for the children too young to understand; food was prepared—the universal comfort in times of trouble. Simon and Hal stood around for a while, offering what they could and feeling awkward until both Molly and Reba shooed them away to 'do their jobs, and make things right'.

They drove back to the Hall in silence. By the time Simon picked up his flyer it was after twentieth hour. Hal wanted to check on Clearwater but was clearly exhausted. Simon almost pulled rank on him, but Hal finally agreed to rest for the night and meet with Simon and what remained of the team at seventh hour in the morning.

Simon slowly guided his flyer back over the Finnegan. Even the docks of Westport held no comfort for him. He knew that Clearwater might be in grave danger. He tried to care, but couldn't think of anything but Ham and of Reba's stricken face and silent tears. Orcs had killed Ham. They'd killed Alira. They'd killed his father. Azeri like Clearwater, bringing their civil war here to his country, to his city. They could all rot in the Seven Hells as far as he was concerned. For the first time, he thought he understood Hal's deep-seated prejudice against Orcs.

He hadn't hated all Orcs after Alira's death, only the one who had killed her. For a while, Azeri became his special targets, but the more he tried to hate them, the more he felt Alira whispering to him, talking to him in his dreams. He didn't understand her words, but her meaning was clear. Forgive. He thought he'd done that, but the last few days had tested him beyond his capability.

He passed over the Old Wall, the ancient dividing line between Westport and Cymbeline proper. He passed the Customs House and then found himself flying low over All Gods Square. He almost turned north toward his own district, intending to open the bottle of Portalis brandy Ham had given him on his last birthday and toast his friend until he drank himself to sleep. Almost. But he turned east and south, spiraling down toward Tanner Street and the cul-de-sac where Clearwater lived.

He sighed. He was still a King's Peacekeeper. If Clearwater was in danger, it was partially his fault. Both decency and duty required him to at least warn the Orc.

Simon parked his flyer at the curb and sat in the saddle for a long moment. Clearwater's house was dark but otherwise looked as neat and trim as it had that morning. Still, something felt wrong. The Stone seemed rotten, as Hal would have said. Simon drew his Bonecleaver and dismounted his flyer. He checked the front garden and both side yards before opening the small iron gate between the sidewalk and Clearwater's garden. It creaked, but no light came on in the house.

Simon stepped carefully onto the front porch, looking left and right to the windows on either side of the front door. They remained dark, shades tightly closed. Something was missing. He looked about carefully, then he noticed it.

The small camel fetish that had been nailed to the doorframe was gone.

He gripped the sword in his right hand and extended his left to knock on the door. "Mr. Clearwater?" he called. "It's Sergeant Buckley. I need to speak with you, sir."

The door moved under his knock. It was open, the latch broken and the doorjamb splintered.

Simon peered inside. Light from the square spilled through the now open door onto a patch of floor. A dark stain covered the patterned Azeri carpet, ending just short of the doorframe. Simon muttered a standard incantation and the glowglobe mounted on a wall sconce just inside the room flared on.

Clearwater hung upside down from a heavy hook that had been forced into an overhead ceiling beam. A long slash under his chin gaped open like a second mouth, dripping with half-congealed blood that trailed down to the jelled lake of red covering the floor. Empty sockets in the Orc's face dripped thin trails of blood where the eyes had been gouged out. Crude Azeri script had been scrawled in the same red on the wall beside him, but Simon couldn't read the words. He stepped cautiously through the door, taking care not to disturb the spreading pool near his feet.

Clearwater's hands had been bound to his sides with self-sticking packing ribbon that completely encased him from chest to ankles. His ankles were bound with a length of heavy hemp rope that looped up through the hook in the ceiling. Simon recognized it as a cargo-belaying hook, common on the docks as a secure point for hoisting heavy crates out of holds.

Simon looked carefully around the room where he and Sylvie had sat with Clearwater only that morning. Nothing seemed to have changed. The normalcy of the low table surrounded by thick cushions clashed with the horror hanging just a few feet away. The jarring contrast distracted him, but something else held him in place.

Something had changed. Something was different. Something he had seen before, but—then he saw it.

He eased around the room, hugging the wall until he reached the small shrine to Durlash. Instead of the blood red lacquer image of the Orc thunder god, with an upraised lightning bolt in his hand, there now sat a black glass figure of the god in his role as the bearded judge of the dead. Simon was certain the statue he'd seen in the morning had featured Durlash in his thunder god aspect.

He reached out and lifted the black figure. It was a larger version of the one he'd found in Hightower's office. Etched on the bottom was the Clearwater Glass logo, but no mysterious numbers. With a pang of disappointment, he started to return it to its place in the center of the altar. Then he noticed the slight depression in the gold cloth covering the statue's raised stand, and lifted the cloth.

The stand was hollow. Inside lay a round black glass cylinder with a screw top. He lifted it out, stuck it in his pocket, and replaced the cloth and the statue.

He edged carefully out of the room, backed out the door, and sheathed his short sword. Out at the curb, he activated the Far-Speaker link in his flyer.

"Central," said the bored voice of a dispatcher somewhere in the depths of Wycliffe House.

"This is Sergeant Simon Buckley, badge number two-two-three-seven, Magic Enforcement. I am reporting a homicide."

"Yes, sir," said the dispatcher, all brisk efficiency now. "Location?"

"Eight-seventy-three All Gods Square," said Simon. "The victim is an Azeri named Clearwater." Simon realized with a twinge of shame that he couldn't recall the Orc's first name. "He's a material witness in an illegal conjuring case. Call Sergeant Francis Killian. This is his headache now."

Simon signed off and settled down on the curb to wait. The scene was as secure as he could make it all by himself, and he doubted Clearwater would be getting any casual visitors tonight.

Less than ten minutes after he'd called it in, a patrol sled pulled up. The Keepers in it recognized Simon and he gave them the basic situation. They unrolled the orange crime scene rope and began marking off the front fence, the garden and side yards. By the time they finished, Killian arrived with the CSA mages; not Kyle Evarts, Simon noted. Killian gave him a dismissive nod before starting to shout orders to the mages and the patrol Keepers.

Simon climbed onto his flyer and left before Killian could ask him any questions. He hadn't mentioned the glass vial in his pocket.

He'd intended to go home. He knew he should go home. Instead, he flew up the King's Road to Sylvie's building. He parked across the street and sat on his flyer for a long time. He thought about Ham. He tried to muster his earlier wave of hatred for the Orcs, or at least for the Azeri, but visions of Gripple cowering on the stone slab merged with Clearwater's empty eye sockets and the blood-soaked carpet beneath him. He shook himself as he dozed off. He wanted sleep. He wanted to get drunk. But most of all, he didn't want to be alone.

He climbed off the flyer, slid the sheathed Bonecleaver into the side holster, then locked it and crossed the street. Hiram stood and greeted him as he entered the lobby.

"Sergeant Buckley," the ex-military man said, his right hand discretely under his desktop. "Good meeting."

"Good meeting, Hiram," said Simon with a nod. "Is Lady Graystorm in?"

"She is. Should I announce you?"

"If it's all the same to you," said Simon quietly. "I'll just go up. I know the way."

Hiram eyed Simon's rumpled uniform and windblown hair for a second. His eyes met Simon's and softened. "Her Ladyship told me you lost a man today. My condolences. I'm sure she won't mind if you go up unannounced."

Simon climbed the stairs slowly. He leaned against the wall outside Sylvie's door, suddenly weak with fatigue and overcome by a sense of despair. Finally, he reached out and knocked softly. She opened the door almost immediately.

"Simon," she said, touching his arm. "I hoped you would come. I'm so sorry. About Ham, about Flandyrs, about everything."

He couldn't look her in the eye. "Clearwater is dead. They gouged out his eyes and slit his throat. They hung him up like a piece of meat to bleed out on his own floor."

She took his face in her hands and forced him to look at her. "That wasn't your fault. Ham's death wasn't your fault." She kissed his closed eyelids and murmured, "Alira wasn't your fault." She pulled him inside, into her arms. He clung to her, sobbing into her neck, and she closed the door.

She let him go, turning him around to gently help him out of his jacket. Simon managed to compose himself a little, before turning to face her. She reached out and took him in her arms again, kissing his hands, his face, his lips, at first gently and then with more urgency.

CHAPTER TWENTY

Simon awoke to bright sunlight streaming through a window somewhere to his right. He lay on his back under soft sheets. Sylvie snuggled into him with her head on his chest. She lifted her head and looked into his eyes before he could say anything.

"You're awake," she said, smiling. "I was hoping you'd sleep for a while longer. It would do you good."

"What time is it?" he asked, acutely aware of her taut breasts pressing into his bare chest.

"Just past sixth hour." She sat up, the sheet falling away from her body.

He drank her in, feeling desire and a soft joy. He noticed that the burns on her legs were nearly healed, the blisters now just patches of pink skin. His own neck was still raw and crusted.

Unsure for a moment, he looked away. "Are we all good?"

She laughed. "Well, we were certainly good last night."

He smiled. It was true, but he still felt uneasy. "It's more complicated than that."

"Is it?" she asked. "You're on suspension and I'm off the Hightower investigation. There's no conflict there. We can do as we please." Her eyes sought his. "But you still feel like you're betraying Alira, no?"

He nodded. "It's stupid. It's been three years, but I do."

"What do your visions tell you?"

He looked at her sharply. "How do you know about that?"

She smiled and shrugged. "I told you before, she left her mark on you."

"They aren't visions," he said. "Just dreams. I only see her in my sleep. Sometimes I hear her voice, as if she's speaking in my ear. But always in Qetchwa, and most times I don't understand what she's saying."

"Are the dreams happy or sad?" Sylvie asked.

"They used to be sad or angry, sometimes frightening. But lately they've been calming." He looked at her. "You're humoring me. You think I'm just a lovesick kid."

She shook her head, her expression serious. "No. If Alira truly loved you, and it's clear she did, she invested a part of her *Ghiras*, her soul, in you. You're still linked to that. I'd say she's telling you to move on. She was a very lucky woman."

"Not so lucky. I felt that Fire spell trigger. I tried to warn her."

"That wasn't your fault, Simon," Sylvie said. "She's forgiven you. She wants you to forgive yourself. Both for her and for all the other unnecessary guilt you're hauling around."

"You sound like you really believe she's communicating with me."

"She is, in a way." Sylvie looked intently at him. "I can see the part of her *ghir* she left behind. She's gone, but that part of her soul that knew yours, that loved you and was loved in return, can never be reunited with the whole. It was given willingly and is part of you now."

"I'm possessed?" said Simon with a shaky laugh.

"I'm serious, Simon. Why do you think Elves take human lovers? For us, you are creatures of abundant energy and freedom. Our souls crave that ephemeral quality. You live such a short time that your souls remain pure and free. An Elf's love for a human is a pure love, an ideal love, simply because it is ultimately a temporary love. But it remains hot and fierce for as long as your human lover lives."

"Alira tried to tell me something like that once. I didn't understand. I think part of me didn't want to admit that she'd remain young for so long that it might as well be forever, while I'd get old and die."

Sylvie touched his cheek. “Yes, but don’t you see? It’s that gift, the gift of mortality, which makes your love so intense, so pure.”

Simon shifted uncomfortably. He didn’t know where to go from here, but found he wanted to go there with her, somehow. But before he could speak, the summons tone from his mirror relieved him of the necessity of saying anything at all.

He rooted through his discarded clothes and found the mirror; Liam’s face appeared as he swiped his hand across the screen.

“Simon, good morning. Sorry to call so early,” said Liam. If he noticed that Simon was not dressed and not in his own flat, he didn’t say anything. “Can you come to Hal’s place? I’m here with Hal and Jack. Jack’s not doing too well. We need to talk.”

“Understood,” said Simon. “Give me forty-five minutes.”

“We’ll be waiting. And I have news about Gran Swampwater for you, once you get here.” Liam broke the connection before Simon could frame a question.

Simon stood and gathered his clothes. He looked around but Sylvie was no longer in the bed.

“Coffee or tea?” she called from the kitchen.

“Coffee, please, black,” he called back. He slipped on his breeches without hose and pulled on his shirt. He stepped out into the front room of the apartment. Sylvie wore a light green robe and was pouring coffee into a pair of fine china cups.

"I have first rights on the shower," she said. "Unless you'd care to join me?"

They made it to Stonebender Hall in forty-two minutes, despite a longer shower than Simon would have taken most mornings. The bright sunlight of the early morning had lasted less than an hour. By the time they crossed the Finnegan Estuary, doubled up on Simon's flyer, low clouds filled the sky and a north wind promised rain, or maybe even snow.

There had been no discussion about whether Sylvie should join him. It was just assumed. They dismounted in Hal's stable and walked together to the big oak door. Hal answered it and showed no surprise that Sylvie was with Simon, either.

"In the kitchen," Hal said. "Molly left tea and oatcakes. She's with Reba at Ham's place."

Sylvie touched Hal on the shoulder. He reached up and took her hand and they walked toward the rear of the hall. Simon followed.

Liam and Jack sat on chairs near the stove, or rather, Liam sat. Jack slumped in that liquid posture that only extreme drunkenness can attain. He'd either gotten an early start on the day, or was at the end of a very long night. Liam supported Jack's head and held a cup of tea in his other hand. He looked helplessly from Simon to Sylvie.

"Leave off," said Hal. "The man needs a good drunk. He'll sober up in good time."

"I'm not so sure," said Liam. "You didn't see him down in Fernhill. He'd go from tears to blind rage to a sort of mindless stare and then back again, over and over. The Medics wanted to cast a sleeper spell on him, but Evarts and I convinced them to let me take him home. We went to a dive tavern down in Westport instead. We were the only ones there who weren't Orcs." Liam tried again to get Jack to drink some tea. The Dwarf took a mouthful, then spat it out, muttered something, and closed his eyes.

"They got here about third hour," said Hal. "A patrol sled dropped them off. Seems Jack tried to tear the place down all by himself. I managed to keep the call off the morning squawk report, but had to call in a couple of favors. I told the night watch Sergeant that we were on Ninety-Six. He knew about Ham. He was sympathetic."

Sylvie went over to Jack and laid her hand on his forehead. He stirred and opened his eyes. She reached up with her other hand and gently closed them, speaking a few words in Qetchwa. Jack seemed to relax then. His head lolled back and he began to snore.

"Let's get him more comfortable," she said. "He'll sleep it off for a few hours."

Hal and Simon managed to lift the now inert Dwarf and move him to a bench seat near one of the cupboards. Liam sipped tea and looked at Sylvie warily.

"How did you do that?" he asked.

'Do what?"

"Put Jack to sleep like that," Liam answered. "He wasn't listening to me or to Hal."

"He just needed a softer touch. He'll be better when he awakens, but it will still be a long hard path for him. He'll need your strength for that."

Liam sipped tea and nodded. "My Gran was an Elf, from the Free People, not from the Havens. She could always get us littles to sleep with just a word or two. You have the same touch."

Sylvie nodded. "But it's just a trick. It only works on children, or on drunks."

"Remind me to stay sober around you," said Liam.

Simon came over with a mug of tea and an oatcake for Sylvie. Hal pulled up a chair and drank from a tankard of small beer.

"Jack's taking this hard, lads," Hal said. "And m'lady." He nodded to Sylvie. "He's owed *were geld* for Ham and it's up to us to collect."

Simon nodded. Liam looked uncertain.

Sylvie shook her head. "We can't let this become personal," she said.

"Lass, it became personal the second those tattooed heathens tried to blow us up at the farmhouse," said Hal. Sylvie frowned but said nothing.

"Evarts confirmed that the Fire grenade that killed Ham was from the same batch as the farmhouse," said Simon. "This is all connected. Where do we go from here?"

"We lean on your glassmaker," said Hal. "He knows more than he told."

"He may have, but we'll never know," said Simon. "He's dead. Barsaka's boys got to him last night.

Hung him from a cargo hook, gouged out his eyes, and slit his throat. He won't be telling us anything."

"Traitor's death," said Hal. "With no eyes, Durlash can't see into his soul and judge his worth. He's condemned to wander as a wraith forever."

"Speaking of Durlash, "said Simon. "I found this hidden in a house shrine to him." He produced the cylinder and looked at Sylvie. "The statue had changed," he explained.

Sylvie picked it up and examined the top. "Have you opened it yet?" Simon shook his head. "May I?" She unscrewed the silver top and poured out the contents into her hand. She held a small wafer of ebony, the thickness of a fingernail, inlaid with a smaller square of aquamarine. Next to it was a round silvery object, the size of a halfpenny coin but devoid of any engraving. Finally there was a small square of tightly folded paper.

Simon recognized the ebony wafer as the spell activation component of a handheld magic mirror. He picked up the paper and unfolded it.

"Flandyrs to Blackpool, Midwinters Day," he read. "There's a string of numbers here, a mirror locus." He took out the parchment he'd salvaged from Hightower's office and compared the locus he'd copied from the Durlash figurine to the one from Clearwater's stash. They matched.

He held up the ebony wafer between a thumb and forefinger. "What do you think, Liam?" he asked.

"Looks like the summoning wood from a handheld," Liam said. "I might get something off of it with a Reveal, but if it's keyed to a specific mirror, it will only activate on that device."

"Clearwater, or someone, wrote a mirror locus on this paper, probably the device that this wafer came from. It's also the locus that was scratched onto the bottom of a small statue in Hightower's office." Simon turned to Sylvie. "Your initial idea may have been better. We should have summoned that locus."

"Maybe," said Sylvie. "But this still connects Flandyrs to both the glass factory and the Brigades. Wasn't Blackpool one of the Orcs who picked up the aquamarine powder from Clearwater's factory?"

Simon nodded. "And he's likely tied to or even related to Hargash Barsaka. I don't know whether he killed Clearwater or not, but he already has a reputation for dirty work. If Clearwater has proof of a connection between Blackpool and Flandyrs, he may have tried to throw a loop around Flandyrs or Barsaka, or both. That would have been enough for Barsaka to kill him."

"So," said Hal. "It's time we talked to Blackpool and Gorski."

"Agreed," said Simon. "Stopping the Brigades has to be our first priority. They've already tried to kill the Crown Prince, and they still have a stockpile of grenades. So how do we find them?"

"We go down to the Hollows, kick some Orc ass, and take names," said Hal.

CHAPTER TWENTY-ONE

Sylvie shook her head. "We should focus on Hightower. She's the key to all of this. She's the link between Flandyrs and the Brigades. She made the Fire grenades. She wouldn't have dealt with anyone but Barsaka or a high-level lieutenant. As satisfying as it might be to strong-arm some Brigade soldiers, it won't get you to the top dogs."

"And where will Hightower take us?" asked Simon. "We have nothing except that she made the grenades and Flandyrs probably set her up in the farmhouse. Why? Why did she make the Fire grenades in the first place? Why did Flandyrs let her use the house? What was in it for Hightower?"

Sylvie remained silent, her arms crossed. She cocked her head expectantly, as if waiting for Simon to continue.

Simon sighed. “You’re right. Hightower is the ultimate key to this. She’s the starting point for us and I think her Portal magic is somehow even more important than the Azeri connection. But we’ve got nothing. We’re not even officially on the investigation. Meanwhile, Barsaka and his Brigade soldiers have gods know how many Fire grenades at their disposal. They’ve already tried to attack the royal family. They’re planning something, and the potential stakes are too high to ignore.”

“So putting a beat-down on some Orcs in the Hollows is going to help you find them?” asked Sylvie.

“I don’t know,” said Simon. “But Hal and Jack are out for blood, and I can’t say I disagree. If we get the Orcs who killed Ham, I’ll count it as a win.”

Sylvie didn’t answer. Her face remained grim as she turned away and went to check on Jack.

“Simon?” Liam stood next to him. “Everything all good?”

“Sure, Liam. All good,” Simon said wearily.

“Well, I don’t know if it’s important anymore,” Liam gestured to where Hal and Sylvie stood over Jack. “But the Marshall down on the Southern Rez, an Orc named Greenmire, wants to talk with you about Gran Swampwater. He didn’t say why, but he left his locus for you to summon when you get a chance.”

“Did he say what it was about?”

Liam shook his head. “Like I said, I don’t know if it’s important, if we’re backing off of Hightower.”

'We're not backing off. I've been relieved and you're on a short vacation, that's all."

"Right," said Liam. "So do you want to reach out to him, or not?"

"Give me the locus," said Simon. He handed Liam the ebony wafer. "Meanwhile, see what you can do with this. Get some of Evart's tech boys on it as well. If there's any information there, get me a copy."

Liam looked hurt. "So you don't want me to come with you and Hal?"

Simon reached out and gripped the young mage's arm. "Think about your career, Liam. Hal's been a Keeper so long, he's untouchable. He knows where whole rooms full of skeletons are buried. I'm probably on the chopping block anyway. We're going off the books with this, and will likely burn for it. You have a future. Don't trash it by getting too close to Hal and me. "

Liam looked at the small bit of black wood in his hand. Then he nodded and turned away.

"And what about me?" asked Sylvie, stepping closer. Simon hadn't seen her approach. "Should I go back to the Havens and be a good little Elf girl while you and Haldron break the law in the name of *were geld* for Ham?"

"No," said Simon. "But think hard about what you do next. For some reason, Flandyrs is lining up with the Azeri. He's a Ranger, too. Do you really want to risk everything and trust that Summerfield isn't part of this, or at least complicit?"

"Flandyrs is playing his own game," said Sylvie. "And yes, I trust Summerfield. His family and mine go back a few centuries and there's *anylas,* obligation, between them. He'll cover me, even if Flandyrs is acting with Haven sanction."

Simon shrugged. "Right, then. We'll start as soon as Jack wakes up. I'd like you to write up everything you learned from your lunch meeting; also, your impressions of the interview with Clearwater. We may be off the case, but I still want it all documented. If the Brigades pull something big, and I think they will, Killian and Gulbrandsen are going to be under the sword for covering this up. We need to be ready to act when the time comes."

"Are you going to get in touch with that Marshall?" asked Sylvie.

Simon nodded and took out his handheld. The mirror locus was already there, sent from Liam's own mirror. He mouthed the summoning incantation.

"Yes?" A dark-skinned Orc peered at him from the mirror. "Who is this?"

"Marshall Greenmire," said Simon. "I'm Simon Buckley, King's Peacekeepers. Liam Aster said you wanted to speak with me?"

"Oh, aye, Sergeant Buckley," said the Orc. He had black hair and eyes that slanted sharply up from his flat cheekbones. His ears were oval and slightly pointed as well. Southron, thought Simon. Nearly pure blood, too. What's he doing outside of the Empire?

Greenmire went on. "Heard about your man," he said. "Bad business. Gran Swampwater told me to give you her sympathies and said that she'd like to talk with you and your Elf woman as soon as possible."

Simon glanced at Sylvie. "What Elf woman?"

"The Gray Ranger who's been shadowing your investigation," Greenmire said as if it were a given. "She said it was important to the both of you."

"How?" asked Simon.

The Orc shrugged. "Don't ask me. I'm just delivering the message." He waved a hand. "And before you ask, yes, I do whatever Gran tells me. Everyone down here on the Rez does, if they know what's good for them."

"All good," said Simon. "We'll be down there before midday."

He waved a hand over his mirror and it went black.

"How does she know about me?" asked Sylvie.

"I don't know. But we need to find out," said Simon. "Hal and Jack can strong-arm the Hollows without us. Snick is Hal's Orc anyway. It might be better if we stayed out of it for now."

Sylvie smiled. "You were looking for a good excuse not to go, weren't you?"

They borrowed Hal's Oxley for the trip down to the Reservation, the distance and the weather making riding double on Simon's flyer impractical. Simon locked his leather bag containing the case notes along with the vial from Clearwater's house, in the rear storage compartment of his flyer. The strange hand weapon, he pocketed in his uniform jacket. He slid a dagger into the sheath in his boot top, but left the Bonecleaver stowed in the flyer's side scabbard. Then he joined Sylvie in the little sports sled.

They reached the main gate about ten minutes before midday. Greenmire met them in the administrative center.

"You'll have to leave that sled here," he said. "Gran lives in the Spirit House. No spells within two *li*. We walk."

Two *li* turned out to be about 200 yards. The Spirit House was a low-walled compound built of mud bricks and living trees. The corner pillars were live oaks, the doorframes and lintels flowering dogwoods. Windows were unglazed but screened by intertwined willow shoots. Two elderly Orc crones stood on either side of the main doorway holding short staves of intertwined Oak and Iron.

Greenmire stopped at the threshold and bowed. The crones nodded and pointed their staves at Simon and Sylvie.

"You are summoned to the House of the Earth Spirit," Greenmire said to Simon and Sylvie in a formal tone. "Will you enter?"

"We will," said Simon. He turned and bowed to the crones. They turned and entered the compound. Simon and Sylvie followed them.

In the center of the square compound a pile of black onyx rocks towered six feet above Simon's head. The crones disappeared behind it and he felt an immense surge of power run down his spine. He turned to look at Sylvie. She stared at the top of the pile of black rocks, and he followed her gaze.

A ragged gash in the fabric of the world rose from the topmost shard of onyx, like a flame from the wick of a candle. Blue fire glowed around a black tear in the gray winter sky. Through it, Simon could see stars glowing in a clear night sky.

"You are looking at the night sky on a world like our own, and yet not," said a voice from behind him. "This is Portal Magic, the way the ancients cast it."

The opening closed, like the snuffing of a candle. Simon felt a rush of air on his face as the blue flames swirled in a tight spiral that funneled down into the black rocks. He and Sylvie turned together to look at the Orc behind them.

She was old but stood upright and tall, almost as tall as a man. Her sparse hair was white and pulled back from her sharp face by a red and orange scarf. Her eyes, so dark that they appeared black, seemed to flash as she looked from Simon to Sylvie and back again. She wore a loose gown fashioned from strips of willow and birch bark, set off by a belt of heavy platinum links that she wore low on her hips. She held a black ebony staff tipped with onyx in her hand.

Sylvie reacted first. She bowed low and said, "Gran Swampwater."

Simon gulped and bowed as well.

The old Orc laughed, a surprisingly youthful sound. "I am Olega Swampwater," she said. "Born for the Marsh People, by *strahk* of the Swamp

Spirit. *Gran* is a title bestowed out of respect. It's been so long since I was called Olega, I doubt I'd answer to it."

She looked Sylvie up and down. "You are Sylvie Graystorm, born for House Graystorm, by *strahk* of the Air Spirits. You have more *ghiras* than your kinswoman, Glendowyn."

"She was a *ghir*-cousin only," said Sylvie. "Not blood."

"Bah! You Elves place too much value on blood. *Ghiras* matters more than blood." She turned her gaze on Simon. "You are Simon Buckley. Born for the Free People, by *strahk* of the Fire Spirits. You have the blood of the Northwest in you."

"My father's people," said Simon.

Gran Swampwater waved a hand. "Yes, but the Fire of the Free People is the *strahk,* the Spirit gift, that lights your *ghiras.* You can feel the tumble and spin of magic as it is cast. That is their gift."

Simon shook his head, as if to clear it. She was talking in riddles. He needed answers. "I am sorry about your son," said Simon. "I feel responsible for his death."

"You should not," Gran said, pounding the tip of her staff on the ground. "His fate was set once Glendowyn learned of his bloodline. Your intervention postponed his death; that is all. There is now hope where before there was only risk."

"Gran Swampwater," said Sylvie. "We are not mages. We don't understand what my *ghir*-cousin was trying to do. We know little about Portals, except that they require Blood to open. You mentioned Gripple's bloodline. Why is it important?"

The two crones reappeared, their arms covered in blood. Between them, they carried the carcass of a sheep, already partially skinned.

"There is much you should know, and, I fear, little time to learn," said Gran. "Come, we will sit and I will try to explain."

Simon and Sylvie turned away from the other women and followed Gran Swampwater through an archway of willow boughs to a cool nook, shaded by a huge oak, the ground covered by soft green moss. Gran seated herself on a russet-colored cushion set directly on the ground. She motioned toward two similar cushions for Sylvie and Simon. A young Orc girl in yellow ribbons and little else stepped from behind an oak tree with a wooden tray. She set it on a low rock table in front of Gran and scurried away. Gran poured tea from an earthenware pot into small clay cups and offered them to Simon and Sylvie.

"You must understand the nature of things before you can understand the Portals," began Gran Swampwater. "They are a manifestation of the Earths, all the myriad number of them. Each time a spell is cast, the world divides. On the one hand is the Earth where the spell changes the world as the caster intended; on the other is the world where the casting failed, or produced a different outcome. All of these worlds are there, existing side by side, each unique, each tied to the world that was." She paused and sipped tea.

"But the world is here, around us. What are you talking about?" asked Simon.

"Actually," said Sylvie. "This is similar to some of the more outlandish consequences of quantum magic theory. Each probability cascade produces a parallel cascade where the outcome is opposite, or at least different. It hasn't found much acceptance, especially at the Academy, but many Human theorists accept it as one possible solution to the Unity paradox."

"Say what?" asked Simon.

Sylvie shrugged. "Each spell, each decision we make, divides the probability stream and creates a separate world. Like I said, it's one of the more outlandish predictions of quantum magic. It seems impossible, but the mathematics are sound."

"Mathematics," said Gran derisively. "You sound like a Human, trying to understand the world with numbers and words. We of the People have always known this. Portals show us the future that might be, the past that never was, worlds like our own but not, and some things so strange even we in the Spirit House cannot understand them."

"You use Blood Magic so casually?" said Simon.

"There is Blood and there is blood," said Gran. "You saw the Black Portal. In a few hours my sisters and I will eat the sheep that died to open it. We waste nothing."

"So any blood will open a Portal? Then why did Hightower try to kill your son?" asked Sylvie.

"Glendowyn never understood the true purpose of Portals," said Gran with a shake of her head. "At first, I believed that she did. We explored the basic spell, observed the results from a safe distance. The Portals are for viewing possible paths, not for travel. Any life's blood, given in reverence, will allow visions to pass the threshold. But the blood of a sentient will open a door to the other side. And the true Blood of an Earthborn will allow solid objects to pass. This was the secret I revealed to Glendowyn."

"Earthborn?" asked Simon.

She looked him up and down, an appraising gesture. "You are different. More Fire than Earth in you. Interesting."

Gran continued. "Each race was born of different elements—Earth, Air, Fire, or Water. Elves are of Air and Fire; Dwarves of Fire and Earth, the elements of the Forge and the Smith; Orcs are of Water and Earth, the elements of green and growing things. The origin of Humans is shrouded in pain and violence. Your kind is of equal parts of all the elements. Some have more of one, some of another, but all in proportion. It is what sets you apart, your great strength and your great weakness."

"Gripple's father was Born of the Loam People, by *strahk* of the Earth Spirit, a true Earthborn. Gripple turned his back on the Spirit Way, choosing the Way of growing things. But the Blood was in him."

"And Hightower knew this?"

Gran nodded. "I swore her to secrecy when she lived here among us. She wrote her Human paper and kept her word. But then I learned of the disappearances and knew she had played us false."

On a hunch, Simon responded. "Orcs began disappearing from the Hollows up in Cymbeline."

Gran nodded. "They were known to us here in the Spirit House. They were all Born by *strahk* of the Earth. They had traces of the Blood. I warned my son. I asked him to come home. But he never really believed in his Blood. He loved his farm and wouldn't leave. I convinced him to be careful, but it wasn't enough."

"Professor Hightower had gloves and a long pole sheathed in lead," said Simon. "If she opened a Portal using blood from one of those Orcs, could she reach through and pull objects into this world?"

Gran looked at him wide eyed. "You have seen such things?" she asked.

Simon nodded. "She had a lead-covered, six-foot pole and some lead-lined gloves with her." He reached into his pocket and drew out the strange weapon he taken from the evidence room. "And she had this."

Gran reached out to the object, then hissed and drew her hand back, as if it were hot.

She shook her head. "Foolish, foolish woman."

CHAPTER TWENTY-TWO

"Why do you say, 'foolish'?" asked Simon.

Gran sighed. "If she retrieved things through the Portal, even with her silly pole, she would have been standing too close. That is why we summoned the vision you saw at the top of the black *stila*. The Portal light can kill if you stand close, but if you stand well away, it has no effect on you."

"Square of the distance," whispered Sylvie. Gran looked at her. "The danger drops off with distance, just like spell strength."

Gran nodded and said to Simon, "You did her a kindness. If she hadn't been an Elf, she'd have died much sooner."

"The coroner said that her bone marrow had failed, like a Human with white blood disease, but Elves don't get that," said Simon.

Gran shrugged. “We don’t know how it kills, but the Portal light is deadly. Some just die; others are burned, as if by a great heat, even though the light itself is cold. Glendowyn always doubted me when I warned her. She had the Elven certainty that she was smarter than my sisters and all those who went before me. Foolish.”

“But what did she hope to gain?” asked Sylvie. “And why take your son?”

“Gripple may have chosen a different path, but he had the true Earth Blood. Glendowyn hoped that his blood would allow a living thing to pass through the Portal it created and survive. She never believed that it was the light that was deadly, not the Portal itself.” Said Gran. “But she wasn’t the real force behind taking my son.”

“Then who was?” asked Simon.

“Just after Gripple was taken, a messenger brought a letter to me.” Gran produced an envelope from the fold of her sleeve. “They threatened to kill Gripple if I didn’t come to Bowater and meet Glendowyn. She and I had parted on good terms, and I thought I knew what she was trying to do, so I did not go. I didn’t believe she would actually try to kill my son.” She handed the envelope to Simon.

Simon opened the envelope and took out a folded square of cheap notepaper. “*We have your son. Glendowyn Hightower requires your assistance. You will comply if you wish to ensure your son’s safety,*” he read aloud. Included in the folded note was a fuzzy image of Gripple Swampwater chained to the stone slab in the farmhouse. The Bowater farmhouse address was scrawled on the image.

"Why did the Azeri attack my team and kill your son?" Simon asked. "We'd already stopped Hightower. We know she made the Fire grenades for them, and they must have a lot of them left. Why kill Gripple?"

"That was to punish me," said Gran. "Hargash Barsaka has tried for years to recruit young people from our community. My sisters and I, here in the Spirit House, have denied him. He tried to take hostages, like my son, to force us to make his weapons."

"So, why did Hightower help him?" asked Sylvie.

"I suspect he paid her in platinum," said Gran. "Platinum augments Earth magic. The stronger the spell, the more platinum it consumes. The amounts are small, but the metal is dear, and repeated spells consume it rapidly."

"And the Azeri Empire has some of the richest veins of platinum in the world," said Simon.

Gran nodded. "Barsaka had my son taken to pressure me into helping Glendowyn. When I refused, he gave Gripple to Glendowyn for her Portal magic. Then you stepped in and saved him. Barsaka couldn't let that pass. I'm sorry your man was killed. This was aimed at me and mine, not at you."

"Well, Barsaka got what he wanted. He has the weapons, Hightower is dead, and with her, the spell she was working. What we need now is to find out what Barsaka is planning and how to stop him."

"No," said Gran Swampwater. "Hargash is the instrument of another, not the source of your danger. He believes in his quest, but doesn't know that his path has been set by someone else."

"There is another mage," said Sylvie quietly.

Gran looked at her and nodded. "You have sensed him?"

Sylvie nodded as well and turned to Simon. "Remember what I said about the probability cascade at the glass factory? I don't think Glendowyn Hightower was capable of that kind of magic. She was a decent Earth mage by all accounts, but didn't have a reputation as a Master."

"Flandyrs?" asked Simon.

Sylvie shook her head. "As far as I know, and per his dossier, he's no mage. I don't see him keeping that kind of ability secret." She turned back to Gran. "Do you know who this other person is?"

"No," said Gran with a sigh. "My sisters and I have felt him, far away at the edges of our castings, but we do not know him. But he knows us. He must have directed Glendowyn to the Orcs of the Earth Blood who have gone missing. He would have known about my son, and his importance to a Blood spell. It is he who moves Barsaka and his people about like pieces in a board game."

"Game piece or not, Barsaka has already made an attack on the Crown Prince," said Simon. "He's got the means to start a war, and the will to do it. We need to find him and stop him."

"You need to find Barsaka and stop his madness, yes," said Gran. "But your danger won't end there. The Portals are the ultimate goal. Barsaka and his revolution, a war between the Empire and your Commonwealth, even the fall of the Gray Havens are all possibilities that my sisters and I have seen through the visions on top of the *stila.* The one who guided and betrayed Glendowyn has seen these things as well, and something else; something that he desperately wants to bring about. He believes the Portals will show him the way."

"We still need to find Barsaka," persisted Simon. "Even if there's someone else behind him, we'll only get to that person through Barsaka. And right now, as interesting as this has been, it hasn't gotten me any closer to him or to the Orcs who killed my teammate."

Gran pursed her lips and blew a shrill whistle. A curtain of willow branches behind her was thrust aside and two large young Orcs stepped through. Between them, they held an older Orc, slim with sparse hair, wearing a rumpled business suit. The older Orc was bleeding from a split lip and had fresh bruises around his left cheek, and his hands were bound in front of him with a thin cord that cut into his wrists. The younger Orcs thrust him forward and he fell on his face at Simon's feet.

"Durking Bogrunner," said Simon. "What's he doing here?"

Gran reached down and grabbed a handful of Bogrunner's thin hair. She pulled his head back so that he looked into her face.

"This one has been luring our young people away to the city with false promises. This one tricked my Gripple into leaving his home and shot him with a sleeping dart and gave him to Hargash Barsaka. This one arranged the ambush that killed my son and your friend. This one has forfeited his life, but he may have information that you can use. Question him. Do not be gentle."

Simon stood and jerked Bogrunner to his feet by the collar, and Sylvie gasped. He pushed the Orc backward onto the flat stone table, scattering the tea service. Bogrunner cried out as he landed flat on his back and his head bounced off of the table edge. Simon placed a booted foot on the Orc's chest, holding him down.

Simon drew his dagger from his right boot and held it in front of Bogrunner's face. "Who did you talk to about Clearwater?"

The Orc chuckled. "What do you care? He were a traitor. Got what he deserved."

Simon slashed with the tip of the dagger, so fast that Bogrunner didn't notice at first. Then the Orc screamed as the tip of his right ear dropped to the moss-covered floor. Blood ran down his neck and scalp, soaking into his hair and pooling behind his head. He thrashed, scattering more blood.

"Simon!" shouted Sylvie, starting forward.

Gran stepped in front of her and placed a hand on her shoulder. "No, child," she said. "This is Blood work."

Simon pressed his weight into Bogrunner's chest and grabbed a handful of hair, holding his head still.

"You're a Peacekeeper," the Orc sobbed. "I got rights."

"We're on the Rez, Sovereign land. King's got no writ here," growled Simon. "I'm just a guy who's lost a friend and found an innocent Orc hung from his own ceiling beam like a slab of meat. Now, who did you tell?"

"No," said Bogrunner. "You can't . . .," He screamed again as Simon's dagger slashed through the left side of his nose. He choked and sputtered as blood drained down his throat.

"Give me a name," whispered Simon as he placed the tip of his dagger against Bogrunner's left eyelid. "Or the next thing you'll lose will be an eye. If I don't like your answers, I'll take the other one. That's what they did to Clearwater. Then I'll fillet you like a mackerel and hang you from the Reservation fence as crow bait. Talk!"

"Gorski!" shouted Bogrunner. "I told Murg Gorski. He'd put it out that there was money for them as ratted on Peacekeepers asking around the Hollows."

"Who killed Clearwater?" asked Simon.

"I don't know," said the Orc. He wailed as Simon applied some pressure to the tip of the dagger. "I don't! It might have been Gorski, or Blackpool, or both. They was Barsaka's enforcers down in the Hollows."

"Why did you set Gripple up? Who told you to lure him out?"

"Barsaka. He sends me a message from a public mirror, tells me to pick up a needle shooter from this address. I go, find the building, an old warehouse off'n Tanner way out in the East End. Cobber meets me at the door, hands me a box and slams the door in my face. Open the box. In't there a needler in it? And a locus, says 'Summon at twenty-third hour.'" He paused for breath and coughed blood. "So I summon it; I ain't no assassin, but what else can I do? No picture, just voice, real low and harsh-like. Like he's talking through a wad of wool. Says to go south, find Swampwater, get him to come out of his house and then shoot him with a needle and leave. 'Don't look back,' says he. 'We'll do the rest,' says he. That's all I know."

"And the ambush on my team?"

Bogrunner rolled his eyes, looking from Simon to Gran. "Please," he said. "I'll tell you, but you gotta take me with you. Don't leave me with her."

"No promises," said Simon. "But I will turn you over to Marshall Greenmire. He's the law down here, not me."

"He ain't Swampwater kin?" asked Bogrunner.

"He's a Southron, no kin to Gran or Gripple."

Bogrunner shut his eyes for a moment, then nodded slightly, careful not to push against Simon's blade. "It were that tall Elf, the one who was with those law crows what shut down Clearwater. He found out where I live, tapped on my door yesterday at the crack of dawn. 'You're going down to

Fernhill,' says he. 'Orders from Barsaka.' Hands me the key to a cargo sledge. 'You drive,' says he. 'Park where the boys in the back of the sledge tell you to. Then you disappear.'

'Can't,' says I. 'Got a business to run, don't I?'

'Mr. Clearwater sends his regards,' says he and he pulls out this fancy mirror and show me a picture of Sanjik Clearwater, upside down, his eyes gouged out and his throat cut. So I drove the sledge like he wanted. There was three Azeri hard boys in the back and a big wooden crate. They told me to park in the middle of the road and skitter. I done as they said."

Simon took his foot off of Bogrunner's chest and slid the dagger back into his boot. He pulled the Orc to his feet. "Give me the address of the warehouse and the mirror locus that you called."

Bogrunner recited an East End address, several miles out the Old Tanner Road. Simon made a note of it on his handheld. He wasn't surprised that the mirror locus Bogrunner gave him was familiar. He'd seen it scratched on the bottom of a Durlash figurine and written on the scrap of paper in Clearwater's stash. Dammit. He should have listened to Sylvie and summoned that locus straight away.

"Let's go, Sylvie," he said, turning his back on Bogrunner. "We need to get back to Cymbeline." He bowed deeply to Gran Swampwater. "I'm in your debt, Gran Swampwater. Please accept my condolences on your loss."

Gran placed a withered hand on his forehead. "May the Spirits of this Earth guide and protect your *ghiras,* Simon Buckley."

"Wait," called Bogrunner. "You promised to take me to the Marshall."

"Marshall Greenmire's just outside the gate," said Simon over his shoulder. "I'll tell him you're here. I'm sure he'll come get you."

They had almost made it across the courtyard when Bogrunner started to scream.

CHAPTER TWENTY-THREE

Sylvie was silent as Simon drove the sled out to the S393 and the main route back to Cymbeline. Once he had settled into cruising mode on the divided highway, she turned to him.

"I don't think I can continue with you in this, Simon," she said. "Hal and Jack strong-arming Orcs down in the Hollows is bad enough, but torturing a suspect is something I can't tolerate. At the least we should have taken Bogrunner with us, but to leave him with those crones is the same as murder."

Simon gripped the steering yoke, controlling a burst of anger. He forced his voice to remain neutral. "We had no jurisdiction down there. It's Sovereign land. Only Greenmire could have detained Bogrunner. And he wouldn't dare defy Gran Swampwater."

"That's your excuse? Orc vengeance trumps Commonwealth justice?" she fumed. "Bogrunner could have given evidence against Flandyrs. He told us who ordered the attack that killed Hamish and Gripple. But now we've got nothing."

"Bogrunner is an Orc and Flandyrs is a High Elf with diplomatic cover," said Simon with a sigh. "He'd claim diplomatic immunity and demand a trial in a Haven jurisdiction. What Elf or Human would corroborate Bogrunner's testimony? You? Based on what? All we have is hearsay, and that obtained under duress after we'd both been taken off the case. Even Justice Severna would laugh us out of court."

"You cut his ear off," Sylvie said.

"I cut the tip of his ear off," Simon corrected. He raised a hand when she began to speak again. "No. Don't tell me he doesn't deserve that. You've never spent any time down in the Hollows. You have no idea how Overseers like Bogrunner abuse their own people. They lure them away from the Rez and trap them in a dead end of drugs and prostitution and virtual slavery. The authorities turn a blind eye to it all. He sold out Sanjik Clearwater. He killed Ham. So no, I don't give two shits what Gran and her sisters do to him."

"Ham and Clearwater weren't your fault," said Sylvie, more softly.

"Yes, they were." Simon's hands tightened on the steering yoke. "I made the decision to go off book to the glass factory. I pressured Clearwater into talking to us. I sent Ham and Jack down to the Rez. I'm the team Sergeant. It's my responsibility."

"You can't save the world, Simon Buckley," Sylvie said, sounding exasperated.

"No, but I can avenge Ham. Maybe I can get justice for Sanjik Clearwater."

"By beating and torturing people?" shouted Sylvie. "How is that different from what you say Bogrunner did? How is that different from what Barsaka did to Clearwater?"

"It's different because I'm a King's Agent. It's different because I don't kill and torture innocents. I don't sell out my own kind for foreign gold." Simon paused to take a deep breath and calm himself—if he could. "If you want to go back to the Rangers, fine. I understand. I'll drop you at your flat, or at Wycliffe House, whichever you choose."

Sylvie looked out her side of the sled and sighed. "I don't want to go back to the Rangers, at least not while Flandyrs is still in the consulate. If we take him down, Barsaka will be on his own. Maybe that will help you find your justice. That, at least, I can do."

Simon glanced at her. "How are we supposed to get to Flandyrs? Bogrunner would be no help without corroboration. Clearwater is dead. No one at that fancy law firm is talking. We have no proof that Flandyrs is involved in this, whatever we may think we know."

"I'm not talking about prosecuting him, only getting him relieved and sent back to the Havens.

I'm a Graystorm. My word is worth something, even if I'm relating hearsay. And Summerfield has no love for the political arm. If I can convince him that Flandyrs is carving his own path, I'm sure he'll have him relieved." At Simon's doubtful look, she quickly went on. "He's not a real consular officer, after all. He's a spy for the Rangers. Threaten exposure and they'll have to send him home."

Simon did not answer her right away, torn between anger and shame. He knew that she was right about Bogrunner. He'd taken an oath to serve and protect, not just the innocent but the patently guilty as well. How many times had he lectured Hal about his prejudices against Orcs?

But damn them to seven hells, Ham was dead. He'd tried to do the right thing and they suspended him for it. What the hells did he owe the Peacekeepers, or the King? And who the hells was she to judge him?

As soon as he thought it, he felt the shame again. He was a Keeper; first, last, and always. It was all he'd ever wanted to be. It was what Alira had wanted him to be. He looked again at Sylvie and realized it mattered to him what she thought of him.

Simon fished in his front pocket, pulled out the key to his flyer, and handed it to Sylvie. She looked at it, puzzled, then at him.

"In the storage box on the back of my flyer is a leather bag. In it are all the case notes up until I was suspended." He shrugged at her sharp look. "I copied them before I turned them over to Killian.

Use them. Take them to Summerfield, or to the Ambassador, someone you trust. Use them to get Flandyrs out of the Commonwealth."

"Come with me, Simon," she said, touching his arm. "We can go to Summerfield together. You can corroborate it all. We can do this. Hal and Jack will get their *were geld*, but you don't have to be part of that. After we get Flandyrs, we can all go after Barsaka."

Simon shook his head. "I can't, Sylvie. I have to see this through; for Ham and for Clearwater. For Alira. And for us, if we have any chance of being together after this. I can't live the rest of my life knowing that I could have done something to stop Barsaka, but hid behind protocols and procedures instead of taking action."

"What are you going to do?" she asked.

"Drop you off at Hal's place. You take my flyer back to Wycliffe House, or to your place, and get that evidence to Summerfield," he said. "I'll check out the address that Bogrunner gave up. If I can reach Hal and Jack, we'll meet up there. After that, it will depend on what I find."

"What about the mirror locus?"

Simon thought for a minute. "I'll talk to Liam. He already has the locus number. It's time to put a back trace on it and see where that leads. He can work with Evarts; maybe bury the request in a batch of routine queries. Hopefully there isn't a Tag and Report spell on it to alert the mirror that someone ran a trace. If Gulbrandsen and Flandyrs know about the number, you can bet they've already done that. You may not have a lot of time after Liam runs the trace to make your case to Summerfield."

Sylvie nodded and they lapsed into silence until the exit for Glenharrow came into view. Simon pulled into the stable at Stonebender Hall and parked the sled. Sylvie turned to him.

"Please come with me," she said. "I do understand what you're doing, but this isn't the way. We can take the evidence we have so far to your Captain Axhart, bypass Gulbrandsen and Flandyrs completely. If we get both Axhart and Summerfield into this, we can stop Barsaka and get Flandyrs out of Cymbeline for good. What you're doing with Hal will burn you both, even if you do get Barsaka."

Simon knew she was right. He sighed and rested his head on the steering yoke. He was tired of fighting. Even if they killed the Orcs who had ambushed the team, it wouldn't bring Ham or Gripple back. It wouldn't get them any closer to stopping Barsaka or Flandyrs.

Gran had said that her son's fate had already been decided and nothing Simon had done could change that. Was that the way of everything? Decisions made could not be unmade, but did that mean the path set by those decisions couldn't be changed?

"What about Hal and Jack?" he asked finally. "I can't turn on my team. Hal and Molly are family."

"I know," said Sylvie. "But even family can make bad decisions. I know only too well how family duty can ruin a life. Don't let that happen to Hal and Jack. Stopping the Brigades and getting the person behind the ambush is better *were geld* than killing the thugs who threw the grenades. Convince Hal of that."

Right. As if it were that easy. He wanted to believe Sylvie. But Hal was his family. Second father, if truth be told. How could he defy him if it was a matter of *were geld*? *Oh, 'Lir, what should I do?* The answer came as a soft caress in his mind; a few words of Qetchwa, and a soft kiss, like a breath of wind, on his lips. Then the presence was gone.

"Right," Simon sighed, hoping he had heard what Alira was trying to say. "Take the evidence to Summerfield. I'll try to find Hal and Jack. Neither one is answering their mirror. We'll scout the warehouse while you work on Summerfield. If the warehouse checks out, I'll meet you back at Wycliffe House in a few hours. We'll go directly to Axhart and try to convince him to mount a raid. If Summerfield is behind us, it will make things easier."

Sylvie smiled and kissed him. "I'll see you in a few hours," she said and got out of the sled.

Simon backed out of the stable and headed for the Glenharrow Bridge across the Finnegan. He summoned Liam's mirror as he approached the Cymbeline side of the estuary.

"Good meeting, Liam," he said. "Any progress on the spell chip?"

"Some," said the Fire mage. "One of Evarts' Fire guys had an idea for a false mirror, sort of like setting up a field expedient. We might be able to bypass the security if the chip identifies the false mirror as the real one. Tricky casting though, and we don't have a locus identification."

"Go ahead and try the locus we got from Clearwater's house. It keeps turning up and I want to know who it belongs to." He quickly reviewed his meeting with Gran Swampwater and the interrogation of Bogrunner. "We may tip our hand, but I think it's time to run a back trace on that locus. See if you can get Evarts to help bury the trace in a batch of routine requests."

"All good, boss," said Liam.

"Have you heard from Hal or Jack?" Simon asked.

"No, but Molly summoned me a few minute ago asking the same thing. They must have shut down their mirrors."

"I'm heading out to the East End. I'll check out the warehouse and get back to you. If Hal reaches out to you, tell him where I am." Simon waved his mirror off and stowed it under the seat.

Cymbeline's industrial East End centered around a network of old canals built in the closing days of the Magisterium. The largest, the Great Cut, crossed a neck of land that formed a long bend in the Finnegan and bypassed a treacherous shoal that used to trap ships at low water. Branching canals ran inland to the farms and factories that supported the modern industrial city. Streets tended to follow the canal grid, but Old Tanner Road cut across the entire district on a diagonal, crossing and re-crossing canals on bridges and causeways of all sizes. The Haverford iron bridge across the Great Cut had once been the highest center span bridge in the world. From the top of its humped roadway, Simon looked down on the maze of warehouses and low-rise spell factories of the far East End.

The address Bogrunner had given him was about two miles from the Haverford Bridge in an area of storage yards, two- and three-story warehouses, and the leather tanneries that had given the main road its name. Simon slowed and checked the street numbers carefully. He pulled over to a curb about two blocks from the building, a warehouse with the name *Smetaka and Co.* painted on the wall. Simon grounded the sled and watched the street. He could see the warehouse easily. It stood three stories tall, higher than the low buildings surrounding it. Street traffic was steady but not heavy as sledges and heavy lorries and tractor sleds with drag trailers attached rumbled past him. Occasional passenger sleds glided by, keeping pace with the larger haulers. He saw no one enter or leave the warehouse and the big roll-up doors that faced the street were shut. A big Hilten six-seat sled squatted at the curb right in front of the front door.

Simon settled behind the yoke of the Oxley, keeping his head low so that he could see the warehouse and the big sled parked in front, but not be noticed by passing traffic. Ten minutes passed slowly. Simon struggled to stay awake, the fatigue of the last two days suddenly making itself felt. He was beginning to nod when the summoning tone of his mirror jerked him back to full alertness. He reached under the seat and found the handheld, activating it with a quick swipe of his hand.

The scarred face of Lieutenant Harold, the security officer he'd met at King Olaf Hall, swam into view.

"Buckley," Harold said simply.

"Lieutenant Harold," Simon said. "Did you call to gloat?"

"No," Harold shook his head. "I heard you'd been suspended. It wasn't my doing. You lied to me, but in spite of that, I recommended to the Minister that you be given a commendation."

Simon smiled. "It wasn't exactly a lie. And this thing is bigger than just a single Azeri with a bomb vest."

Harold nodded. "I realized that when the Minister told me to turn the bomber over to your Lieutenant for processing. I protested to my Commander, but the Minister himself signed the order."

Simon said nothing, momentarily stunned. He shook himself. "Minister Alorton had the bomber turned over to the Peacekeeper Force?"

"Aye," said Harold with a sigh. "I don't know what kind of shit you've gotten yourself into, Buckley, but it goes a long way above my rank."

"It makes some sense," mused Simon. "Alorton sided with Tintagel when they claimed diplomatic immunity for my suspect."

"Immunity? Buckley, who the hells are you?"

"Just a simple Keeper, in over his head," said Simon. "Why did you call, LT?"

"To pass on some information, in case it made a difference to your investigation." Harold held up a hand. "I know you've been relieved, but if I read you right, I doubt that would stop you. Am I right?

Simon just shrugged.

"Anyway," continued Harold. "I did manage to get a few minutes with that bomber before he was moved to Wycliffe House. He's a true believer, Snake clan, recruited out of the Western Provinces by Barsaka's people."

"Not surprising. I saw his tattoos."

"Perhaps not," Harold agreed. "But he was recruited for the attack on the Crown Prince by Barsaka himself. Right here in Cymbeline. He wouldn't or couldn't tell us where Barsaka is, but he met him in a Brigade safe house down in the Hollows just before the attack. We think Barsaka is still in the capitol."

"Any idea where?" asked Simon.

"Nothing firm. We hear rumors of a major Brigade base in the East End, but have no real leads."

Simon looked up at the warehouse. "I may have some information for you on that," he said. "Give me a few hours. Thanks for reaching out."

Harold nodded. "Summon this locus when you have new information. It's my private mirror, I'll respond, day or night." He signed off without waiting for Simon's reply.

After another thirty minutes with no activity from the warehouse, Simon activated the sled and pulled out into light traffic. He cruised past the building. The black Hilten hadn't moved in the time Simon had watched the building, and as he slid past he saw two Orcs seated in the front. They didn't turn their heads as he passed but their eyes tracked him. Simon kept his gaze straight ahead, but still recognized the Orc in the right-hand seat from the arrest record Hal had sent him. It was Wadelok Blackpool.

Simon drove on for several blocks, then turned down a side street and backtracked. A block north and two blocks east of the warehouse he parked by an abandoned lot. In the middle of the block, he found the utility alley behind the buildings and followed it to the rear of the warehouse.

A tall steel fence separated the alley from the rear of the building with a gap of about ten feet. Simon saw no guards on the rear or on the roof. This side of the warehouse was a blank wall for the first two stories with only a single door set near the east corner. Tall windows lined the third story, probably to give light to the interior. Simon touched the fence, but withdrew his hand quickly. There was a Warding on the fence that would likely trigger an alarm inside the warehouse if it sensed anything other than a light touch. No way in by stealth, although a breaching team could assemble here undetected if they stayed away from the fence.

He walked farther down the alley, past the corner of the warehouse. The fence turned there, too, and ran down the narrow space between the building and its neighbor.

The next building appeared to be a transfer center of some kind. There were large roll-up doors facing the alley and a raised tower in one corner for a dispatcher's office. The doors were shut and Simon saw no one in the tower. He walked to the far end, just below the tower which stood in the corner nearest the three-story warehouse. An exterior ladder ran up the side of the building to the roof. The lower six feet of the ladder was retracted up on a pulley system so that it did not reach the ground.

Simon glanced around, but saw no one watching. He took three running steps, jumped and caught the lower rung. With a squeal, the pulley turned and he rode the ladder to the ground. He climbed up to the roof and again looked around.

The place looked deserted. The roof ran around three sides of a loading yard that opened onto the street. Several cargo sledges and a heavy lorry sat motionless in the yard and the gate to the street was closed. Simon crouched and ran along the slight peak in the roof until he reached the foot of the tower. The stairwell rose through an opening in the roof that was closed and secured with a heavy lock, but the upper part was open. He climbed the single flight to a trap door in the bottom of the dispatcher's cage. He feared this would be locked as well, but when he pushed up, it opened easily. He pulled himself up into a small room containing a swivel chair and a small writing desk. Old shipping bills littered the desk and a few clipboards hung from the half wall that looked out over the working yard.

Simon forced open a side window and leaned his head out. He could just see through the third-floor windows of the warehouse to a small patch of concrete floor. Stacks of wooden crates covered most of the spot that he could see. A single open aisle, wide enough for a man, ran between the stacks. Simon clung to the side of the tower, his head as far out the window as he could force it, and watched.

Minutes passed. Traffic rumbled by on the street. The window faced away from Tanner Road, so Simon had little fear of being seen from there, but the alley and the yard were right below him. Anyone walking by there would surely notice him.

He was about to give up and climb down when movement inside the warehouse caught his eye. A broad-shouldered Orc walked down the aisle between the crates, a paper in his hand. He appeared to count each stack carefully and then write a notation on the paper. Suddenly he looked up as if something had caught his attention, and Simon recognized Murg Gorski. Someone else stood at the end of the aisle, but in the poor light there, all Simon could make out was a shadow. Gorski spoke to the other figure, someone tall and lean. After a few seconds, the other figure walked away and Gorski followed.

Gorski and Blackpool in the same place, heavy Warding and a pair of guards out front?

Nothing conclusive, but enough for a search. Time to go.

CHAPTER TWENTY-FOUR

Simon descended to the roof. Too far to backtrack to the ladder. He swung over the edge and hung from the eaves for a second before dropping to the ground. He rolled to absorb the shock, came up and looked carefully around before starting back up the alley toward Hal's sled.

He reached for his mirror, then remembered that he'd left it in the sled. He quickened his pace. He'd keep trying to reach Hal, but would also summon Liam and Sylvie to try to coordinate a raid on the warehouse. Now that he'd found the place, he didn't want to leave it unwatched.

He turned the corner onto the larger side street and stopped short. Murg Gorski leaned against the fender of the Oxley, a wicked smile on his face.

Simon felt, rather than heard, two more Orcs coming up behind him.

Gorski levered himself off the fender and started toward Simon. "Snooping, Bluebelly?" he said. "That ain't healthy. A body could get hurt climbing that old tower."

Simon heard a rattle of metal and ducked as a chain mace swung over his head and smashed into the wall above him. He pulled the dagger from his boot and slashed upward with it, catching the forearm of the Orc with the mace. He scuttled sideways as the Orc howled and dropped the weapon.

Simon stood, his back now to the wall. Gorski continued to approach, pulling a curved Azeri longknife from a sheath at his waist. The Orc Simon had slashed held back, trying to stop the bleeding with a dirty handkerchief. He was hurt, but not incapacitated. The third Orc eyed Simon's dagger warily. He held a short cudgel studded with spikes.

"Kill him, Murg," said the Orc with the injured arm.

"Nah, Boss wants him alive, at least long enough to tell what he knows. Then you can kill him."

Simon gripped the dagger at low ready. He looked for an opening around Gorski. If he could get to the Oxley, he might be able to get the strange weapon Hightower had brought through the portal. He didn't understand how it worked, only that it did. If Gorski didn't slice him to ribbons first, he could take both of the Orcs down.

He feinted left at the Orc with the cudgel, hoping to make him step back. The Orc was an experienced brawler and stood his ground, cudgel held in close where he could use it to deflect Simon's blade. Simon pulled back as Gorski rushed him.

He managed to dodge Gorski's first thrust at his neck and deflected a slash at his belly with the flat of his blade, but that left him half-turned and open to a blow from the other Orc. He raised his shoulder as the cudgel came down at his head and managed to take much of the force of the blow on his back and deflect the swing. Still, the club caught him on the back of his head and made him stagger. Blood welled from a cut in his scalp. He barely twisted away from another thrust from Gorski's blade.

He pressed his back to the wall and shook his head to clear it. Gorski and the other Orc had switched places. Gorski was now on his left, harder to defend against with the dagger in his right hand. Simon wished he'd listened to Hal years ago and trained in two-bladed combat. It would have made it easier to use the dagger in his off hand. He swiveled his head back and forth, watching both Orcs as they shifted around, looking for an opening in his guard. The third Orc finished knotting the handkerchief around his arm and picked up the mace in his left hand. The three of them exchanged a look and Simon settled his weight on the balls of his feet.

Gorski moved first, as Simon had expected. He aimed a cut at Simon's groin. Simon parried, swiveling to his right and using Gorski's momentum to pull him forward, between himself and the Orc with the mace. Gorski was fast. He ducked and rolled, evading Simon's blade. The second Orc stepped left and swung the mace.

A black Keeper sled careened around the corner and Jack Ironhand jumped out of it before it had completely stopped. He was in tactical gear and held a D'Stang at his shoulder. His first bolt hit the Orc with the mace in the back, knocking him down. The mace continued its arc in the Orc's now lifeless hand and hit Simon squarely on the forehead. Most of the force of the blow was spent, but it was enough to knock him down. His vision narrowed and almost went black. Simon saw Hal leap from the sled. Jack's D'Stang whined again and the bolt erupted from the third Orc's neck. Hal shot Gorski in the thigh as he tried to get up, and the Orc collapsed to the ground.

Using the wall, Simon struggled to his feet. Jack ran forward, dropping the D'Stang. He picked up the mace and brought it down on Gorski's head with a wet crunch. Simon swayed and watched, his head foggy, barely able to understand what was happening. Jack struck again and again, shouting and sobbing. Hal ran to Jack, gripping him around the chest and forcing him back.

"Stand down, Jack," Hal shouted. "They're dead. Stand down."

Jack continued to struggle for a second; then he dropped the mace and held onto Hal, sobbing into his shoulder. Simon leaned his aching head against the wall. Blood trickled down his neck from the cut on his scalp and his forehead pounded with each heartbeat. He reached up and gently probed the egg-sized swelling there. His vision started to clear and he surveyed the scene at his feet.

Gorski's head was an unrecognizable mass of blood and bone. A red stain spread from the neck of the second Orc, who still held the cudgel. His eyes stared sightlessly at Simon. The third Orc lay face down, Jack's bolt buried to the fletching in his back. Simon looked up at Hal. His friend's expression was grim but satisfied.

"Good timing," said Simon.

"We were in the neighborhood," said Hal. "Looks like you were in a spot of trouble."

Simon nodded. "You weren't answering your mirror."

Hal shrugged. "Off the book, didn't want to have to explain anything."

"How did you know to come here?"

"Checked in with Liam when you didn't respond to a summons. He told us about this place."

Jack stepped back from Hal and turned to face Simon, his face still streaked with tears. "If you want my badge and weapon, Sarge, I won't fight it. This was for Ham."

"Shut up, Jack," said Simon. "We don't have time for that shit now. It's done. But we can't be tagged with this; not yet anyway. Pull your bolts and help me move these three into the alley."

Jack nodded and wiped his eyes. He bent to pick up his bolt thrower and slung it from his tactical vest. Then he drew the bolts from the bodies and tucked them into his vest.

Simon, Hal and Jack dragged the bodies into the alley. They weren't concealed but at least they wouldn't be obvious from the street. Simon scuffed loose dirt from the vacant lot over the blood on the ground, concealing it from any casual observer. He joined Hal and Jack in the alley.

"What's the tale here, lad?" asked Hal, indicating the three dead Orcs.

"The warehouse over there," said Simon, pointing to the large building. "I'm pretty sure the Fire grenades are in there. I don't know how many Azeri are in there as well. There was a big black Hilten parked out front when I first got here. Blackpool was at the yoke, but I couldn't see who else was in it. I didn't see guards on the front or the roof, but the fence is Warded and I'll bet there's a locking spell on the back door."

"That Hilten was just pulling away as Jack and I came up," said Hal. "What about these three? Think they'll be missed?"

Simon nodded. "Someone spotted me when I was up on the roof of the next building down. They know I'm here. Gorski said his boss wanted me alive. They'll be expecting him any time."

"Right then." Hal hefted his D'Stang. "We're on our own. Jack, cover the back. Drop anyone who comes out that door. Simon and I will take the front. Get up on the FS net, listen for the signal and be ready."

Jack nodded and trotted off down the alley. Hal activated the FS net and handed an ear clip to Simon.

"Com test," he said. Simon heard it clearly and gave Hal a nod.

"Loud and clear," came Jack's reply over the net. "I'm in position across from the back door."

"All good," said Simon. "Wait for our signal."

Hal walked over to the Keeper sled and opened the rear compartment. He pulled out a D'Stang and three magazines.

"Two cold Iron and one Fire," he said, handing the weapon and the ammunition to Simon. "I don't have another vest, so stay on my rear and be careful."

Simon nodded. He thought for a second, then clipped a Fire magazine into the D'Stang's receiver and flipped the safety off. He shrugged at Hal's raised eyebrow.

"We're off book," he said. "We don't know what's in there and I'm too tired to worry about niceties like rules. We go in fast and hard and blow the place up if necessary."

"Just control your aim," said Hal. "If those grenades are in there, one of those rounds could send us to the Green Lands in an eye blink." He bent and grunted slightly as he lifted a three-foot breaching ram. The black iron rod was about six inches in diameter and ended in a blunted cone of hardened steel. A handle welded to each side allowed it to be carried by two men and swung back and forth.

Simon took one handle and Hal the other. Simon had to stoop slightly because of their height difference. He felt a twinge in his back and hoped it wouldn't get worse before they hit the door.

They walked quickly to the corner, hugged the wall of a low building there, and looked up Tanner toward the warehouse. Simon eased his head out, far enough to see the larger building.

The Hilten was gone. In its place a big cargo sledge was backing up toward the roll-up door closest to where he stood. He tapped Hal on the shoulder and signaled that he should drop the ram. Hal crouched, looked around the corner, then nodded. They both stood and brought their bolt throwers up to their shoulders.

"Jack," said Simon on the FS net. "We're going in."

"Ready," came the reply.

"I'll take out the sledge," Simon whispered to Hal. "You rush the door and keep them from closing it."

Hal grunted in reply and stepped in front of Simon. "Stay behind me," he said. Simon tapped him on the shoulder and they stepped out into the street. They moved forward at a rush, sighting along the barrels of their weapons, Simon a step behind Hal and slightly to his left to give himself a clear field of fire.

The sledge had just backed up to the loading dock. Two Orcs stood on the raised dock watching the bed of the cargo carrier. An Orc at the steering yoke reached down and dropped the loading jacks from the underside of the sledge and, looking up, saw Simon and Hal. His mouth opened just as Simon sent a Fire bolt into the bed of the sledge.

The near side of the sledge exploded in a fireball, shattering half of the cinnabar rods under the cargo bed and collapsing the loading jacks on that side. It tipped sideways, throwing the Orc from the driver's cab ten feet to the street, where he lay still. Hal's first two bolts took out the Orcs standing on the dock, and he rushed up the access stairs next to the burning sledge. Simon followed, the intense heat searing his already burned neck. Two more Orcs rushed from the interior of the warehouse. Simon shot one with a Fire bolt. His chest exploded and the body was flung back into the interior. Hal shot the second Orc in the groin and he fell screaming.

They rushed inside, still in their combat stance. Crates like the ones Simon had seen earlier had been positioned in the loading dock, waiting for the sledge. Hal moved up behind them, using them as cover. Simon lifted the lid from one of the crates. Nestled in a bed of wood shavings were half a dozen Fire grenades like the ones they had found at the farmhouse. He grabbed Hal's shoulder and pulled him back.

"Not here," he said. "They may be rigged to go off."

Hal looked to his right. "That way," he said. He sent bolts left and right and ran at a crouch toward the front of the warehouse. The screams of the wounded Orc echoed in the cavernous space.

Simon felt totally exposed as they crossed the open floor. They needed cover. He tapped Hal's shoulder and pointed to a cargo lift parked near the front of the warehouse. Hal veered left toward it, keeping his D'Stang on the rear of the building. Shouts and the rattle of feet on stairs echoed from that direction, growing louder.

At the rear of the warehouse stood a raised section that rose two stories above the concrete floor, walled off with a wooden frame. The first level was a solid wooden wall with a single, wide opening in the center. The second level had a row of windows looking down on the warehouse floor, clearly an office of some kind. The windows were covered with fabric shades. Behind them, shadows moved.

They reached the cargo lift as a half-dozen Orcs rushed from the opening in the wooden wall. Bolts rang off the cab and fork of the cargo lift, and one buzzed past Simon's left ear, causing him to duck. Hal grunted as a bolt hit him in the chest. He waved off Simon's hand when he reached out to support him.

"Just a bruise," Hal gasped. "Vest stopped it. We can't stay here. They'll flank us."

Simon nodded. "Cover that door," he said, pointing at the opening where the Orcs crouched. Already they were moving left and right to get around their flanks.

Simon stood, drawing fire from several directions. He aimed his D'Stang at the windows, loosed a bolt, then ducked behind the lift. Glass shattered and a roar of flame erupted from the office. Orcs shouted and ran out into the open as flaming debris fell. Hal swung left and right, sending bolts into the fleeing Orcs.

Simon turned and sent a Fire bolt into the front door, blowing it outward but starting another fire in the wall around it. He tapped Hal and pointed to the back door, straight across from where they crouched.

"I'm going to take out those crates." He pointed at the stack he had seen from his perch in the tower. "Break for the back door as soon as I do."

Hal nodded as bolts rang off the lift. Several came in from their left, glancing off the floor. One tore through the sleeve of Simon's jacket, slicing a gash in his upper arm. He swiveled left and loosed a bolt. He slapped Hal on the back of his vest and pointed to the door. Hal loosed two more bolts, emptying his last magazine. Then they both ran.

"Jack, two coming out," Simon shouted into his FS. "Hold your bolts."

The Fire bolt hit the grenades and exploded with a loud whoosh. The secondary explosion was a palpable wave of raw sound. Simon was picked up and dashed to the floor, sliding helplessly on his face until the back wall stopped him. Hal slammed into him, thrown by the same shockwave. A geyser of fire roared up to the roof and spread outward, igniting everything it touched. Orcs screamed, and three of them ran blindly across the warehouse, living torches. One fell over the stacked crates near the roll-up door, setting them ablaze.

Simon staggered to his feet and kicked at the back door. The frame held. He kicked again and again; the air around him was burning. Smoke filled his vision. He felt Hal stir at his feet and reached down to pull him to his feet. They kicked together and the frame splintered. One more kick and the door flew open. Cool air rushed in and blew away the smoke for a second. Simon shoved Hal through and dove after him as the backflash from the fresh air feeding the flames erupted from the door behind them.

Simon rolled on the ground, extinguishing his smoldering jacket. Hal sat off to one side, gasping for breath, his tactical vest smoking. Jack stood over him, still covering the door with his D'Stang.

The ground shook with another explosion as the rest of the Fire grenades ignited. The windows above them shattered, raining glass and debris on them. Black smoke billowed through the door as flame spouted from the roof. Jack grabbed Hal by the back of his tactical vest and dragged him back through a hole he had cut in the fence. Simon got to his feet to follow but turned as an Orc crawled through the door behind him.

The Orc was an Azeri, blue snake tattoos showing through the ragged holes that had been burned in his shirt. Much of his hair was gone, his scalp a mass of blistering burns. Still Simon recognized him from the Arrest on Sight alerts he saw on his mirror every morning. He reached down and lifted the Orc under his arms. Simon dragged him through the fence and dropped him at Jack's feet.

"Hargash Barsaka," said Simon, his voice hoarse with smoke and fury. "This is the bastard who ordered Gorski to kill Clearwater. He had Flandyrs set up the ambush on you and Ham. He sent the Orc that killed Alira."

Simon reached down and drew the dagger from his boot. He turned the Orc over with a vicious kick and knelt, pressing the blade into Barsaka's neck. The Orc opened his eyes, startled for an instant, then felt the blade. He lay rigidly still, watching Simon with cold eyes.

"Time to die," whispered Simon.

"No!" Hal shouted. "Stop it, Simon. Not this way."

"He killed Ham," Simon snarled. "He killed Clearwater. He killed Alira."

"I know, lad. I know," Hal said gently, now standing at Simon's side. "But *were geld* won't bring them back. You are as much my son as any that Molly bore me, but you aren't a Dwarf. This isn't the Keeper's way. It isn't the Human way. It will poison the good that Alira and Sylvie have both seen in you." He sighed. "We've done enough killing for one day. We'll bring him in to Axhart. Then we'll get after Flandyrs and Gulbrandsen."

He reached down and took the dagger from Simon's hand. Simon didn't resist. Barsaka started to move, but Hal placed a boot on his chest and pointed his D'Stang in the Orc's face.

"I won't let the lad kill you, but that doesn't mean I won't do it myself," he said. "On your belly, hands behind your back."

Simon sat back on the ground, his head in his hands, as Hal pulled manacles from his tactical vest and secured Barsaka's wrists. His head throbbed, his burned neck screamed with renewed heat and blood trickled from his lacerated arm and swollen scalp. He was tired, so tired. He wanted nothing more than a little quiet so that he could sleep for the next month.

Jack touched his shoulder. "You all good, Sarge?"

Simon rubbed his eyes and wiped his face on his sleeve. "All good, Jack," he said. Sleep would wait. He looked at Hal. "Thanks."

Hal grunted. "Just keeping you out of trouble. Like always."

Simon struggled to his feet. "Let's get the hells out of here."

CHAPTER TWENTY-FIVE

It was after seventeenth hour by the time they got back to Wycliffe House. Hal and Jack took Barsaka in the Keeper sled, and Simon drove Hal's Oxley. They pulled into the stables to a flurry of activity. Hal had called ahead and a security team was waiting to take Barsaka to the holding cells and guard him against both reprisals and any Brigade attempt to break him out.

Simon slid the Oxley into a stall near the rear and made his way to the stairwell, largely unnoticed. Jack and Hal were the center of attention. Keepers slapped them on the back and congratulated them on the capture. Simon knew their superiors would be less sanguine about the afternoon's events, even if they appreciated the outcome. The entire operation had been off-book and illegal. The Arrest on Sight warrants for Barsaka would hold up, but the destruction of the Fire grenades and the burning of the warehouse were not things the King's Prosecutors office would want to tout to the newsies or to a Magistrate.

Simon stopped at the First Aid station on the detention level. The Healer on duty cleaned and dressed his arm, applied a salve to his forehead and burned neck and gave him a green potion to drink. It helped the pain. Simon thanked him and headed up the stairs toward the squad room.

Killian met him at the top of the stairs, blocking his path. "What the hells is going on, Buckley? This was my case. You're on suspension. I ought to have the KP's office arrest you for interfering with an active investigation."

"Go ahead," said Simon. "Take it to Gulbrandsen like a good lapdog. I'm sick of the whole mess. But while you played around here, my team took down Barsaka and half his Brigade." He shoved Killian aside. "I'm hurt and tired. I've seen two Orcs butchered who wanted only to be treated like Men. I've lost a friend to this damned case and likely will be out of a job by tomorrow. Get out of my way before I forget we're on the same side."

Killian stepped back, real fear in his eyes. He watched Simon pass then started up the stairs to the Command level, no doubt to report to Gulbrandsen. Simon didn't care. He crossed the squad room, ignoring curious stares from the day watch. The large mirror on the squad room wall was full of news reports about a huge warehouse fire in the far East End. Arson was suspected, the solemn-faced newsreader intoned, more details in the next hour. Simon almost laughed out loud. Arson was one way to put it.

He slumped behind his desk, noting with some irritation that Killian had changed the screen image on his mirror and had set pictures of his wife and sons on the desk. He closed his eyes for a moment and must have dozed. He awoke with a start to find Killian sitting on the couch, his face pale, and his expression fearful.

"There's a security team in Gulbrandsen's office," said Killian. "Axhart is in there with some Gray Rangers. Gods, Simon, what's going on?"

"You may need to find yourself a new patron, Frank," said Simon. His tone was sarcastic and he regretted it immediately when Killian's face grew even paler. "It looks like Sylvie Graystorm came through. We had evidence that Gulbrandsen was suppressing evidence and passing confidential information to Galen Flandyrs, the Tintagel consular rep. Flandyrs used it to try to thwart any leads that might reveal he was connected to Barsaka and the Brigades. Hal and Jack just delivered Barsaka, and Sylvie took our reports to Senior Ranger Summerfield. I imagine Axhart and Summerfield are making things uncomfortable for Gulbrandsen right now." Simon looked at the pictures of Killian's family on the desktop. "You need to cover yourself, Frank. What did you give to Flandyrs? I know Gulbrandsen told you to keep him informed."

"Only the notes you turned over," said Killian, wiping sweat from his face. "And the stuff from that murder scene you called in."

"What exactly?" Simon asked carefully.

"The crime scene images, the coroner's report, and the notes we found."

"What notes?"

"A file of bills and notations one of my guys found in a desk," said Killian with a shrug. "It didn't seem important, just bills of lading for stuff like glass quality sand, coal, and aquamarine dust. That one had a couple of names noted in pencil on the side margin, which is why I thought he'd want to see it."

"What names?" asked Simon.

"Flandyrs, of course. That's why I turned it over to him. The other name was Blackpool. I gather from your notes, he's some kind of lowlife from down in the Hollows."

"Not just a lowlife," groaned Simon. "He's an Azeri, an enforcer for Barsaka. We saw him at the warehouse today. That bill was evidence directly linking Flandyrs to the Brigades. Where is it?"

Killian actually sobbed. "Oh shit. I gave it to Flandyrs. I didn't make any copies."

"You'd better hope he destroyed it and that your guy didn't see the names," said Simon grimly. "You could be looking at obstruction charges if Axhart finds out. I think you should get yourself to a good Advocate." Simon softened his tone. "Go home, Frank. Talk to Moire. She'll need to know what you could be facing."

Killian stood to leave, but stopped dead as Gelbard Axhart stood in the doorway.

"Sergeant Killian, wait for me in the squad room," the Captain said. "I'll be wanting a word with Sergeant Buckley before I talk to you."

"Aye, sir," squeaked Killian. He shot one glance of appeal at Simon and left.

Axhart stepped in and Simon came to attention. Although a Dwarf, Axhart had a presence that seemed to fill the tiny office.

"At ease, Sergeant," said Axhart. "Sit down. You look like you could fall down at any minute."

"Aye, sir." Simon eased back into his chair, fighting a wave of nausea, whether from fatigue or fear, he didn't know. Axhart sat on the arm of the battered old couch, perfectly at ease.

"You've had a busy couple of days for an Agent on suspension," said Axhart. He raised a hand when Simon started to speak. "No, no excuses. The facts that you and your team captured Barsaka, uncovered a diplomatic scandal, and likely destroyed a terrorist arsenal, if that fire in the East End is what I think it is, are the only things keeping me from tossing you in a cell right now. What in the name of Stone did you think you were doing?"

"My job, sir," said Simon.

Axhart blew out an exasperated breath. "Don't take that attitude with me, lad. I'm trying to be on your side here. That fool Stonebender won't shut up about *were geld* for Agent McPhee. He thinks he's untouchable, but if the KP's office gets the idea that you lot were on some kind of revenge quest, he'll find he's down a blind tunnel with no lamp."

"It wasn't like that, Captain. I was the one who pushed it." Simon rubbed his temples. "I gave Hal and Jack their orders. I took Sylvie Graystorm down to the Rez. I was the one who left Bogrunner there with Swampwater's mother. This whole thing got out of control when Ranger Graystorm and I went off book to that glass factory. This is on me, not Hal."

"And yet Stonebender claims he was the one who pushed you to stay on the case." Axhart laughed. "The two of you are like an old married couple. Gods, you deserve one another." Axhart stood. "There will be no official inquiry into your conduct. You can thank Summerfield for that. He made a case for keeping this under the rocks until he can get Flandyrs into custody and out of the Commonwealth. Any official investigation would uncover some dirty knickers that the Havens and this Department would rather not air, not to mention the fact that the Foreign Minister himself could be implicated. None of which means that there won't be consequences. You won't lose your badge, but you will take your medicine and smile. Am I clear?"

"Aye, sir," said Simon, once again standing and coming to attention.

Axhart nodded. His face softened a degree. "Good work, lad," he said.

"Thank you, sir. If I may, where is Ranger Graystorm?" asked Simon.

"I haven't seen her," replied Axhart. "Summerfield brought me the files she had given him, but she didn't accompany him to my office."

"But we were supposed to meet here if she succeeded in getting Summerfield to act."

"Maybe the lady had other plans," said Axhart. "She isn't in the House, to my knowledge." He turned and strode out into the squad room, shouting for Killian.

Simon pulled out his mirror and sent a summons to Sylvie's handheld. The screen flipped directly to her message scroll. He waved it off and summoned Hal.

"Aye, lad," Hal said in answer. He was still in the stables, but now standing at the entrance to the holding cells.

"I can't reach Sylvie," said Simon. "She was supposed to be here with Summerfield. We arranged to meet."

"Maybe the lady had other plans," said Hal, echoing Axhart.

"No," insisted Simon. "We had a deal."

"Maybe she went back to her place," suggested Hal. "There wouldn't be much need for her here once Summerfield took over. He may have sent her home so that she wouldn't be noticed. She did go off her own books for us."

"Maybe," said Simon. "But she didn't answer my summons."

"She might be asleep. The two of you have done a lot of running around the past few days."

"Something's not right, Hal. Check your sense of Stone on it. Why would she sleep through my summons if she's expecting to see me here, even if Summerfield sent her away?"

The Dwarf stroked his beard. "You have a point. What do you want to do?"

"I need to borrow your Oxley again," said Simon. "I'll go over to her place first."

"Take it," said Hal. "I'm handling the booking on Barsaka. Do you want Jack to come with you?"

Simon shook his head. "No. It may be nothing and I don't want to draw too much attention to her if Summerfield wants her out of sight."

Hal nodded. "Tell me when you find her."

Simon swiped his hand over the mirror and summoned Sylvie again. Again no answer. He pocketed the mirror and walked quickly across the squad room and down the stairs. He stopped at the sled Hal and Jack had driven and pulled a D'Stang from the back along with a cold iron magazine. Back at Hal's Oxley, he pocketed the weapon from Hightower's Portal, before muttering the incantation to activate the sled.

The drive to Sylvie's flat took only minutes. He turned the corner into her cul-de-sac and immediately noticed his flyer parked by the entrance to the building. The rear compartment was open and empty. His Bonecleaver wasn't in the side sheath and the keys still dangled from the yoke.

Simon picked up the bolt thrower from the seat beside him, clipped in a fresh magazine and flipped the safety lever off. He approached the door slowly, the D'Stang held at his side next to his leg. It was too bulky to really conceal that way, but it wasn't overtly threatening there, either. He didn't want Lester or Hiram or whoever was on duty in the lobby to shoot him as soon as walked through the door.

He stepped into the lobby, expecting a challenge from the guard. The concierge's desk was empty. He brought up the D'Stang.

"Lester? Hiram?" he called. No answer. He stepped closer and froze. A booted foot stuck out from behind the desk. He crouched and swung the bolt thrower left and right but saw no one. He moved quickly to the desk and crouched behind it.

Lester lay on his back, still clutching the heavy bolt thrower he kept under the desktop. Half a dozen cold iron bolts protruded from his chest and abdomen. His eyes stared blankly at the ceiling.

"Shit," muttered Simon, surveying the lobby again. It remained empty and silent. He checked Lester's weapon. There were only three bolts left. Where were the rest? Another careful sweep and he finally saw one, stuck in the far wall, high up near the ceiling as if Lester had gone down shooting. He reached down and gently closed the man's eyes.

Simon pulled the D'Stang up and sighted along the barrel. He rushed forward to the stairs, then moved to one side, against the wall and walked up backwards so that he kept eyes on the landing above. It, too, was deserted. He made it to Sylvie's door. The jamb was splintered and the door stood slightly ajar.

"Sylvie," he called. "It's Simon. Are you in there?"

He pushed the door open with his foot and moved in, checking left and right through the sights of the bolt thrower. The security spell was deactivated, he felt no tingle of magic and there was no glow around his weapon. Sylvie's bookshelf lay on its side, most of the volumes scattered across the floor. Under it, Simon saw the body of an Orc, an Azeri by the tattoos on his arm. Blood stained the ashwood floor from a rapier wound in his groin.

Near the kitchen he found a second dead Orc, this one with a wide slash across his throat. He still clutched a needler in his hand. Simon nudged it out of reach with his foot, then crouched to examine it. The needler was a high-end Czech and Hawley, blackened steel barrel, extra-large magazine; a military grade weapon. This Orc was no common Azeri hard boy.

In the bedroom, he found the third body. Simon saw no wound but the bedclothes were soaked maroon and several iron bolts were buried in the wall up to the fletching.

"Sylvie," Simon shouted. "Are you here?"

He checked the bathroom and the kitchen but found nothing else. No dead Elf, for which he was grateful, but no clue as to where Sylvie had been taken. He checked the dead Orcs in the front of the apartment. They were both Azeri, Snake clan by their tattoos. Their clothing was cheap and nondescript, but their weapons were first rate. They carried no documents or identification.

He went back to the bedroom. The Orc on the bed lay face down with his right hand under his chest, the left flung out toward the wall. Simon grabbed his arm and rolled him over, examining him carefully. The Orc clutched a needler in his right hand. The muscles had barely begun to stiffen. Dead no more than four hours, then.

Simon took the needler from his hand. Again it proved to be a high-quality Czech and Hawley, probably from the Free States judging by the polished aluminum grip. He checked the magazine—six out of eight needles left. He ejected one and checked the color. Blue for sleep.

He knelt and looked at the Orc. There was a single wound in his lower chest, right below and just left of the breastbone; a perfect heart thrust. He'd have gone down quickly, died within seconds, but not before getting off two rounds.

Simon made a more careful sweep of the apartment. Sylvie's Ranger jacket, shirt and breeches lay in a heap on the floor of the bathroom. Her rapier was gone, but Simon's leather bag lay on the couch, empty. Likely she had left his notes with Summerfield, but the glass vial and slip of paper from Clearwater's house were gone as well.

He stood in the hallway leading to the bedroom and surveyed the front of the flat. He imagined the attack. They'd come as a team, at least five of them. They'd taken Lester by surprise, quietly enough that they hadn't alerted the rest of the building.

They'd smashed the door with a ram, just like the one he and Hal had carried at the warehouse. He recognized the damage pattern on the doorjamb.

Sylvie had been coming out of the shower. She'd been able to take the first two before the others got completely into the flat, and had retreated to the hall where they'd have to come at her one at a time. Pneumatic bolts had forced her back into the bedroom where she'd killed the third Orc. He'd managed to put two needles into her and the rest of the team had taken her. Simon had no clue as to where.

He took out his mirror and summoned Hal, but got no answer. *Damn, he's probably in the cells. No mirrors in there,* thought Simon. He swiped the face of his mirror to clear it and summoned Liam.

"Sarge," cried Liam. "Where are you? Hal said you'd gone to look for Sylvie."

"Sylvie's in trouble," said Simon. "Azeri hit her flat, killed the concierge and took her. Are you still with Evarts' people?"

"Aye, we cracked the code on that ebony chip. That's why I wanted to talk to you. Where did they take Sylvie?"

"I don't know," said Simon. "Get Hal. He's probably down in the cells booking Barsaka. I need him and Jack at Sylvie's place. Tell Evarts to send his best team, too. We'll need them to help us figure out were Sylvie might be."

"Will do, Sarge," answered Liam. "I don't know if it helps, but that chip is registered to an outfit called *Smetara and Company.* They owned the warehouse where you captured Barsaka. Its image gallery held a dozen pictures of Flandyrs meeting with Blackpool. And from the way Flandyrs is reacting, it looks like Blackpool's the one in charge."

"Thanks, Liam," said Simon. "But we already linked Blackpool to Flandyrs. And I don't see an Elf like Flandyrs taking orders from a lowlife like Wadelok Blackpool."

"No," said Liam urgently. "Not Wadelok. Joby Blackpool, the janitor. He's the one who was pushing Flandyrs around."

"But—" Simon started to object, then stopped. *Oh, shit.* "Liam, get Hal now. Tell him to meet me at Caledonia University, Hightower's office. Tell him to bring Jack and scramble an armed response team."

Simon swiped his mirror off, cutting short Liam's, "Aye, Sarge."

Pieces fell into place. Joby had done time for illegal conjuring with an Earth spell. He was a known mage with a blood connection to Hargash Barsaka. They had thought Joby was just another Azeri, caught in the backlash created by the Brigades, but what if he was more? What if he was the super mage that Gran and Sylvie had suspected was behind Barsaka?

As a custodian, he'd have full access to Noyes lab and to Hightower's office. He could have met her there, talked Earth magic with her. She had an interest in the old Orc traditions. He could have used that. He could have fed her knowledge that

Gran Swampwater and her Spirit sisters had held back.

Both Sylvie and Gran Swampwater had said there was a mage behind the scenes, a very powerful one. Liam's images implied that Joby had some sort of hold over Flandyrs. Could he have forced the Elf to set Hightower up in the farmhouse? Had closing down Clearwater's factory been Joby's idea, or was it just Flandyrs covering his tracks? Probably the former, since the golems had been set to attack anyone who checked out the factory and Flandyrs wasn't capable of magic at that level. But maybe Joby was. Simon didn't wait for the CSA team or for Hal's reply. He was certain that he knew where to find Sylvie.

He slung the D'Stang from his back, checked his boot dagger and settled Hightower's Portal weapon in his back pocket as a backup. He ran down the stairs and out of the lobby. He opted for the flyer over Hal's Oxley. It would be faster, especially if he ignored the restrictions on flying over the University and went directly to Hightower's building.

More pieces came to him as he flew over the High Street. Hightower would never have dealt directly with Barsaka. That would be too much even for the most rebellious High Elf. She would have let Flandyrs handle the transfer of the grenades in return for the platinum. But that made Flandyrs vulnerable once Hightower had been killed. He'd covered his own trail under the guise of protecting the Steward's family reputation. Joby would have known that and it would have given him a loop to throw around Flandyrs. That was why Flandyrs had been willing to threaten Bogrunner and force him to participate in the ambush. Gripple would have known Hightower, but could he have seen Joby as well? Was that the real reason he was killed?

Simon stayed high as he flew over North Anna and the colorful lights of the Guild Market. He didn't start his descent until he was over the University fence, bringing the flyer down in a steep spiral to land on a patch of lawn next to the entrance to Noyes lab. It was full dark as he bounded up the stairs to the main door and found it locked.

Simon didn't have time for his lock picks. He went back down the stairs and found a rock in the shrubbery near his flyer. He hefted it and ran back to the door. He threw the rock as hard as he could at the glass next to the lock. It cracked, but held. A second blow with the rock shattered it, and Simon reached gingerly through the hole to release the lock.

The lobby was dark. The staircase to the second floor was lit only by reflected light from the lamps outside and a wan thread of moonlight coming through a skylight. He brought the D'Stang up to his shoulder, wishing he had a seeing stone. He started up the staircase, keeping close to the wall, watching the hallway to the left at the top of the stairs.

He reached the second floor and checked quickly right, then up, but there was no one in the second-floor hallway or on the third-floor landing. He went right until he reached Hightower's office. It was locked and dark, a Foreign Office wax seal stuck to the doorframe near the lock. The seal was intact.

Liam had said that Hightower's lab was on the same floor, farther down the hall. Simon crept along, peering into the dark but seeing nothing other than a faint light coming from around the corner up ahead. The main hallway ended in a right-angle turn. To Simon's left was the closet where he had seen Joby Blackpool getting out his cleaning supplies the first time he had checked out the building. To his right, a second hallway ran down along the north wall of the building. Narrow windows cast faint light through cracks between their drawn shades. Halfway down this second passage, a brighter light shone through the space under a closed door.

Simon reached it and saw only a number stenciled on the door; nothing to identify what was behind it. He looked left and right along the passageway, and saw no one. None of the other doors showed any light.

He reached out and laid a hand on the doorknob. He felt no hint of a Warding, no tingle of magic as he gently tried to turn the knob. The door was unlocked. He slowed his breathing and cleared his mind, groping for any hint of a spell but felt none. He turned the knob and pushed the door open, sighting along the barrel of the bolt thrower as he checked left and right, and went in. He stood in an eight-by-ten-foot room filled with rows of shelves. They were crowded with the raw materials of spell casting, separated by substance; woods in one section, powdered gems and stones in another, and bright ingots of metal stacked against the wall to his right. A single glowglobe hung in the middle of the ceiling, the only one of six that was illuminated. The light it cast was feeble, but bright compared to the dark hallway.

Directly across from him, he could see faint red light streaming from beneath another door, this one heavy oak bound with round cold iron bolts. He started forward, the D'Stang tucked tight to his shoulder, and staggered as the spell struck him.

Pain lanced through his hands and arms. His right calf felt as if it were on fire. He recognized the blue mist that blossomed around the D'Stang and around his boot. He crouched and pulled the dagger from its sheath. Immediately the pain in his calf stopped but his hands burned where they touched the dagger or the stock of the bolt thrower. He set both on the floor and the pain ceased immediately.

"Why, Sergeant Buckley? Is that you?"

Simon recognized Joby Blackpool's voice, but it was different. He spoke with an educated, cultured, Havens accent, all trace of the folksy Country Orc now gone.

"You will leave the weapons there. The particular security spell on this room can be most unpleasant should you bring them across the threshold. Far more painful than the one you have just experienced," Blackpool said. "I have Ranger Graystorm in here. The security spell is also tied to a Blood curse on her. Attempt to bring a blade or weapon into the room and she will die. Come within five feet of either Ranger Graystorm or myself, and she will die. Do you understand?"

"My team is on the way," said Simon. "We know about Flandyrs. The Fire grenades are gone, along with the warehouse. Your cousin Hargash is in custody. It's over. Let Sylvie go and we can talk."

Joby laughed. "By all means, Sergeant. Let's talk. Leave your weapons there and come in."

Simon reached down and touched his dagger. The pain shooting through his hand was even worse this time. That was enough to convince him that Blackpool's security spell was both active and powerful. He stood and faced the heavy oak door. As he started forward, it occurred to him that he'd felt no pain in his back pocket, where he held the slug thrower he'd taken from the evidence room. He reached back and touched it, confirming it was still there.

He stopped and took the thing out. There was no blue glow and he felt no pain. Evarts had said it had no magical aura, no spell signature. Maybe because of that, Blackpool's security spell didn't recognize the thing as a weapon. Simon tucked it into the back waistband of his breeches and reached out to open the oak door.

CHAPTER TWENTY-SIX

The room beyond was bathed in bright light from overhead, high-intensity glowglobes, but underlying the strong white light was a reddish glow emanating from runes and symbols etched into the floor. Sylvie lay on a marble topped table in the center of the room, her eyes closed. She was naked and bound tightly to the four corners with braided wire cords of some shiny silver metal.

On a similar table next to her lay a naked Orc, bound in the same fashion and gagged with a leather strap. His eyes were open and he looked over as Simon entered the room. He struggled against his bonds and tried to speak, but the gag stopped him. Simon recognized him. It was Wadelok Blackpool.

Joby Blackpool stood between the tables wearing a heavy coverall of dark green canvas. A hood and rigid helm were slung from the back of the outfit, clearly intended to be raised to cover his head and neck at some point. He held a long dagger with strange symbols etched into the blade.

Simon approached him slowly, both hands held out in plain sight. Blackpool watched him with a smug half smile.

"That's far enough, I think," said Joby when Simon was about ten feet away.

"Whatever you say," Simon replied. "You're in charge here."

Blackpool laughed. "Did you learn that in Hostage Negotiation class?" he asked. "Establish trust by allowing the subject to feel in control of the situation. Right?"

"What do you want, Joby?" Simon asked. "Like I said, my team is on the way. Even if you kill Wadelok and Sylvie, we'll get you. There's no way out of this room except through me."

"So you think," said Joby with a smile. "You're forgetting why we are here. I plan to open a Portal."

"You'll die," said Simon. "The Portal light is deadly. Give me the knife. I'll guarantee you a fair trial in a Commonwealth court."

"The same Commonwealth that locks my people on Reservations? The Commonwealth that promises equality, as long as you're Human or Elf? Your precious court offers no justice for Orcs, only more degradation."

"Save me the speechmaking, Joby," said Simon. "You're smarter than that. Nobody has to die today."

"Actually, they do, if I'm going to open a Portal. I need the blood of an Earthborn." Joby pointed to Wadelok. "Wade here has Earth Blood. He'll do nicely."

"You'd kill your own cousin?"

Joby shrugged. "We're not that close. And only Earth Blood will work for a Portal that will pass physical objects."

"Then why Sylvie?" asked Simon. "She's not an Orc. Gran Swampwater said she was of Fire and Air. She has no Earth Blood."

"So you've been talking with that Swampwater crone, have you?" said Joby, smiling. "Too bad about her son. That was petty of Hargash."

"But why kill Sylvie?" Simon asked again.

"Swampwater didn't tell you everything, or perhaps she doesn't know," said Joby. "She and the rest of them only saw the Portals as some sort of mystical fortune telling trick. They never saw the potential."

"That's not what I asked, Joby. You don't have to kill Sylvie to open your Portal."

"Not to open it," said Joby. "To enlarge it. That's what Swampwater missed. Once the Portal is open, more blood, especially sentient blood, makes the opening wider. Why do you think I was working so hard to start a war between the Commonwealth and the Empire?"

Simon looked at him, nonplussed for a second. Play for time, he thought. Hal's on his way. Got to keep him talking.

"Flandyrs, I understand," said Simon. "He wanted a war to weaken the Commonwealth and give the Havens an advantage. But why were you working for Barsaka? What good would a war do you?"

Joby laughed harshly. "Me? Working for that self-deluding zealot? I thought you were smart, Sergeant."

"Then what is the real story?" asked Simon. "You're obviously a mage of considerable ability. That probability cascade at the glass factory was something only a select few could have managed."

"Ah, now it's flattery, is it?" said Joby. "Is that step two in the negotiation? Gain trust, then flatter the subject to reduce his antagonism." He laughed again. "Thank you for the compliment, anyway."

Play for time. "Seriously," said Simon. "Why help the Brigades if you don't believe in Barsaka's cause?"

"I never said I didn't believe," said Joby. "I just don't expect his brand of action to bear any fruit. The Empire is too corrupt to change, and the Havens would rather exterminate my kind than grant us the same respect they do to Humans. I once thought the Commonwealth was different, but I saw firsthand how your legal system treats Orcs. I know there's a better way. I've seen it."

Wadelok started banging his head against the marble tabletop and trying to shout through the gag. Joby turned his back for a second, speaking a few words in Qetchwa and passing his hand over the other Orc's eyes. Wadelok stopped moving and seemed to have fallen asleep. Simon took a step toward Sylvie but stopped when he felt a tingling burn start near the base of his spine. He stepped back and the burning went away.

Joby looked at him and smiled. "Testing, testing," he said. "You are rather remarkable, Sergeant Buckley. I think I shall miss you."

"You were saying about Barsaka?" Simon prompted.

"Hargash thinks bombs and political manifestos will change the world," said Joby. "He's dedicated and ruthless, but in the end he's naïve. Orcs will never be free of racial prejudice. At least the Dwarves are honest about their hatred. Humans claim that all the races are equal under the law, and yet not too long past, Orcs were confined to their own communities by that same law. We need a world of our own, free from interference by any of the other races."

"And that world can exist?" asked Simon. "How? Do you think the rest of the races will take genocide lying down?"

"I said nothing about genocide," Joby said sharply. "That's the Elvish way, or the Dwarfish. I'll give credit where it is due: it was Humans who stood in the way of that after the Wars of the Races. No, the Portals have shown me. Out there, among the myriad worlds, is one where Orcs are alone, where we rule ourselves and are masters of our own destiny."

"And you plan to go there?" asked Simon. "Through a Portal? What makes you think you can survive it?"

"Weren't you listening, Sergeant? I told you just a minute ago that any sentient blood will make a portal wider."

Simon cocked his head, remembering something Sylvie had said. "The square of the distance," he whispered.

"Very good," said Joby. "The Portal light is what kills, not the passage through the gateway. And that danger decreases as one removes oneself from the source."

Simon glanced around the room and noticed the scorch marks on the walls that Liam had mentioned. He took a couple of steps back, beyond where the marks reached the wall nearest him.

"Very astute," said Joby with a small laugh. "But futile. Once I add the Elf's blood to the spell, the Portal light will flood this entire space."

"Then how will you survive?" asked Simon.

"The light is generated by the edge of the gateway. Make it large enough and there is a safe zone in the center; a way through which I can pass to that other world. That, and this suit, are how I will survive."

"The suit is lined with lead," said Simon. "Like the gloves Hightower had." Joby nodded. "So this whole time, you simply planned to leave. Why go to all the trouble of recruiting Hightower and Hargash and Flandyrs? Why the attack on the Crown Prince? Why start a war if all you wanted to do was leave this world for another one?"

"Glendowyn was invaluable in proving the feasibility of Portal transportation. As an Elf, she was less susceptible to the light's effects and showed that lead could protect the flesh. Hargash provided the platinum in return for the Fire grenades. And Flandyrs provided a location for making the grenades and for Glendowyn's research. He kept us updated on the movements of the royal family and the security services." Joby paused to tighten Wadelok's bonds when he started to move again. "Of course, the original plan was to gather a cadre of like-minded Orcs to accompany me. Olega Swampwater was on that list, although I hadn't approached her yet. With a big enough Portal, the entire group could have passed through without protective suits. I estimate that the blood of a thousand or so would suffice to create one that large."

"You would have sacrificed a thousand people?" asked Simon, horrified.

"Don't take that self-righteous tone, Sergeant," scoffed Joby. "Your government would have sacrificed a hundred times that in a war with the Empire and called it honorable."

"War is different," protested Simon.

"Is it?" asked Blackpool. "Each of those deaths would have been no less real, for all that you believe your cause noble. One death is a tragedy, a thousand deaths is just a number. And what cause could be nobler than freeing hundreds from tyranny? With Flandyrs' help, we'd have had enough prisoners from the battlefield to accomplish the task. He'd get his war, Hargash would sate his blood lust, and I and my followers would be free."

Simon fell silent, struck by the ruthlessness of the plan and bothered by the injustice that had spawned it. He'd never been comfortable with Hal's bigotry where Orcs were concerned and knew the statistics on Orc imprisonment. Was the Commonwealth really no better than the Havens? At least the Elves were honest about their prejudice. He knew that it was the Commonwealth's manufacturing might that commanded respect from the Steward and his followers, not its stand on the rights of sentients. The Azeri Empire, the Ironlands, and the Free States were only safe because the Commonwealth provided a check on the Havens, a balance of power that allowed the rest to flourish.

Blackpool regarded Simon for a second more before turning away. He lifted his arms and started to chant an incantation. The metal bonds on Sylvie's wrists and ankles started to glow, and the faint smell of burning flesh wafted up from the table. The symbols on the floor glowed red. Blackpool's knife glowed blue, and Simon felt that same disorientation he'd felt in the farmhouse when they'd first encountered Glendowyn Hightower.

Simon reached back and gripped the handle of the strange weapon at his waist as Blackpool brought the blade down in a long sweeping slash. The knife cut cleanly through Wadelok's neck. The

Orc jerked once as blood spouted from the wound and ran down the table. A shallow gutter in the tabletop funneled the blood to the corners where it dripped to the floor. Red light flared through the runes and symbols etched there, and a glowing blue line appeared in the air above Wadelok.

With a sound like tearing linen, the Portal grew from a thin line, to a narrow crack, to a gateway, as tall as a man and twice as wide. Through it, Simon could see another room, darker than the lab, with a concrete floor and walls of bare stone. A workbench of some kind stood near the Portal, filled with tools. Some were recognizable, a coping saw, a screwdriver, a small hammer, but others were strange and he had no clue as to their purpose.

Joby pulled up the hood of his suit, covering his head except for a rectangle of smoked glass where his eyes would be. He turned to Sylvie and raised the knife.

Simon pulled the weapon from his waistband and raised it in a two-handed grip. Joby turned slightly, glancing Simon's way. Simon squeezed the trigger, this time anticipating the recoil and the noise. Blackpool staggered and stepped back, leaning against the table where Wadelok continued to bleed out. He pushed back the hood and stared down at the hole in the suit, centered over his chest.

Simon pulled the trigger again and a second hole appeared below the first. Blood filled Blackpool's mouth and he spat it out on the floor. More blood dribbled from his lips. He tried to take a step toward Simon, but his knees buckled and he fell.

He rolled slowly onto his back and looked up at Simon.

"Should have seen that coming," he said. His eyes seemed to focus on something far away. "Oh my," he whispered. Then his eyes glazed over and saw no more. The Portal wavered and winked out of existence with a rush of hot air.

Simon felt a ping and a tingle at the base of his spine. He took a tentative step forward. There was no burn. The security spell and the Blood curse had both died with Blackpool.

Simon ran forward to Sylvie's side. The braided wire had burned her skin almost black in several spots. It was still uncomfortably warm to Simon's touch as he struggled to untie it. He checked the pulse at Sylvie's neck. It was still strong and regular.

"Sylvie," he said gently. She didn't respond. "Sylvie!" he called more loudly. She moaned lightly. Her breathing seemed regular and strong, as if she were sleeping, but he couldn't awaken her.

He picked up Blackpool's knife, ignoring Wadelok's blood on the hilt and sawed at Sylvie's bonds. The metal was fairly soft and the steel blade cut through quickly. He pulled her into his arms and lifted her. He left the lab and walked slowly down the stairs and out of the building.

Outside, he sat down in the grass next to his flyer, under the light of an ornate lamp. He could hear the whooping sound of a Keeper siren as Hal and the team sped through the campus gate.

He cradled Sylvie in his arms and waited for the medics.

INTERLUDE:
Phoenix Sky Harbor Airport
TSA Confiscated Property Room
May 23, 2015

"Henry," roared Special Agent Jim Zacker. "Silence that damned alarm, will you. It's making me nuts."

The electronic whoop of the radiation alarm cut off a second later. Henry Johnson, the electronics technician on duty for the day, came out of the utility locker where he had been struggling with the alarm circuit.

"Thank you," said Zacker. He looked around the property room. The door behind him had been locked and secured when he and Johnson had responded to the alarm. There was no sign of forced entry and nothing seemed amiss in the room itself.

Wire rack shelves filled most of the space, arranged in four rows running from front to back. Bar codes on the front of each row identified them by date and priority.

Johnson checked the security camera mounted just above the door and gave a low whistle.

"What is it?" asked Zacker.

"Camera's been fried. The memory card and circuit board are dead. That's why the image cut out as soon as the alarm went off."

"But what set off the alarm?" asked Zacker. Eighteen months ago, in response to some disturbing information about ISIS efforts to obtain nuclear material, gamma ray detectors had been installed in the baggage handling areas and property rooms all over the airport. They had never gone off, until today.

"I don't know," said Johnson. He held a small, boxy radiation detector and checked the readout one more time. "Whatever it was, it isn't here now."

Zacker grunted at that. "A malfunction?"

Johnson shrugged. "Maybe, but something fried the camera. An EM pulse would do it, and that might have triggered the detector."

"How would an EM pulse get triggered in here?"

"I don't know that, either," said Johnson. "A small nuke going off?"

Zacker laughed. "Right. I'm reporting this as a system malfunction. Get someone down here to replace the detector and the camera. I need to wrap this up quickly before some reporter gets ahold of it and starts a panic about a dirty bomb in the airport."

Zacker took one last look around. He noticed some stains, like scorch marks, on the walls and ceiling, and wondered when there had been a fire in the property room. It must have been before his time, because he hadn't seen any report of it. As the ranking FBI agent assigned to Phoenix TSA, it would have been in his daily brief.

He waited while Johnson took down the security camera and placed it in his toolbox. He closed the utility locker and they left the room. Zacker carefully locked the door and set the alarm.

It was another week before the thefts were noticed. A routine inventory of the property room came up several items short. Most were inconsequential, a few knives, a cell phone, a studded dog collar. But among the items missing were a nickel-plated .38 caliber Smith and Wesson revolver and a box of ammunition. The serial number of the handgun had been duly recorded when it had been logged in.

Zacker assigned one of his junior guys to run a routine check on everyone who had accessed the room since the weapon had been confiscated, but didn't expect much from that. He reviewed his notes on the gamma alarm malfunction the previous week and ran through Johnson's report as well. He didn't think Johnson had taken the stuff. The guy was a geek, but honest. He reported it to the National Database as a stolen weapon and said a short prayer that it wouldn't turn up in connection with some crime.

Then he promptly forgot the whole thing.

EPILOGUE:

"She's awake, Sergeant," the Healer said. "You can come in."

Simon stepped tentatively into the hospital room. Sylvie sat up in the bed and smiled at him. Her platinum blond hair was plastered to her scalp by sweat. Her face was swollen, her left eye surrounded by a purple bruise. Her wrists were bandaged where the cords had burned into her flesh.

She looked beautiful.

"Good meeting, Sylvie," he said. He wanted to kiss her, but something held him back.

She frowned at him. "That's all you can say?" she asked. "Good meeting? Like we were strangers?"

Simon shrugged. “Never was very good with words.” As soon as he said it, he regretted it. He tried another tack. “How are you feeling?”

“Embarrassed,” she said, turning away from him.

“Why?” he asked, puzzled.

“Because I had to be rescued,” she said, sounding disgusted. “Just like some damsel in distress from an old saga story.”

“You took down three Azeri soldiers with a rapier. It took two sleeper darts to put you down. You persuaded Summerfield to go after Flandyrs, and you made me remember who and what I was.” Simon took her hand. “You’re the kind of damsel I’d be proud to have fight at my side.” He grinned. “And I’ll never tell anyone how I carried you out of that lab like a babe in arms.”

Sylvie punched his arm. “You’d better not!”

Simon winced. “Hey, I took a bolt in that arm.”

She smiled at that, finally, and gave his hand a squeeze. “How are you, Simon?”

He shrugged. “I’ve been reinstated. I’m still a Peacekeeper. I’ve been fined a week’s pay for going off book with this investigation, and I’m stuck on desk duty for a month, but I kept my badge. Minister Alorton has resigned. He’s too well-connected to be prosecuted, of course, but Gulbrandsen is under house arrest until the King’s Prosecutor decides what charges to file. And Hal and Jack have been cleared of any wrongdoing. It’s all good.”

“How is Ham’s family doing?”

Simon sighed. "Reba's holding everything together. There's a life ceremony for Ham the day after tomorrow."

"Would it be all good if I came?" asked Sylvie. "I didn't know him, or his family, but I feel like I was part of your team, at least for a while."

Simon nodded. "I think Reba would like that. I know Hal and Molly would. Will you be out of here by then?"

"I'm pretty tough for a girl," Sylvie said. "Even if I do need the odd rescue now and then."

Simon laughed and squeezed her hand.

"And Flandyrs?" asked Sylvie quietly.

"In the wind," said Simon. "But Summerfield has the Rangers watching the Borderlands and the Peacekeepers are watching the Azeri border. We'll get him."

"He's mad, you know," said Sylvie. "He wanted a war between the Empire and the Commonwealth. While you bled yourselves white fighting the Azeri, he and his cronies back in the Havens were going to take the weird technology from Hightower's Portal and replicate it. They wanted to bring down the Commonwealth and set up a new Magisterium."

"We know," said Simon. "Summerfield searched his living quarters and his office after you tipped him off and found a list of names. There'll be trouble in the Havens for a while."

Sylvie was silent for a moment. She looked away from him and said, "I still have those orders to report to the Borderlands."

Simon nodded. "I know. Summerfield wants you out of the way until this thing with Flandyrs is resolved. No sense in you being a target, or worse, a hostage."

She turned to face him again. "The Borderlands station is a long way from Cymbeline."

"Two days by commercial coach," agreed Simon. "But only eighteen long hours with a fast sled."

"You'd have to break a lot of speed laws to do it that fast," Sylvie said, her eyes fixed on his.

"I'm a Peacekeeper." Simon smiled and squeezed her hand again. "The job comes with certain prerogatives."

Sylvie laughed, just a small laugh, then sighed, settled back on her pillow and closed her eyes.

Simon stayed at her side and held her hand as she slept.

ACKNOWLEDGEMENTS

Thanks to T.L. Smith, John Bowers, Russell Davis, and Garvin Anders for their help with beta reading and plot development. Special thanks to Bob Nelson and Sharon Skinner for compelling me to write this story in the first place, and believing in it enough to publish it.

Made in the USA
Columbia, SC
22 February 2019